SATELLITE FALLING

IDW

Facebook: **facebook.com/idwpublishing**
Twitter: **@idwpublishing**
YouTube: **youtube.com/idwpublishing**
Tumblr: **tumblr.idwpublishing.com**
Instagram: **instagram.com/idwpublishing**

ISBN: 978-1-63140-803-8   21 20 19 18   1 2 3 4

COVER ARTIST
STEPHEN THOMPSON

COVER COLORIST
LISA JACKSON

COLLECTION EDITORS
JUSTIN EISINGER
and ALONZO SIMON

COLLECTION DESIGNER
CHRISTA MIESNER

PUBLISHER
TED ADAMS

Originally published as SATELLITE FALLING issues #1–5.

Ted Adams, CEO & Publisher

Greg Goldstein, President & COO

Robbie Robbins, EVP/Sr. Graphic Artist

Chris Ryall, Chief Creative Officer

David Hedgecock, Editor-in-Chief

Laurie Windrow, Senior VP of Sales & Marketing

Matthew Ruzicka, CPA, Chief Financial Officer

Lorelei Bunjes, VP of Digital Services

Jerry Bennington, VP of New Product Development

WRITTEN BY
STEVE HORTON

ART BY
STEPHEN THOMPSON

ART BY
MARTIN MORAZZO
(Issue #5)

ADDITIONAL INKS BY
AUSTIN JANOWSKY
(Issue #4)

COLORS BY
LISA JACKSON
AND
ALEX LOZANO
(Issues #4 and 5)

SERIES EDITS BY
SARAH GAYDOS

LETTERS BY
NEIL UYETAKE

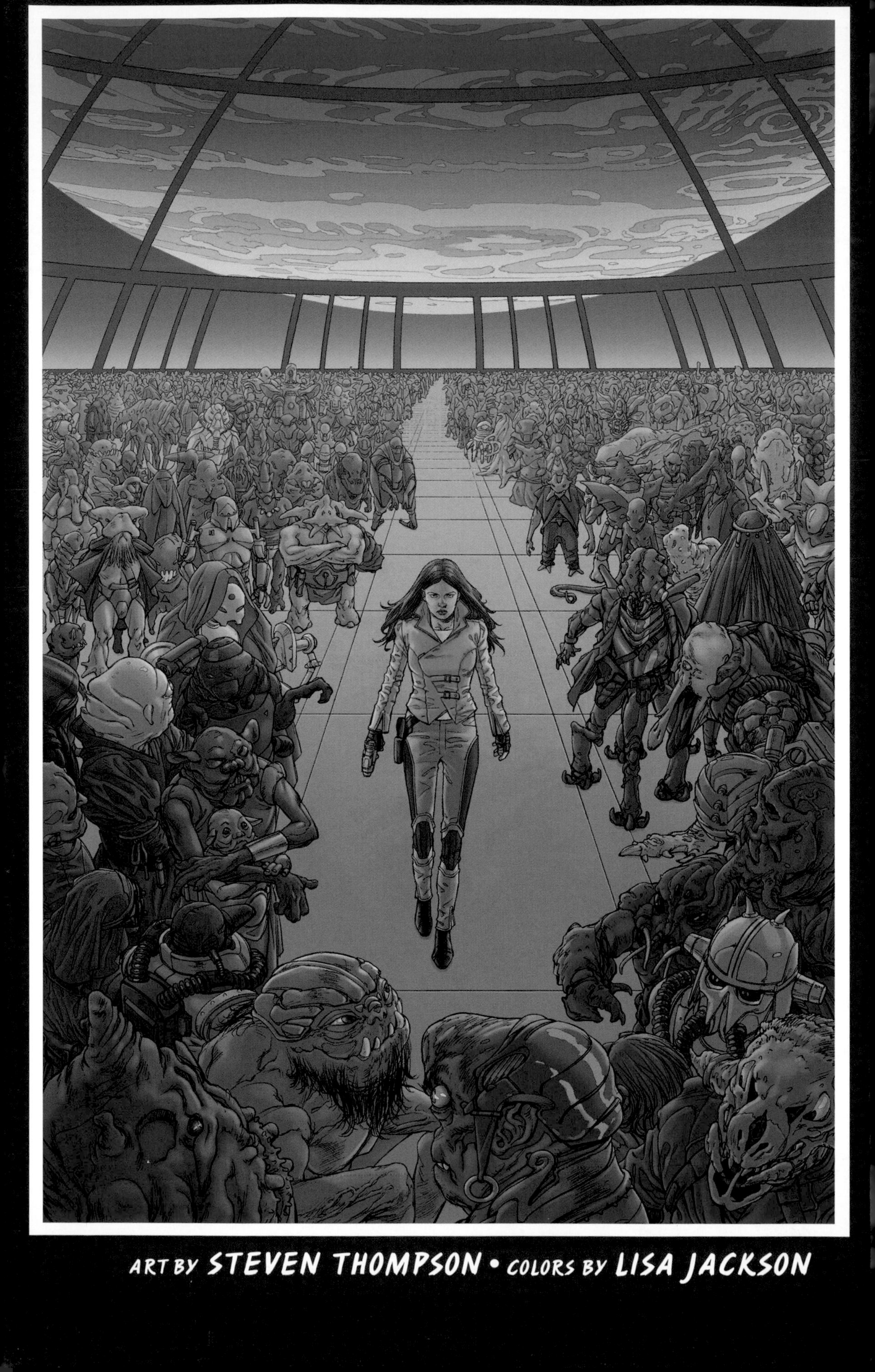

ART BY STEVEN THOMPSON • COLORS BY LISA JACKSON

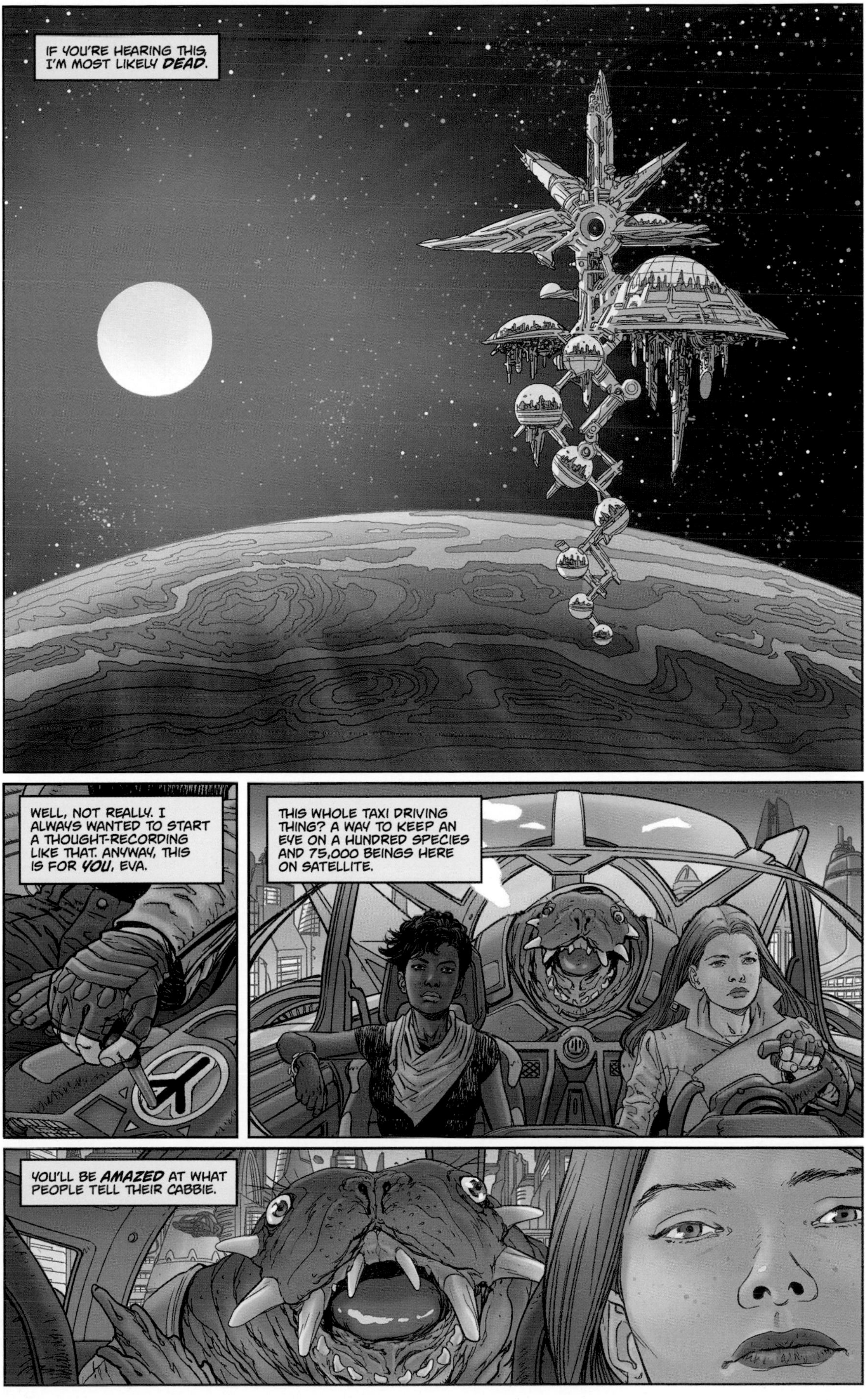
IF YOU'RE HEARING THIS, I'M MOST LIKELY DEAD.
WELL, NOT REALLY. I ALWAYS WANTED TO START A THOUGHT-RECORDING LIKE THAT. ANYWAY, THIS IS FOR YOU, EVA.
THIS WHOLE TAXI DRIVING THING? A WAY TO KEEP AN EYE ON A HUNDRED SPECIES AND 75,000 BEINGS HERE ON SATELLITE.
YOU'LL BE AMAZED AT WHAT PEOPLE TELL THEIR CABBIE.

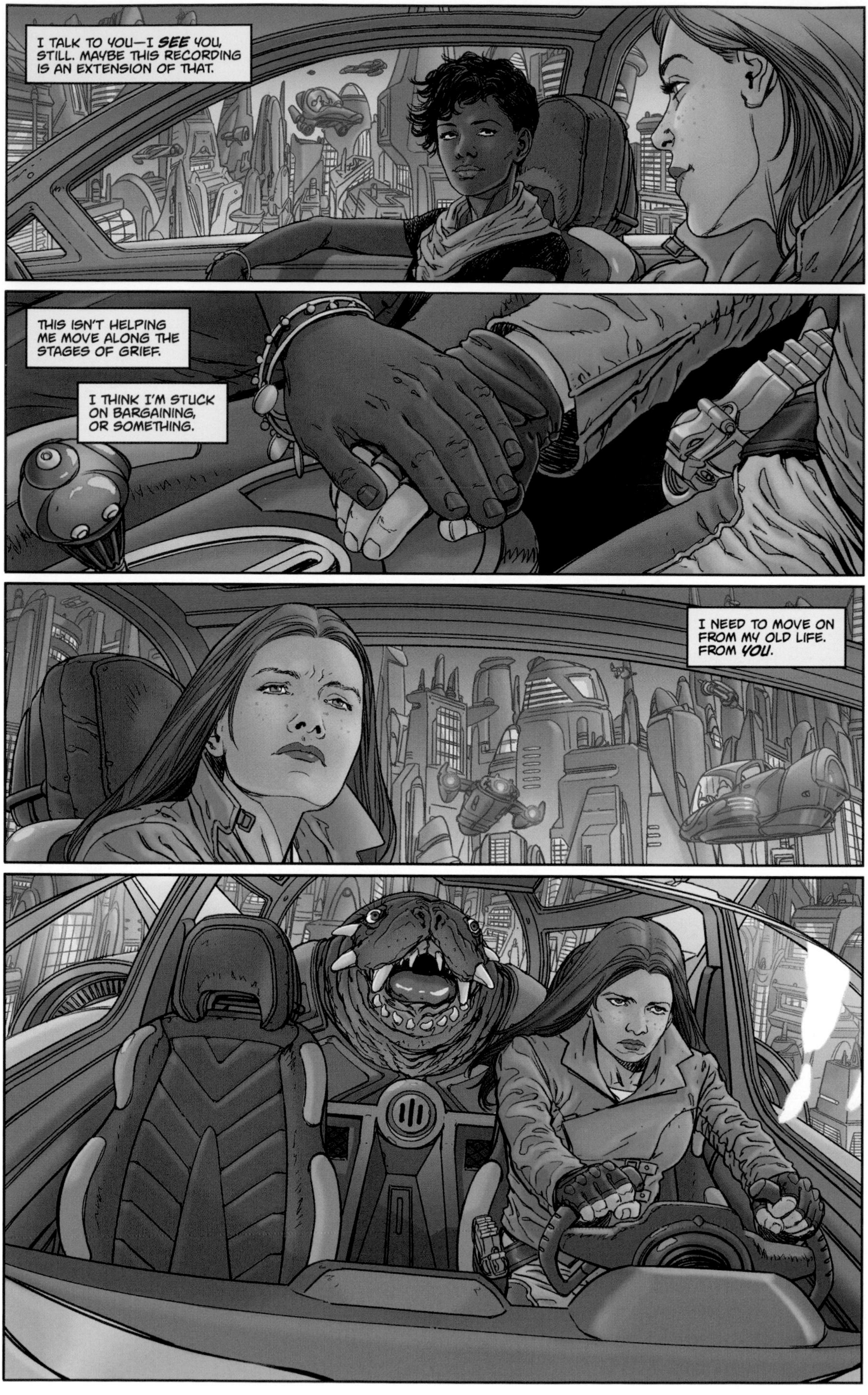
I TALK TO YOU—I SEE YOU, STILL. MAYBE THIS RECORDING IS AN EXTENSION OF THAT.
THIS ISN'T HELPING ME MOVE ALONG THE STAGES OF GRIEF.
I THINK I'M STUCK ON BARGAINING, OR SOMETHING.
I NEED TO MOVE ON FROM MY OLD LIFE. FROM YOU.

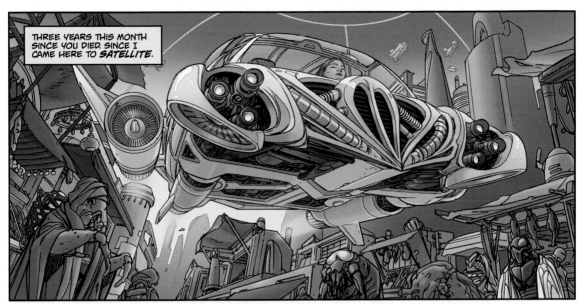

THREE YEARS THIS MONTH SINCE YOU DIED. SINCE I CAME HERE TO *SATELLITE*.

SINCE I MADE THE BIGGEST CHANGE I COULD POSSIBLY MAKE.

THERE *STILL* AREN'T ANY OTHER HUMANS HERE. IF ANYTHING, WE'RE EVEN MORE XENOPHOBIC. MORE *RACIST*. THEY STAY EARTHBOUND.

I CAME HERE BECAUSE THIS WAY, I DON'T EVER HAVE TO SEE ANYONE THAT REMINDS ME OF *YOU*.

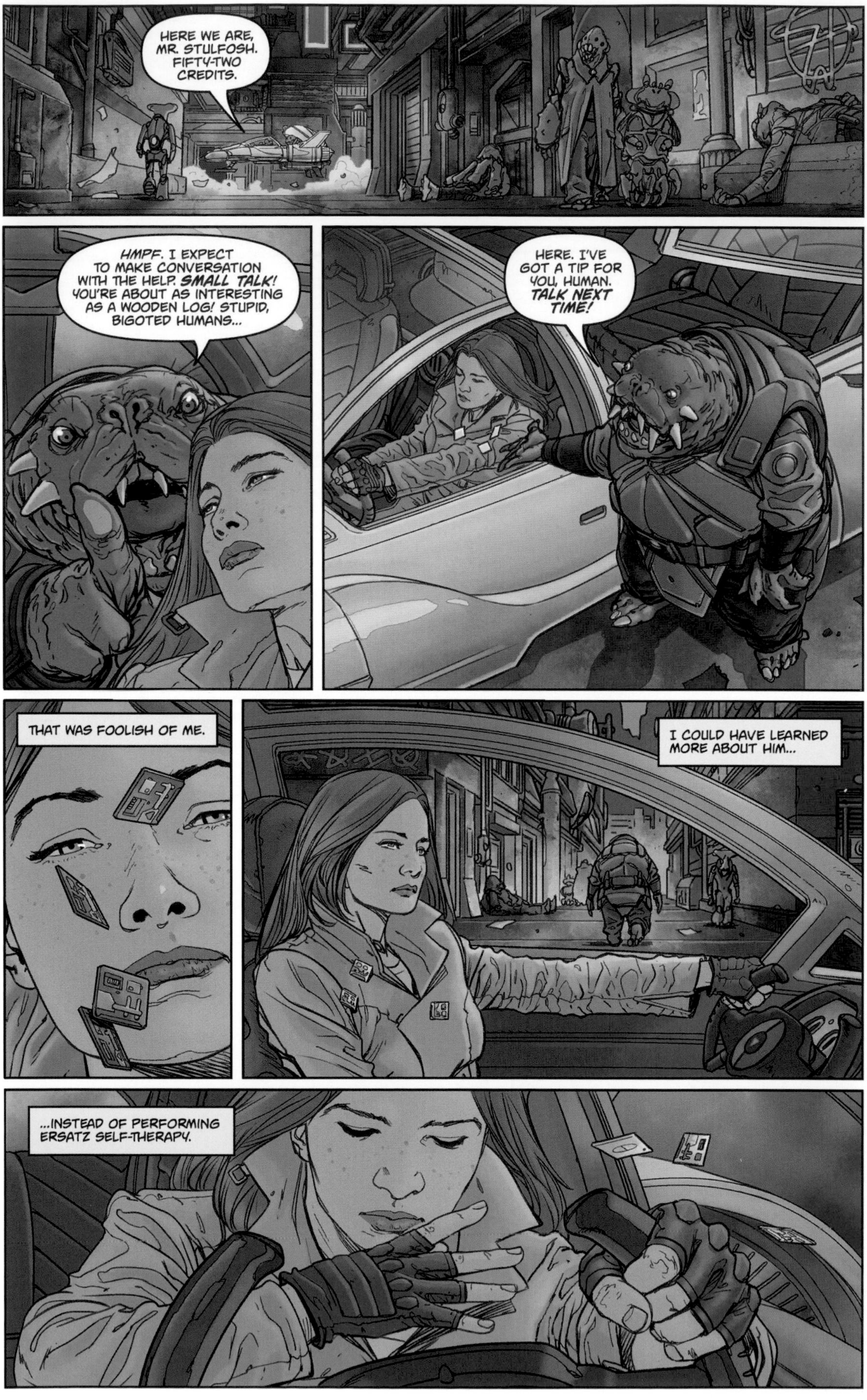
HERE WE ARE, MR. STULFOSH. FIFTY-TWO CREDITS.
HMPF. I EXPECT TO MAKE CONVERSATION WITH THE HELP. SMALL TALK! YOU'RE ABOUT AS INTERESTING AS A WOODEN LOG! STUPID, BIGOTED HUMANS...
HERE. I'VE GOT A TIP FOR YOU, HUMAN. TALK NEXT TIME!
THAT WAS FOOLISH OF ME.
I COULD HAVE LEARNED MORE ABOUT HIM...
...INSTEAD OF PERFORMING ERSATZ SELF-THERAPY.

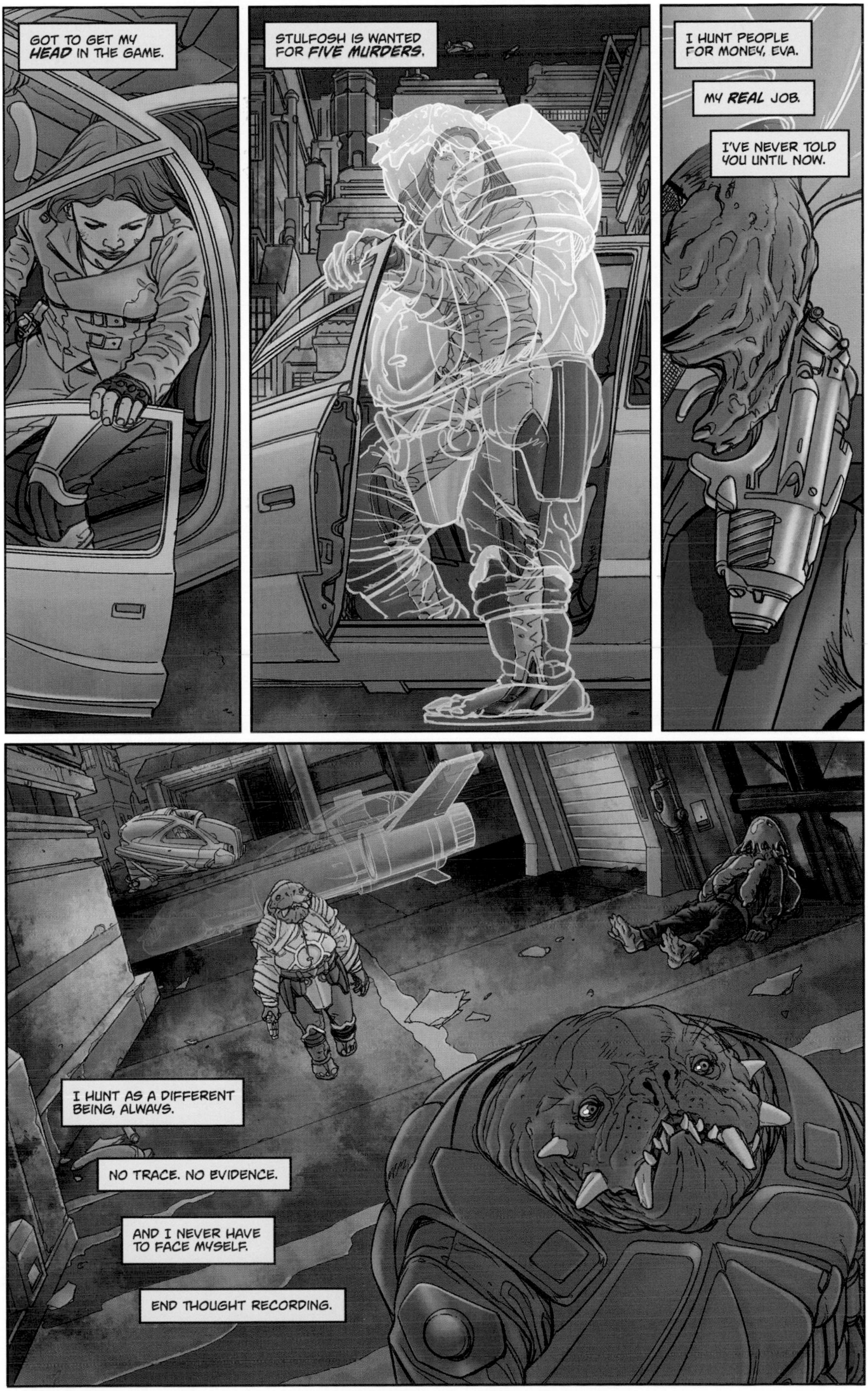
GOT TO GET MY HEAD IN THE GAME.
STULFOSH IS WANTED FOR FIVE MURDERS.
I HUNT PEOPLE FOR MONEY, EVA.
MY REAL JOB.
I'VE NEVER TOLD YOU UNTIL NOW.
I HUNT AS A DIFFERENT BEING, ALWAYS.
NO TRACE. NO EVIDENCE.
AND I NEVER HAVE TO FACE MYSELF.
END THOUGHT RECORDING.

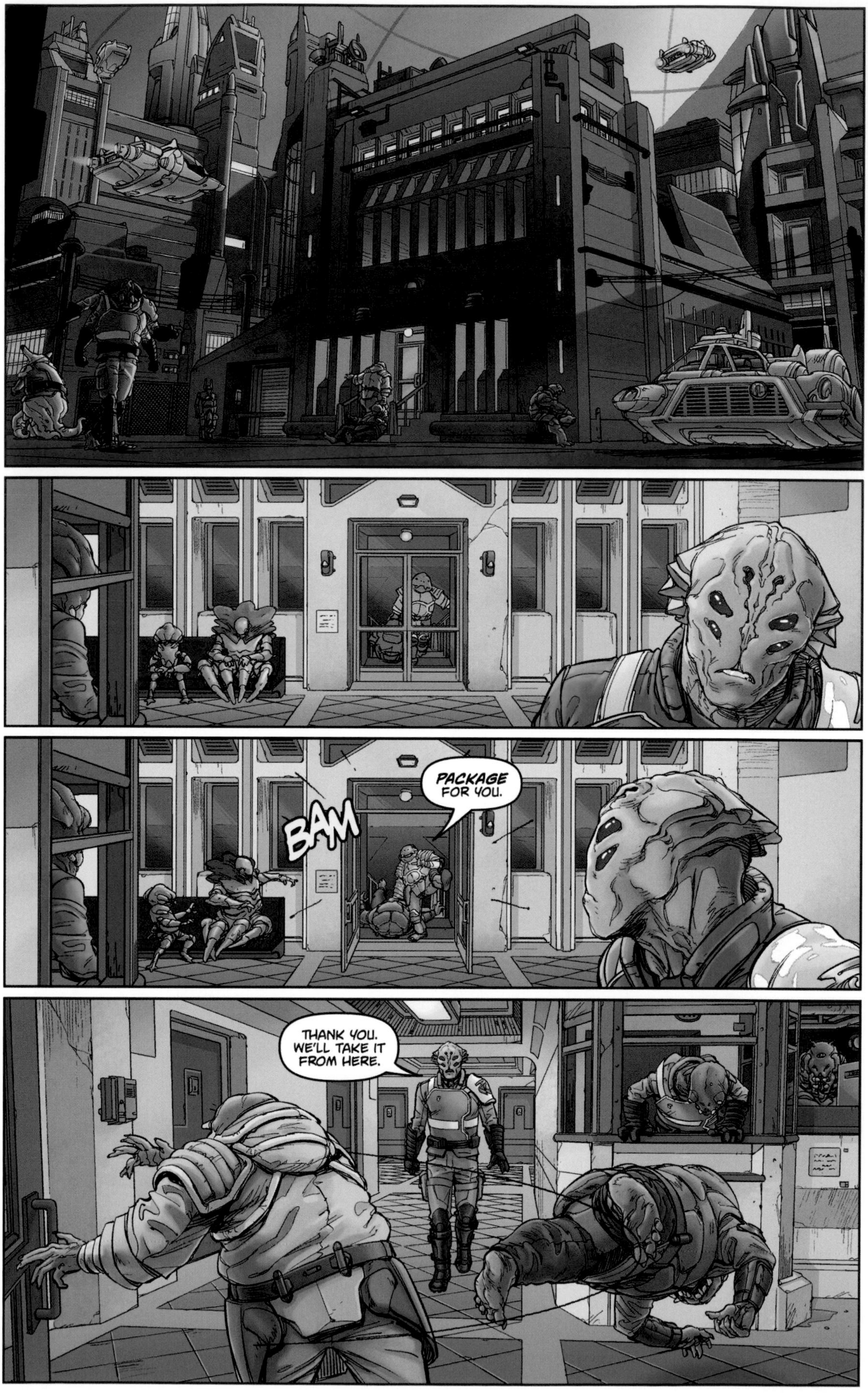
BAM
PACKAGE FOR YOU.
THANK YOU. WE'LL TAKE IT FROM HERE.

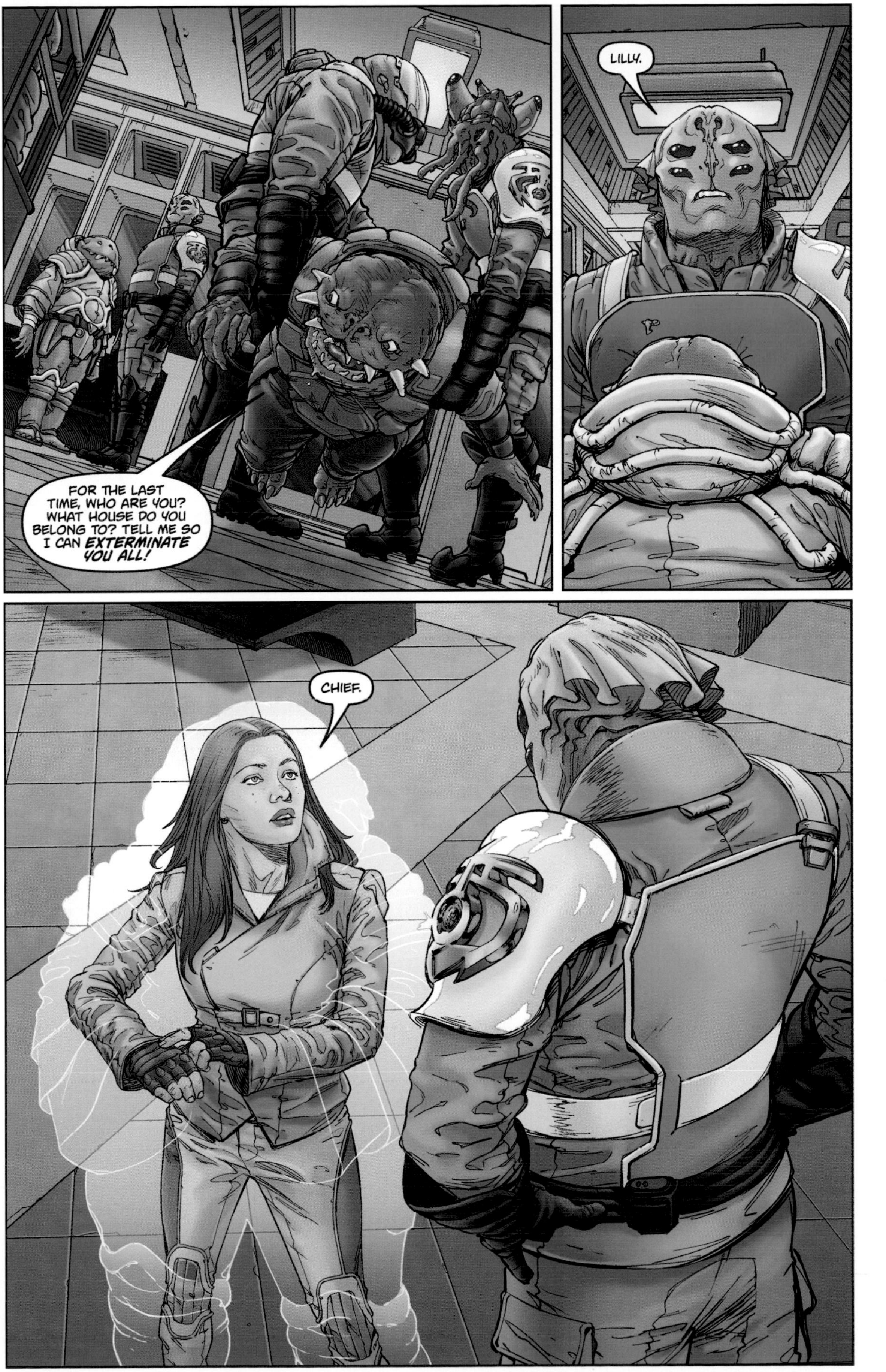
FOR THE LAST TIME, WHO ARE YOU? WHAT HOUSE DO YOU BELONG TO? TELL ME SO I CAN *EXTERMINATE YOU ALL!*
LILLY.
CHIEF.

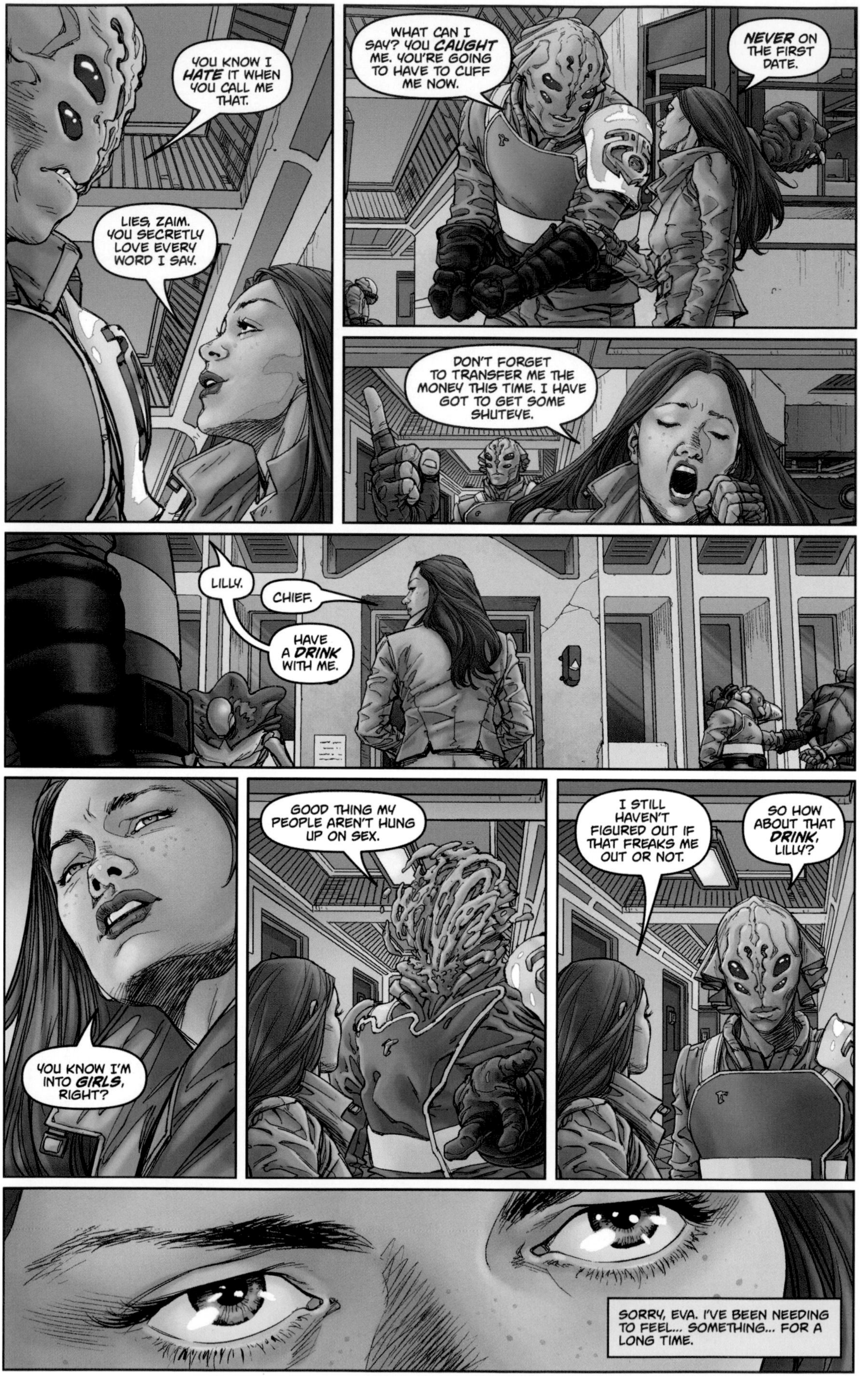
YOU KNOW I HATE IT WHEN YOU CALL ME THAT.
LIES, ZAIM. YOU SECRETLY LOVE EVERY WORD I SAY.
WHAT CAN I SAY? YOU CAUGHT ME. YOU'RE GOING TO HAVE TO CUFF ME NOW.
NEVER ON THE FIRST DATE.
DON'T FORGET TO TRANSFER ME THE MONEY THIS TIME. I HAVE GOT TO GET SOME SHUTEYE.
LILLY.
CHIEF.
HAVE A DRINK WITH ME.
YOU KNOW I'M INTO GIRLS, RIGHT?
GOOD THING MY PEOPLE AREN'T HUNG UP ON SEX.
I STILL HAVEN'T FIGURED OUT IF THAT FREAKS ME OUT OR NOT.
SO HOW ABOUT THAT DRINK, LILLY?
SORRY, EVA. I'VE BEEN NEEDING TO FEEL... SOMETHING... FOR A LONG TIME.

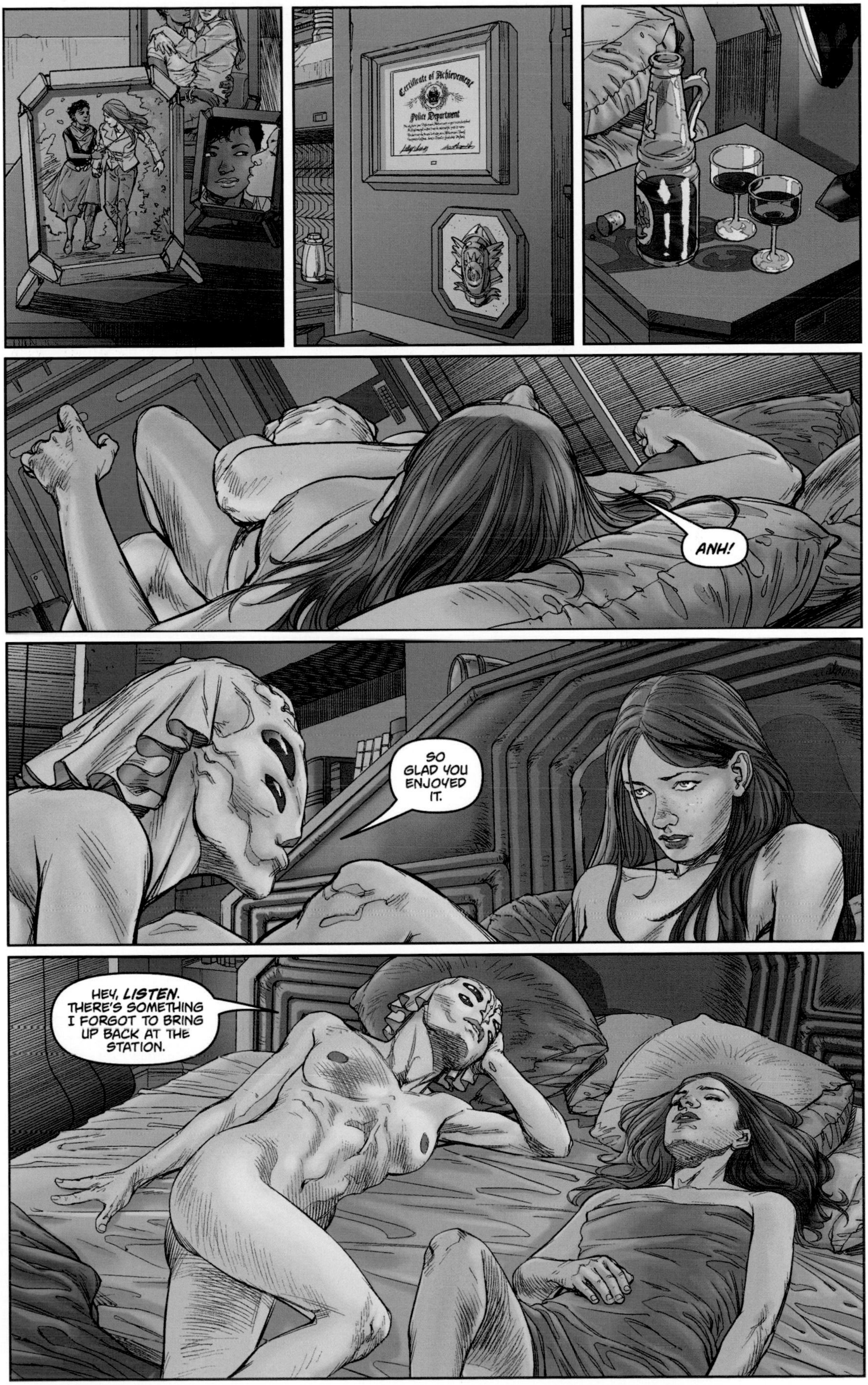
Certificate of Achievement
Police Department
ANH!
SO GLAD YOU ENJOYED IT.
HEY, LISTEN. THERE'S SOMETHING I FORGOT TO BRING UP BACK AT THE STATION.

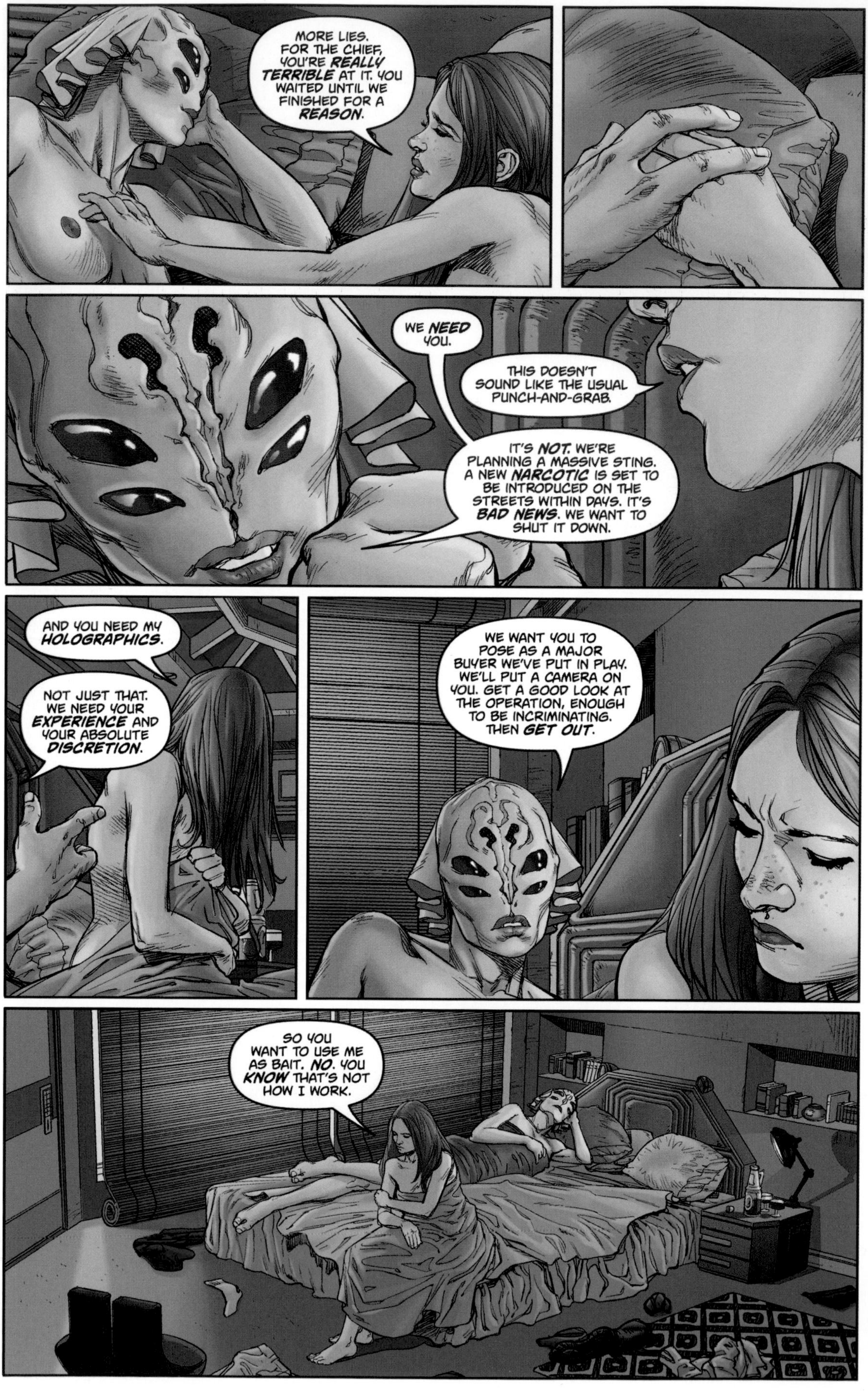

MORE LIES. FOR THE CHIEF, YOU'RE REALLY TERRIBLE AT IT. YOU WAITED UNTIL WE FINISHED FOR A REASON.
WE NEED YOU.
THIS DOESN'T SOUND LIKE THE USUAL PUNCH-AND-GRAB.
IT'S NOT. WE'RE PLANNING A MASSIVE STING. A NEW NARCOTIC IS SET TO BE INTRODUCED ON THE STREETS WITHIN DAYS. IT'S BAD NEWS. WE WANT TO SHUT IT DOWN.
AND YOU NEED MY HOLOGRAPHICS.
NOT JUST THAT. WE NEED YOUR EXPERIENCE AND YOUR ABSOLUTE DISCRETION.
WE WANT YOU TO POSE AS A MAJOR BUYER WE'VE PUT IN PLAY. WE'LL PUT A CAMERA ON YOU. GET A GOOD LOOK AT THE OPERATION, ENOUGH TO BE INCRIMINATING. THEN GET OUT.
SO YOU WANT TO USE ME AS BAIT. NO. YOU KNOW THAT'S NOT HOW I WORK.

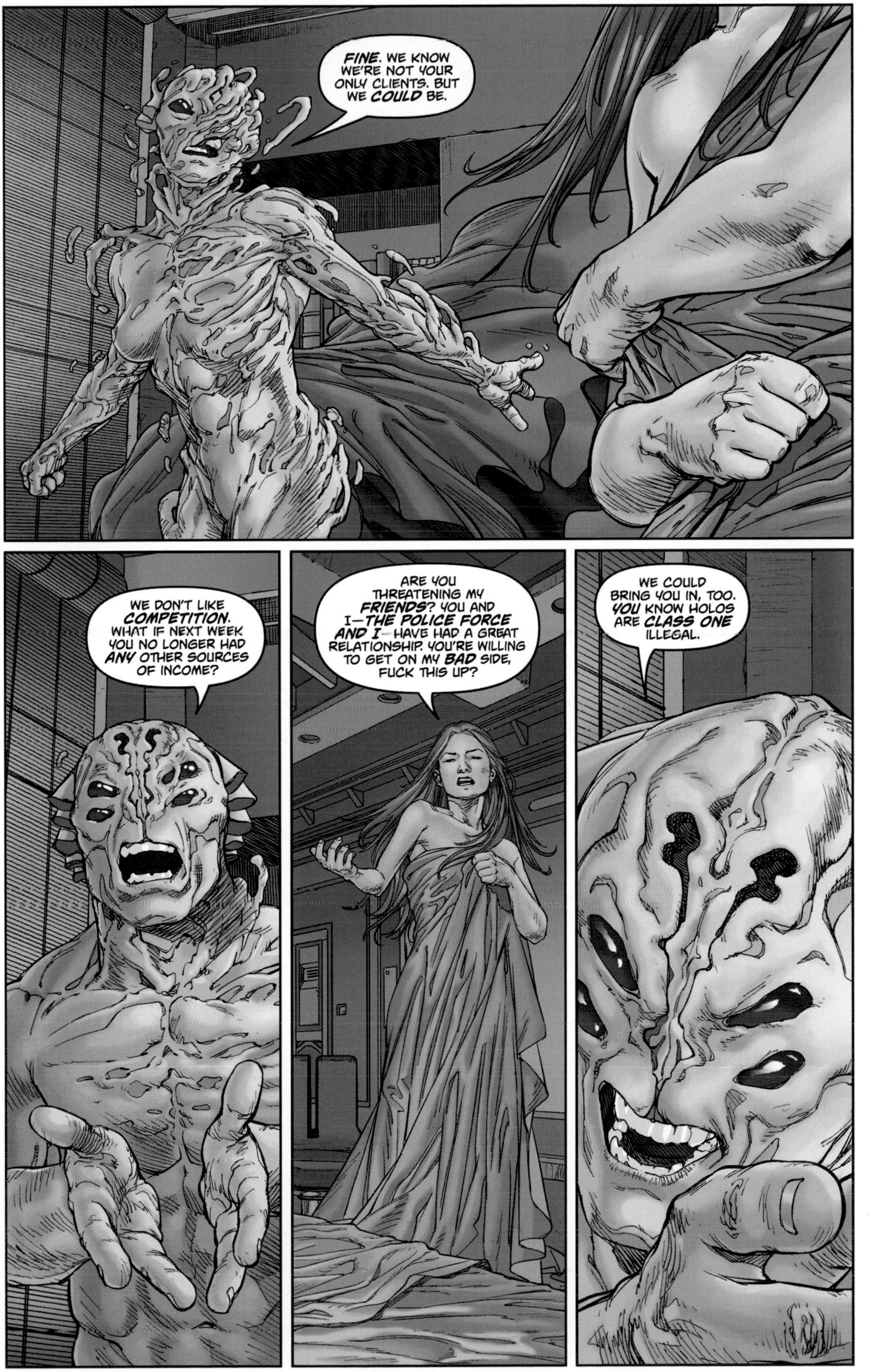
FINE. WE KNOW WE'RE NOT YOUR ONLY CLIENTS. BUT WE COULD BE.
WE DON'T LIKE COMPETITION. WHAT IF NEXT WEEK YOU NO LONGER HAD ANY OTHER SOURCES OF INCOME?
ARE YOU THREATENING MY FRIENDS? YOU AND I—THE POLICE FORCE AND I—HAVE HAD A GREAT RELATIONSHIP. YOU'RE WILLING TO GET ON MY BAD SIDE, FUCK THIS UP?
WE COULD BRING YOU IN, TOO. YOU KNOW HOLOS ARE CLASS ONE ILLEGAL.

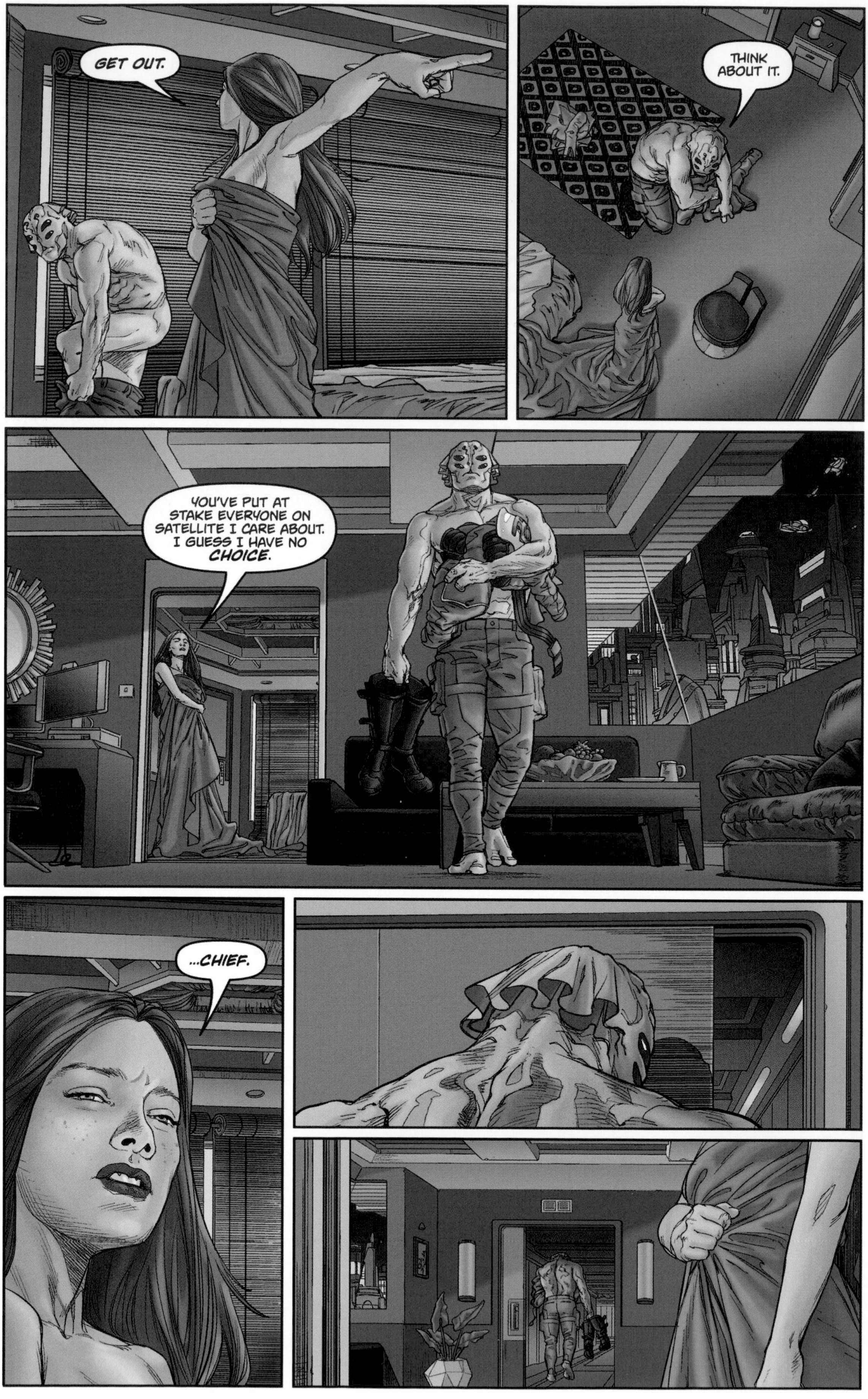
GET OUT.
THINK ABOUT IT.
YOU'VE PUT AT STAKE EVERYONE ON SATELLITE I CARE ABOUT. I GUESS I HAVE NO CHOICE.
...CHIEF.

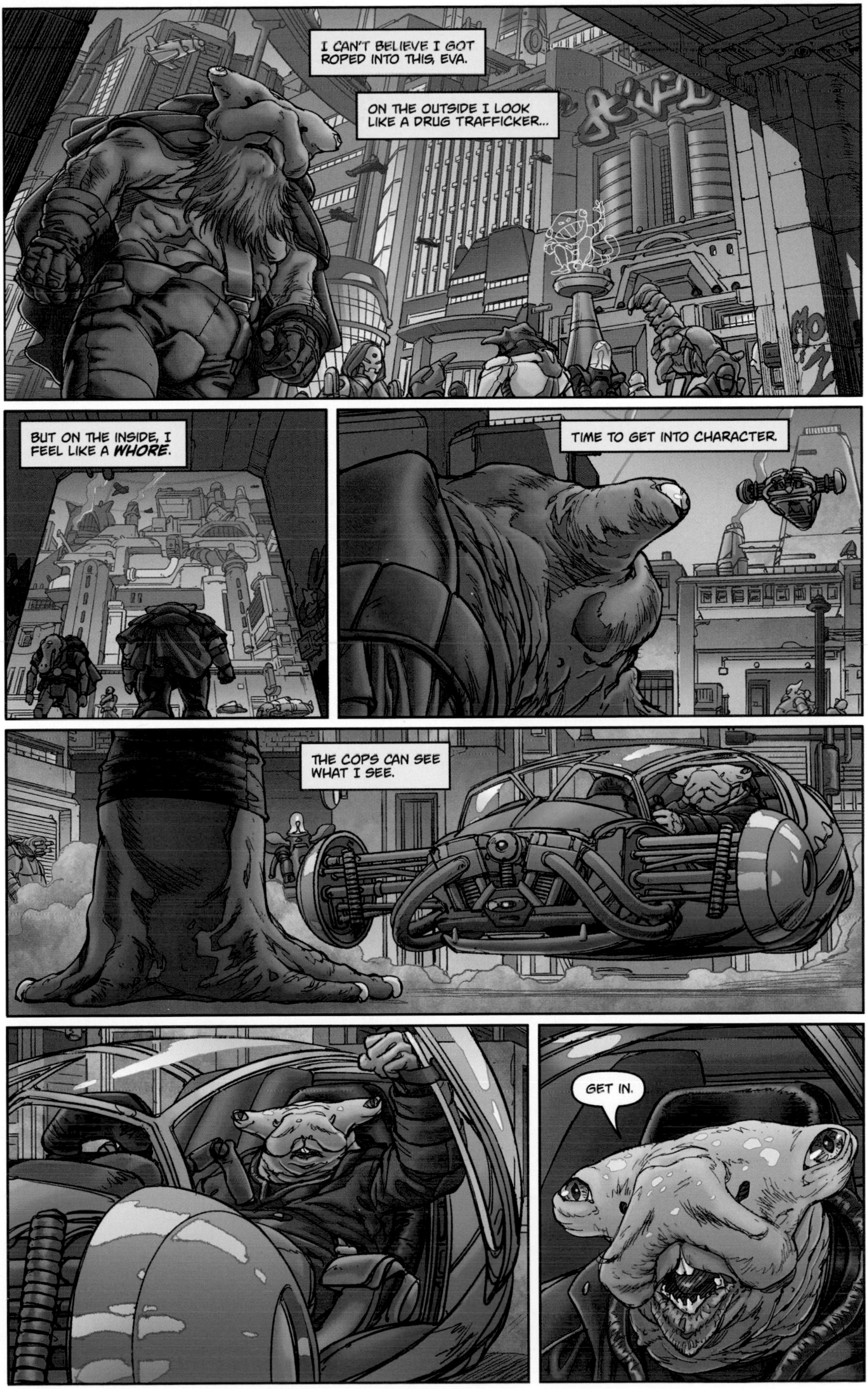
I CAN'T BELIEVE I GOT ROPED INTO THIS, EVA.
ON THE OUTSIDE I LOOK LIKE A DRUG TRAFFICKER...
BUT ON THE INSIDE, I FEEL LIKE A *WHORE*.
TIME TO GET INTO CHARACTER.
THE COPS CAN SEE WHAT I SEE.
GET IN.

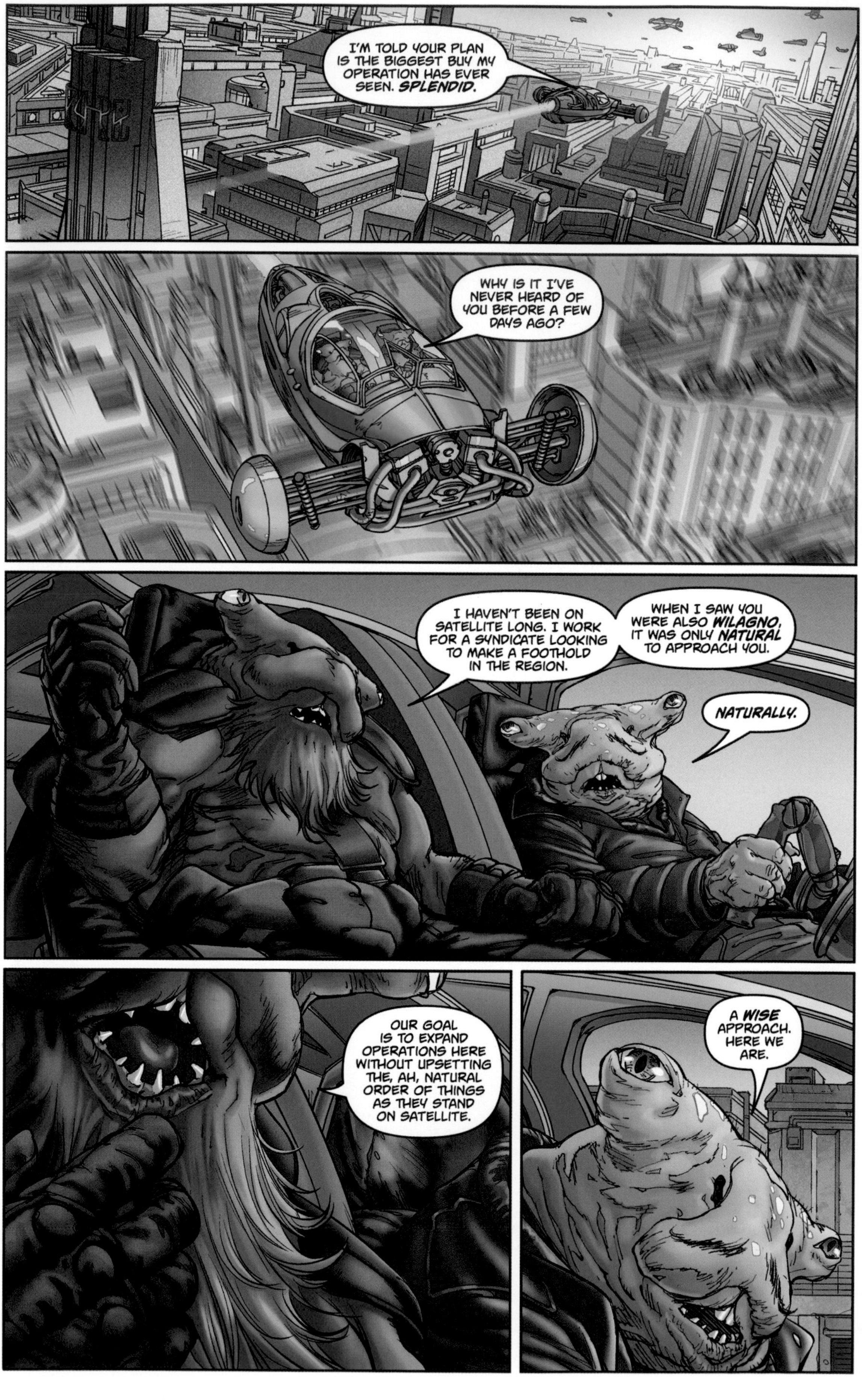
I'M TOLD YOUR PLAN IS THE BIGGEST BUY MY OPERATION HAS EVER SEEN. **SPLENDID.**
WHY IS IT I'VE NEVER HEARD OF YOU BEFORE A FEW DAYS AGO?
I HAVEN'T BEEN ON SATELLITE LONG. I WORK FOR A SYNDICATE LOOKING TO MAKE A FOOTHOLD IN THE REGION.
WHEN I SAW YOU WERE ALSO **WILAGNO**, IT WAS ONLY **NATURAL** TO APPROACH YOU.
NATURALLY.
OUR GOAL IS TO EXPAND OPERATIONS HERE WITHOUT UPSETTING THE, AH, NATURAL ORDER OF THINGS AS THEY STAND ON SATELLITE.
A **WISE** APPROACH. HERE WE ARE.

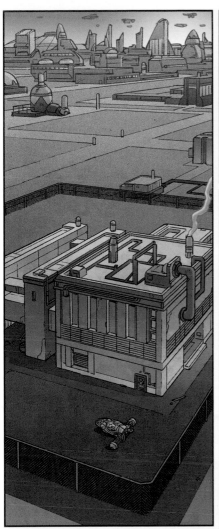

I THINK YOU'LL FIND ALL TO YOUR SATISFACTION.

I SHOULD *HOPE* SO. MY EMPLOYERS WON'T BE KEPT WAITING FOREVER

AS YOU CAN SEE, WE HAVE THE *MANPOWER.* WE'RE PRODUCING AROUND THE CLOCK IN TWELVE-HOUR SHIFTS. WE'VE GOT *QUITE A BIT* OF PRODUCT READY TO SHIP ALREADY.

OUR GOAL IS TO CONTINUALLY IMPROVE WORKFLOW TO MAXIMIZE PRODUCTION AND MINIMIZE OVERHEAD.

SLAVES, THEN.

CERTAINLY *NOT!* THESE ARE THE FAMILIES OF HARDENED CRIMINALS, WHO HAVE CONSCRIPTED THEIR PARENTS AND CHILDREN IN ORDER TO REDUCE THEIR SENTENCES.

WITH FULL COOPERATION FROM LOCAL *GOVERNMENTS,* OF COURSE.

WHETHER THEIR FAMILIES WANTED TO GO OR NOT.

THE *CHOICE* LIED IN WHETHER TO COMMIT THE INITIAL CRIME. WHAT YOU SEE IS SIMPLY... *CONSEQUENCES.*

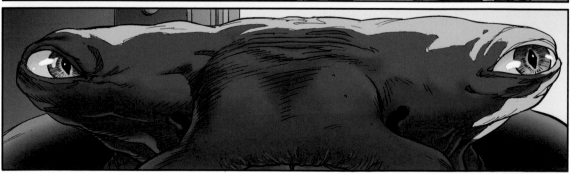

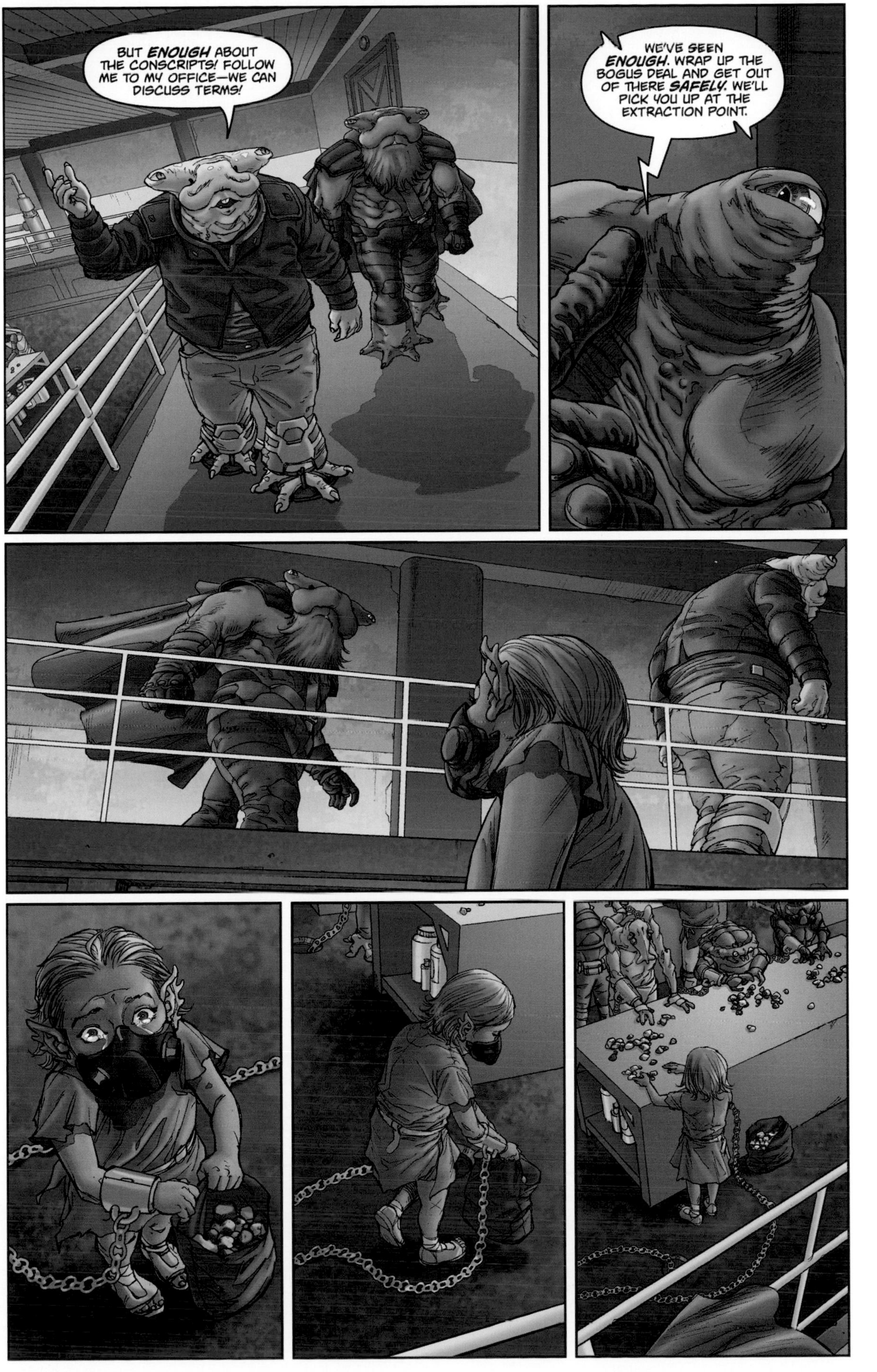
BUT ENOUGH ABOUT THE CONSCRIPTS! FOLLOW ME TO MY OFFICE—WE CAN DISCUSS TERMS!
WE'VE SEEN ENOUGH. WRAP UP THE BOGUS DEAL AND GET OUT OF THERE SAFELY. WE'LL PICK YOU UP AT THE EXTRACTION POINT.

THIS WAY.

NO NEED FOR THEM. I VALUE OUR *PRIVACY.*

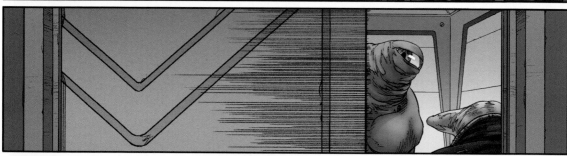

NOW THEN. YOU'VE SEEN WHAT WE CAN DO. LET'S TALK *TERMS.*

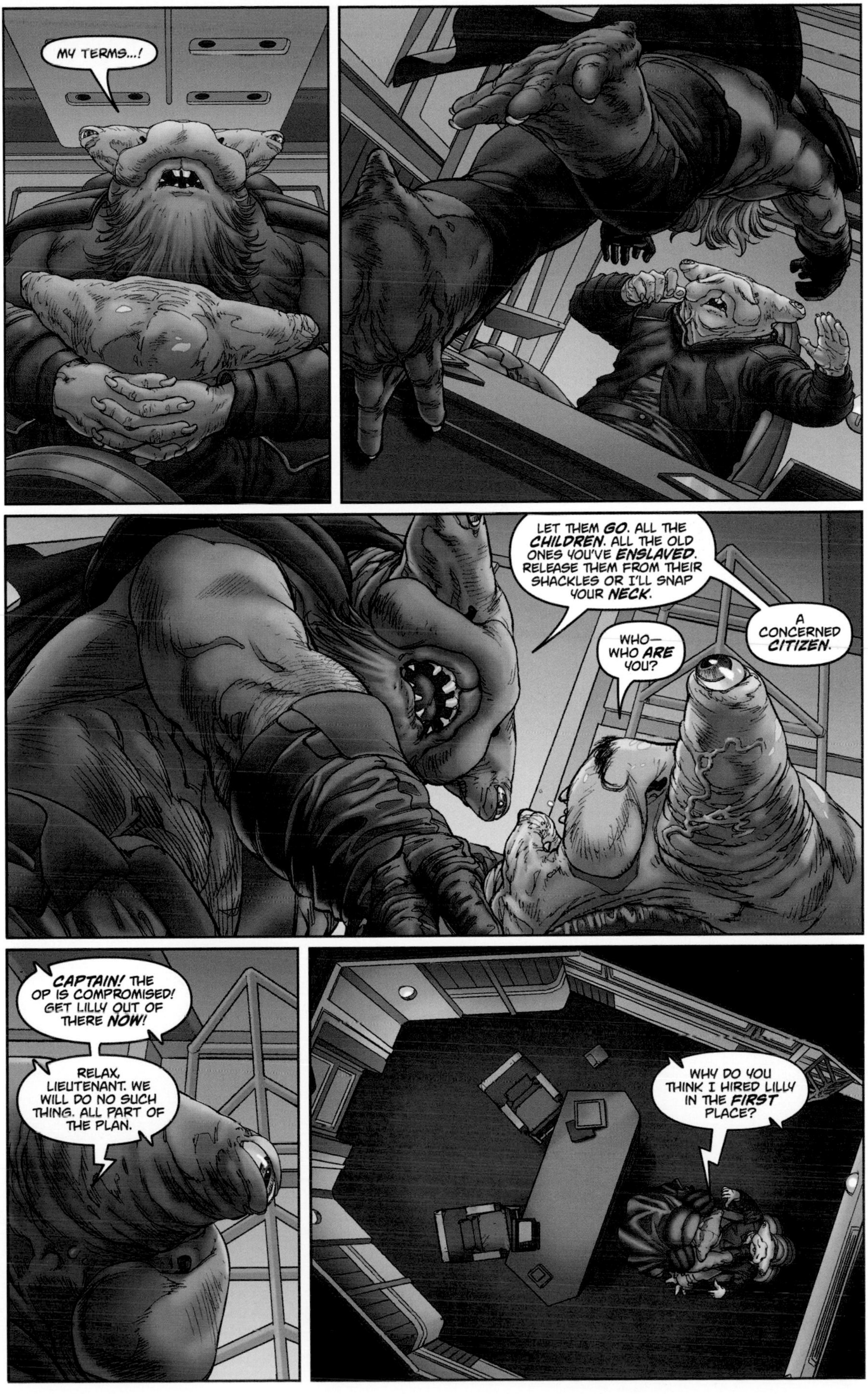
MY TERMS...!
LET THEM GO. ALL THE CHILDREN. ALL THE OLD ONES YOU'VE ENSLAVED. RELEASE THEM FROM THEIR SHACKLES OR I'LL SNAP YOUR NECK.
WHO— WHO ARE YOU?
A CONCERNED CITIZEN.
CAPTAIN! THE OP IS COMPROMISED! GET LILLY OUT OF THERE NOW!
RELAX, LIEUTENANT. WE WILL DO NO SUCH THING. ALL PART OF THE PLAN.
WHY DO YOU THINK I HIRED LILLY IN THE FIRST PLACE?

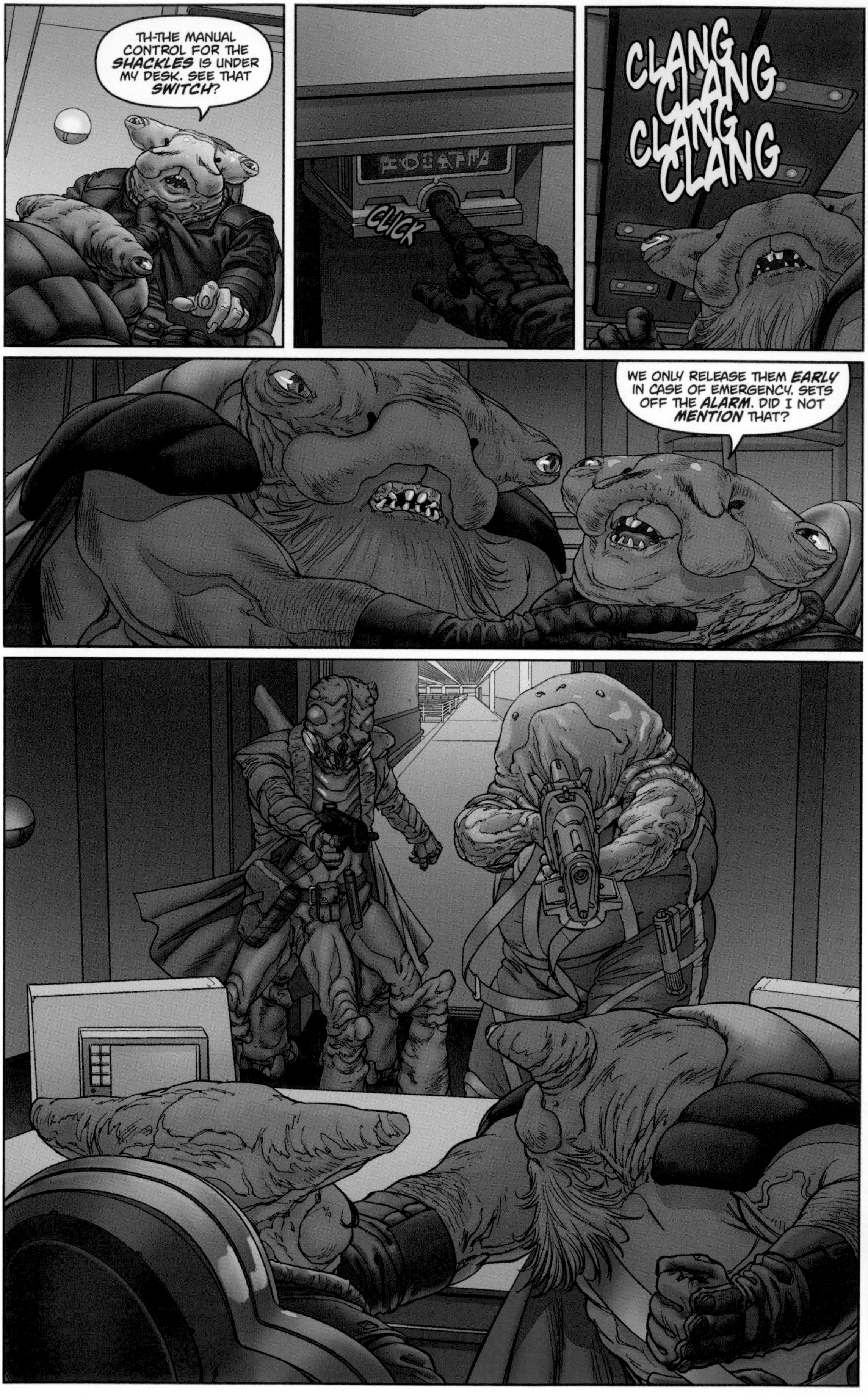
TH-THE MANUAL CONTROL FOR THE SHACKLES IS UNDER MY DESK. SEE THAT SWITCH?
CLICK
CLANG CLANG CLANG CLANG
WE ONLY RELEASE THEM EARLY IN CASE OF EMERGENCY. SETS OFF THE ALARM. DID I NOT MENTION THAT?

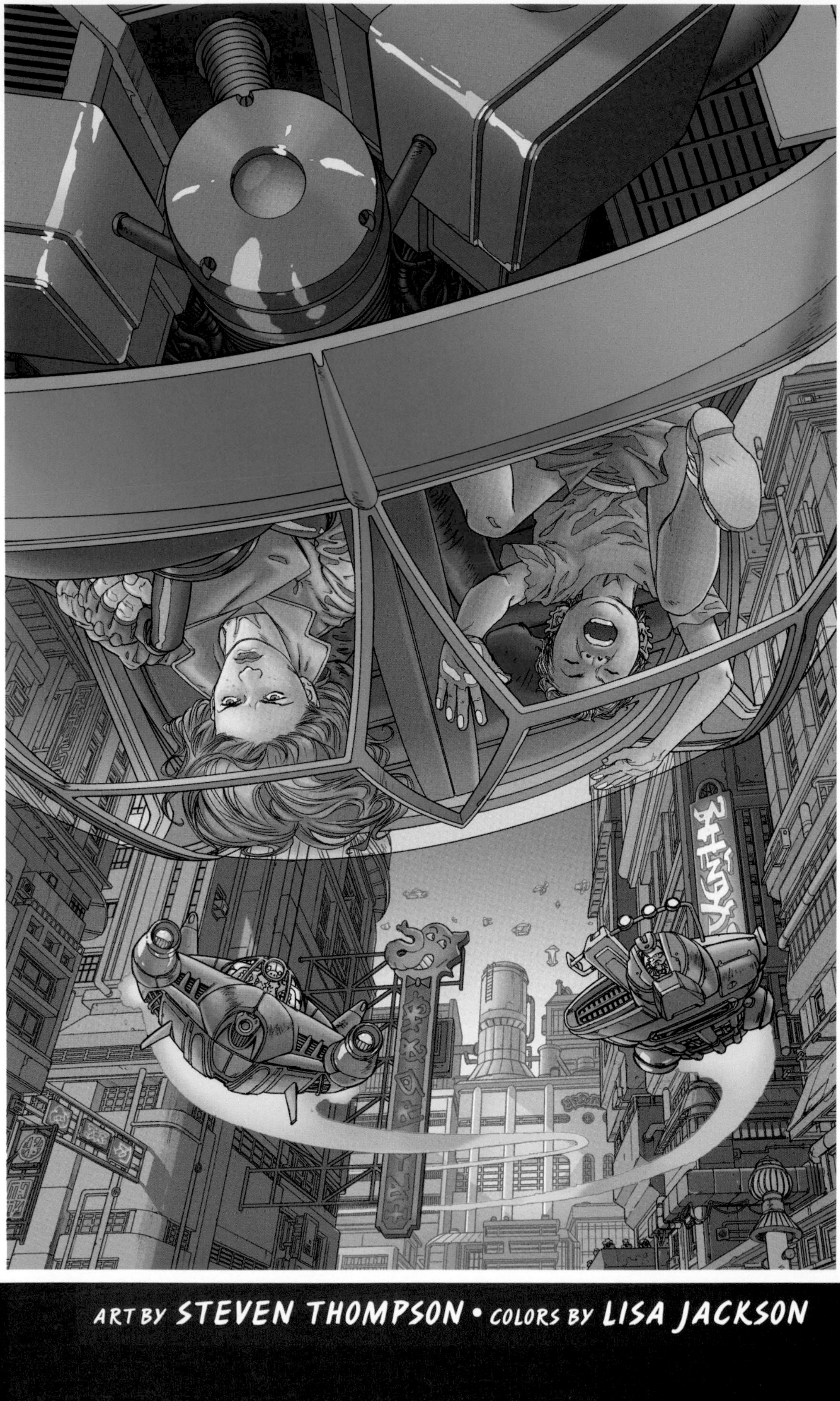

ART BY STEVEN THOMPSON • COLORS BY LISA JACKSON

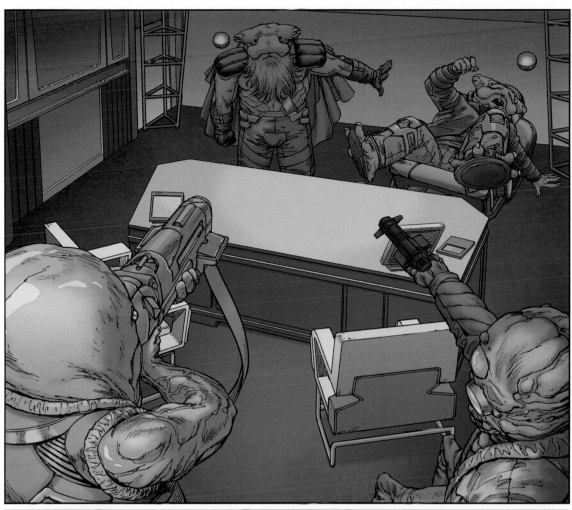

YOU ARE NO *WILAGNO*. FREEING SLAVES. *CONCERNED CITIZEN*. HAH! I'LL FEED YOUR BODY TO MY PET *GRAKH*. OPEN FIRE.

I'VE GOT *ONE* CHANCE AT THIS, EVA.

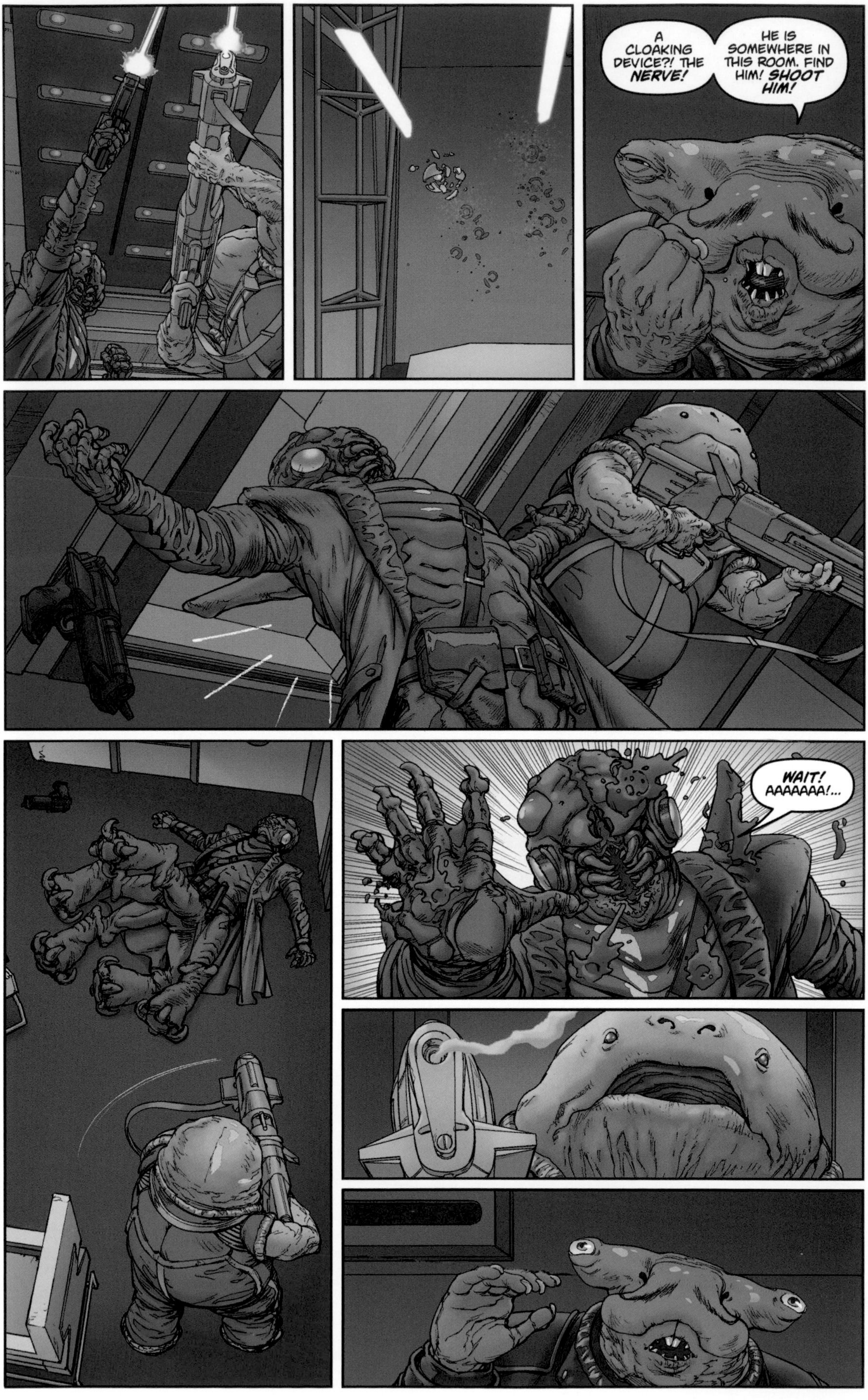
A CLOAKING DEVICE?! THE *NERVE!*
HE IS SOMEWHERE IN THIS ROOM. FIND HIM! ***SHOOT HIM!***
WAIT! AAAAAAA!...

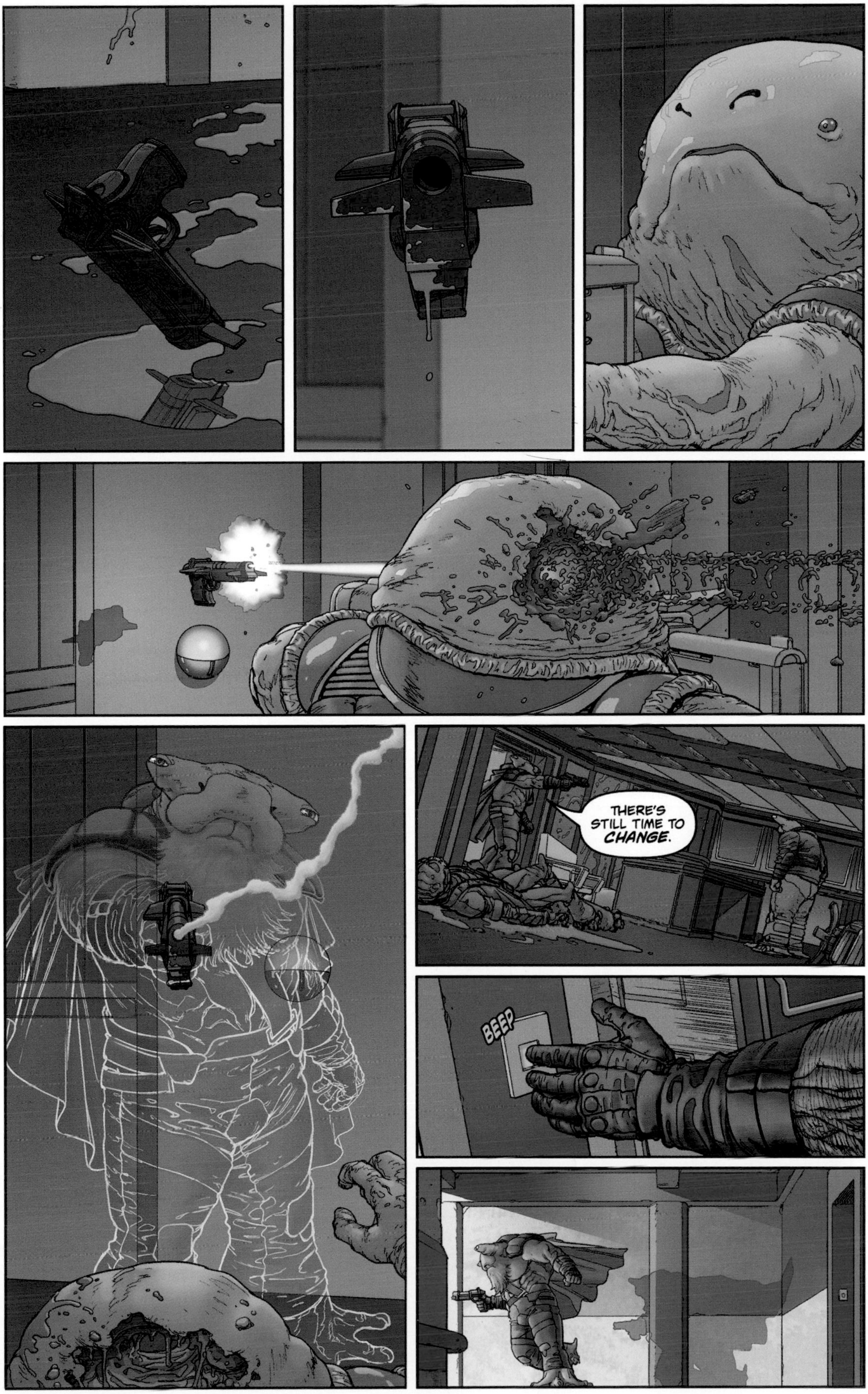
THERE'S STILL TIME TO CHANGE.
BEEP

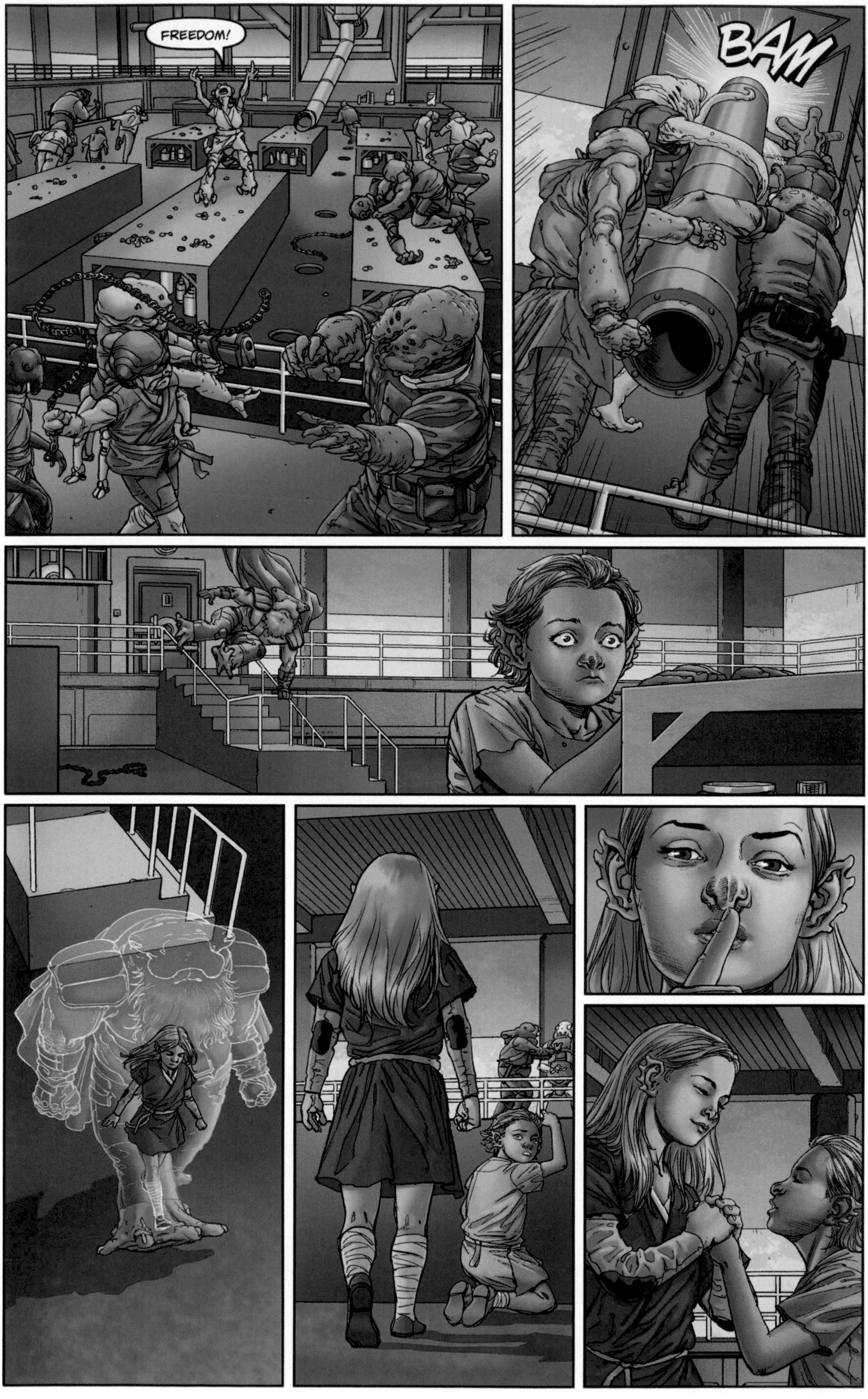
FREEDOM!
BAM

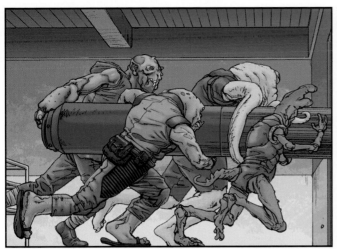

CRACK

CHIEF. CHIEF!
COME IN.

CHIEF!

...

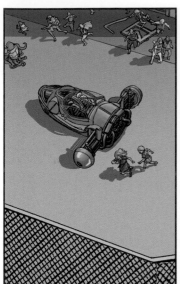

DON'T BE ALARMED.

FINE *MOTOR SKILLS* ARE DIFFICULT WHEN YOU CAN'T SEE YOUR OWN *HANDS*.

SHIT. SHOULDA *KILLED* HIM.

BUT YOU *DIDN'T*.

NO. HE WAS UNARMED. I—I'M NOT READY TO CROSS THAT LINE. NOT *YET*.

I KNEW I TRUSTED YOU FOR A REASON.

ZZT

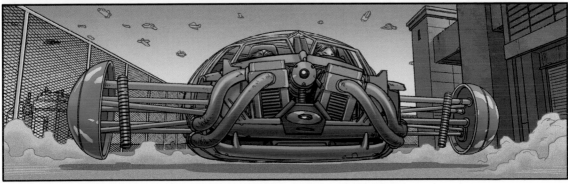

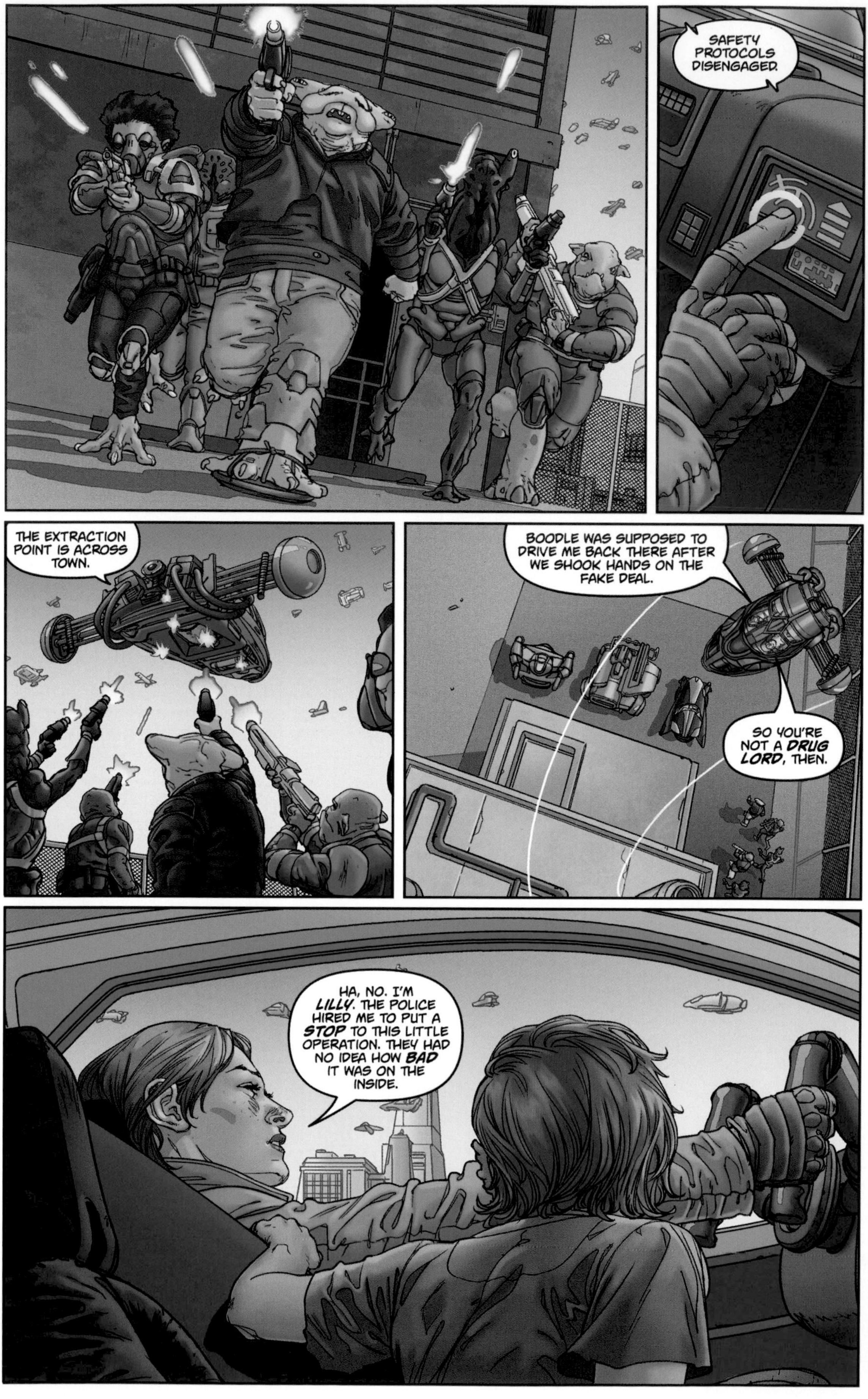
SAFETY PROTOCOLS DISENGAGED.
THE EXTRACTION POINT IS ACROSS TOWN.
BOODLE WAS SUPPOSED TO DRIVE ME BACK THERE AFTER WE SHOOK HANDS ON THE FAKE DEAL.
SO YOU'RE NOT A DRUG LORD, THEN.
HA, NO. I'M LILLY. THE POLICE HIRED ME TO PUT A STOP TO THIS LITTLE OPERATION. THEY HAD NO IDEA HOW BAD IT WAS ON THE INSIDE.

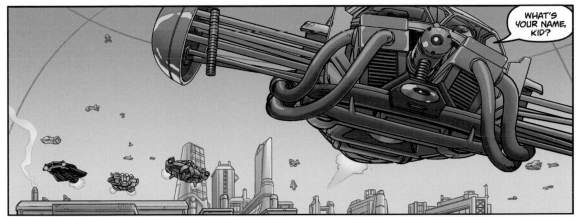

WHAT'S YOUR NAME, KID?

JOULYA.

I REMEMBER YOU. YOUR AUNT PAHT AND UNCLE DE'VON ARE *FRIENDS* OF MINE.

I DROVE THEIR *WEDDING* TAXI. THEY THOUGHT THE TIN CANS I TIED ON THE BACK WERE *COOL* AND *EXOTIC*.

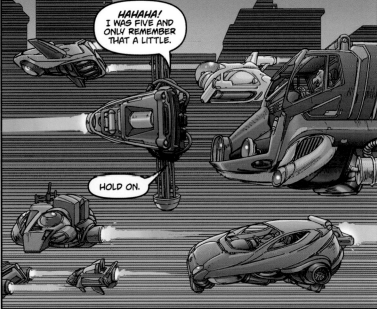

HAHAHA! I WAS FIVE AND ONLY REMEMBER THAT A LITTLE.

HOLD ON.

BOOM

THAT'S ONE.

LILLY!

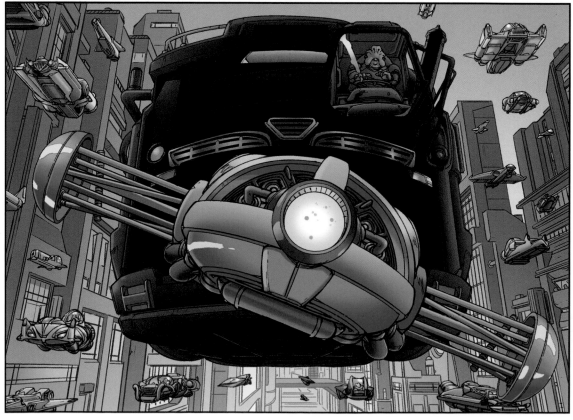

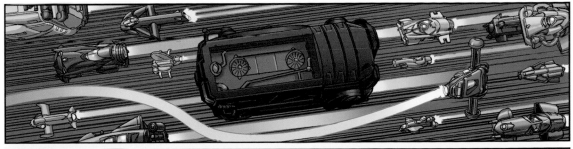

OW! FUCK!

ARE YOU *OK*, LILLY?

YEAH. WHY COULDN'T BOODLE HAVE HAD BETTER TASTE IN CARS? MODELS WITH *GUN-PROOF GLASS*, THAT'S WHAT I'M INTO.

I'VE GOT A PLAN.

IS IT *SCARY*?

ALWAYS. HOLD ON.

HEY. I'M NOT GOING TO LET ANYONE SHACKLE YOU AGAIN, OK?

I HOPE YOUR NIGHTMARES ARE *BETTER* AFTER THIS.

I GET NIGHTMARES. I'M IN CHAINS THERE, TOO.

I'M STILL WAITING FOR THEM TO GET BETTER MYSELF.

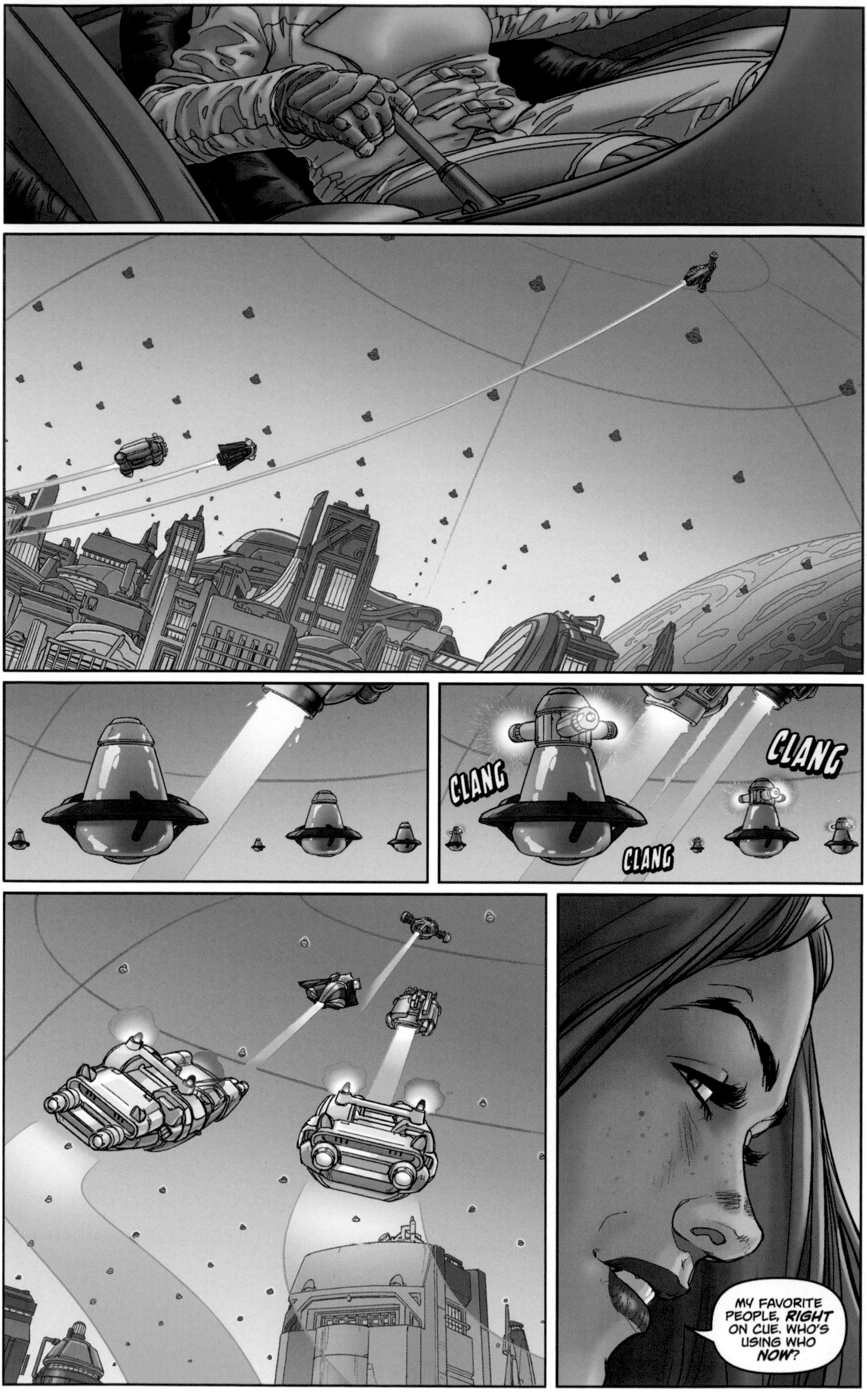
CLANG
CLANG
CLANG
MY FAVORITE PEOPLE, RIGHT ON CUE. WHO'S USING WHO NOW?

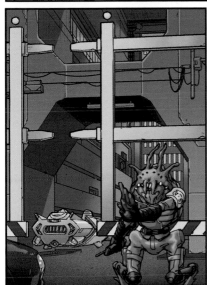

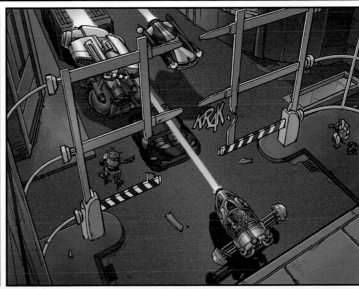

HOLY *SHIT!* CHIEF, ACTIVATE IT. *NOW!*

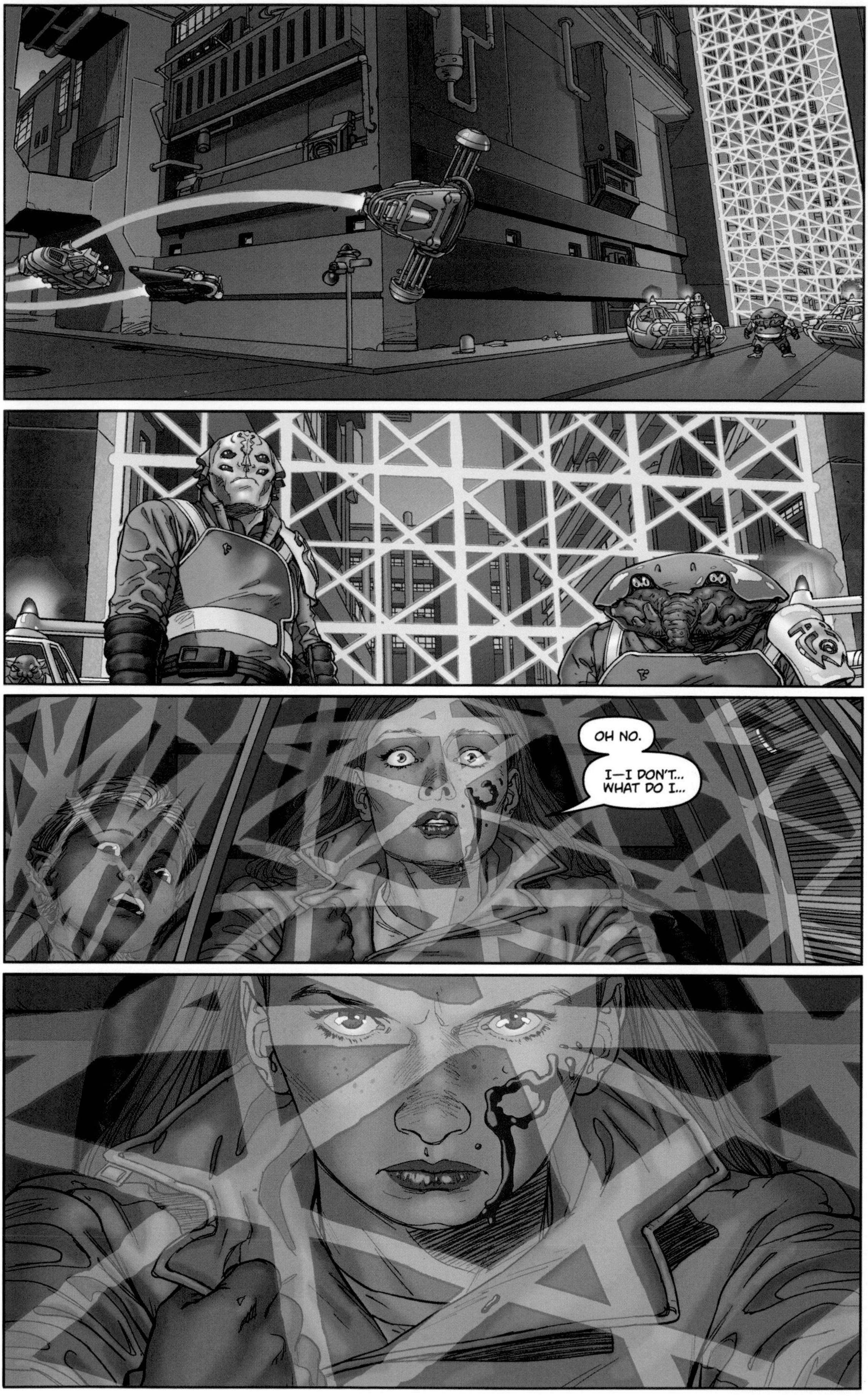
OH NO.
I—I DON'T... WHAT DO I...

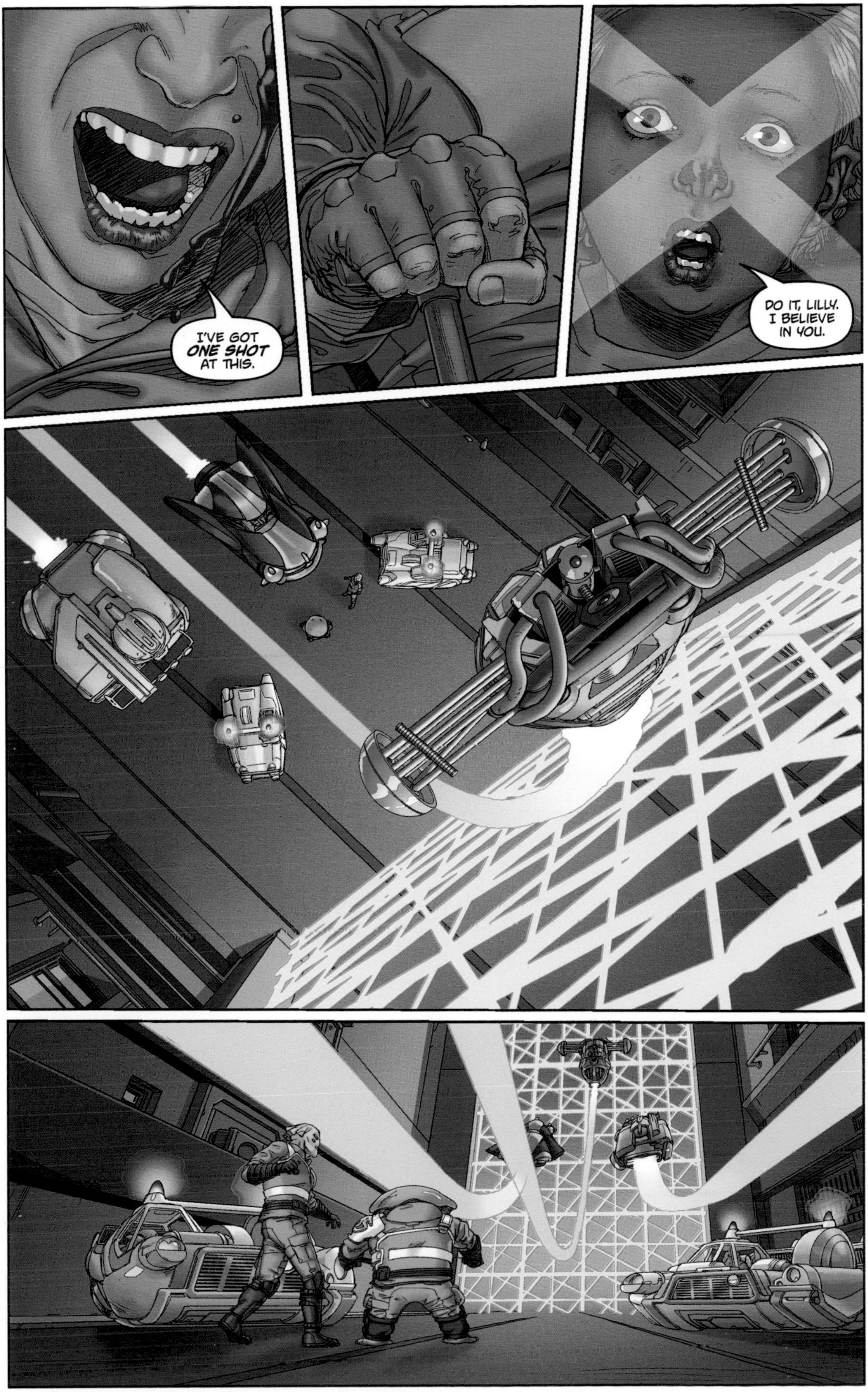
I'VE GOT ONE SHOT AT THIS.
DO IT, LILLY. I BELIEVE IN YOU.

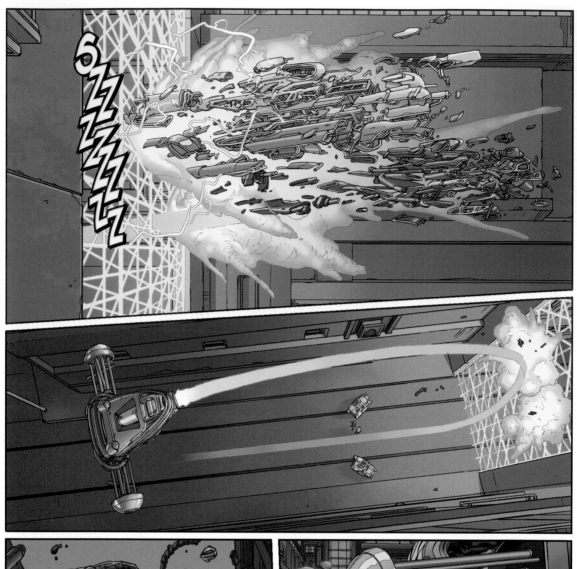

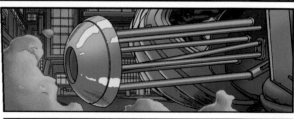

YOU DIDN'T *WASH UP* FOR ME? *SHOCKING.*

LILLY. WHAT... DID YOU *DO*?

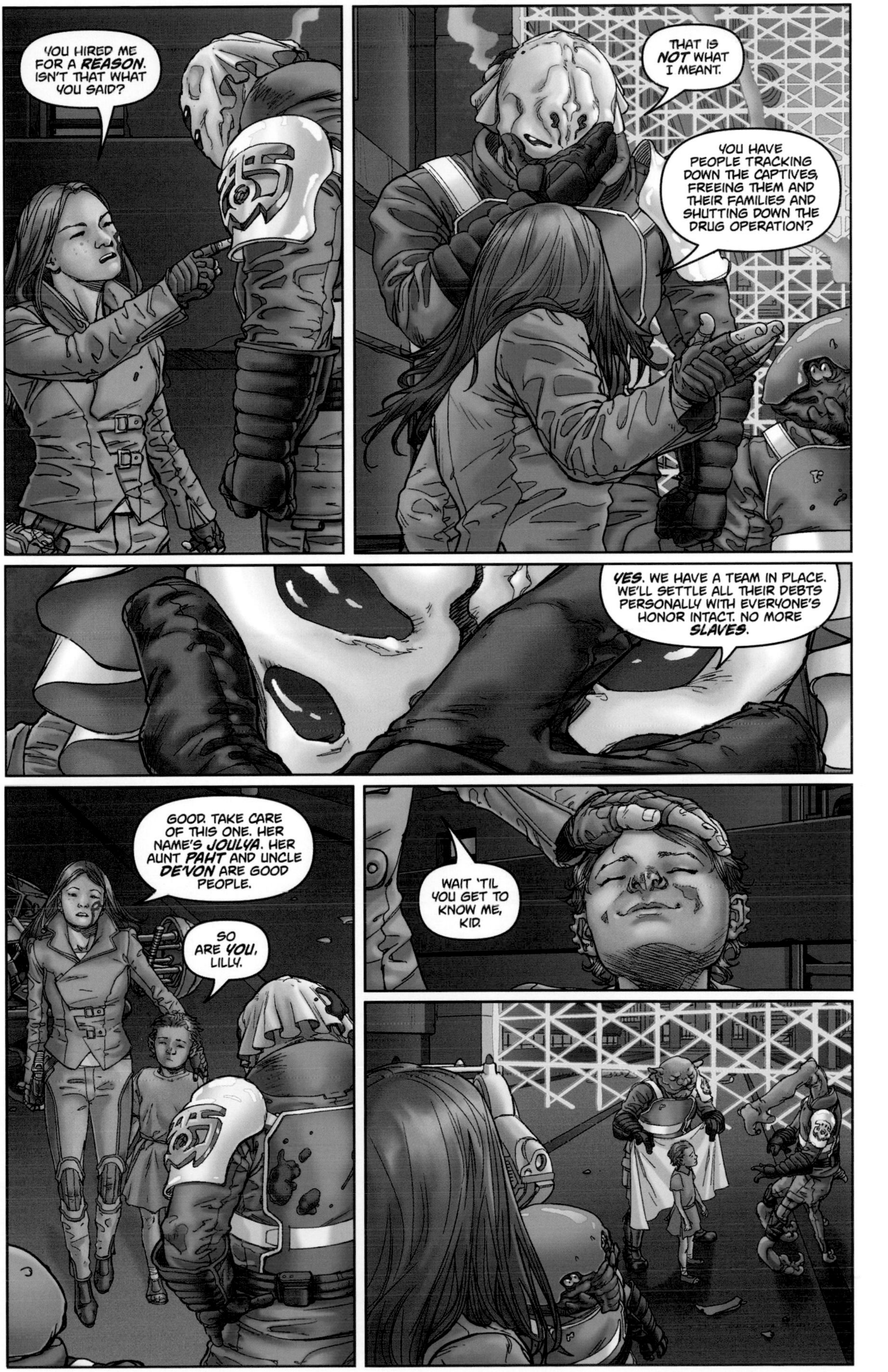
YOU HIRED ME FOR A REASON. ISN'T THAT WHAT YOU SAID?
THAT IS NOT WHAT I MEANT.
YOU HAVE PEOPLE TRACKING DOWN THE CAPTIVES, FREEING THEM AND THEIR FAMILIES AND SHUTTING DOWN THE DRUG OPERATION?
YES. WE HAVE A TEAM IN PLACE. WE'LL SETTLE ALL THEIR DEBTS PERSONALLY WITH EVERYONE'S HONOR INTACT. NO MORE SLAVES.
GOOD. TAKE CARE OF THIS ONE. HER NAME'S JOULYA. HER AUNT PAHT AND UNCLE DE'VON ARE GOOD PEOPLE.
SO ARE YOU, LILLY.
WAIT 'TIL YOU GET TO KNOW ME, KID.

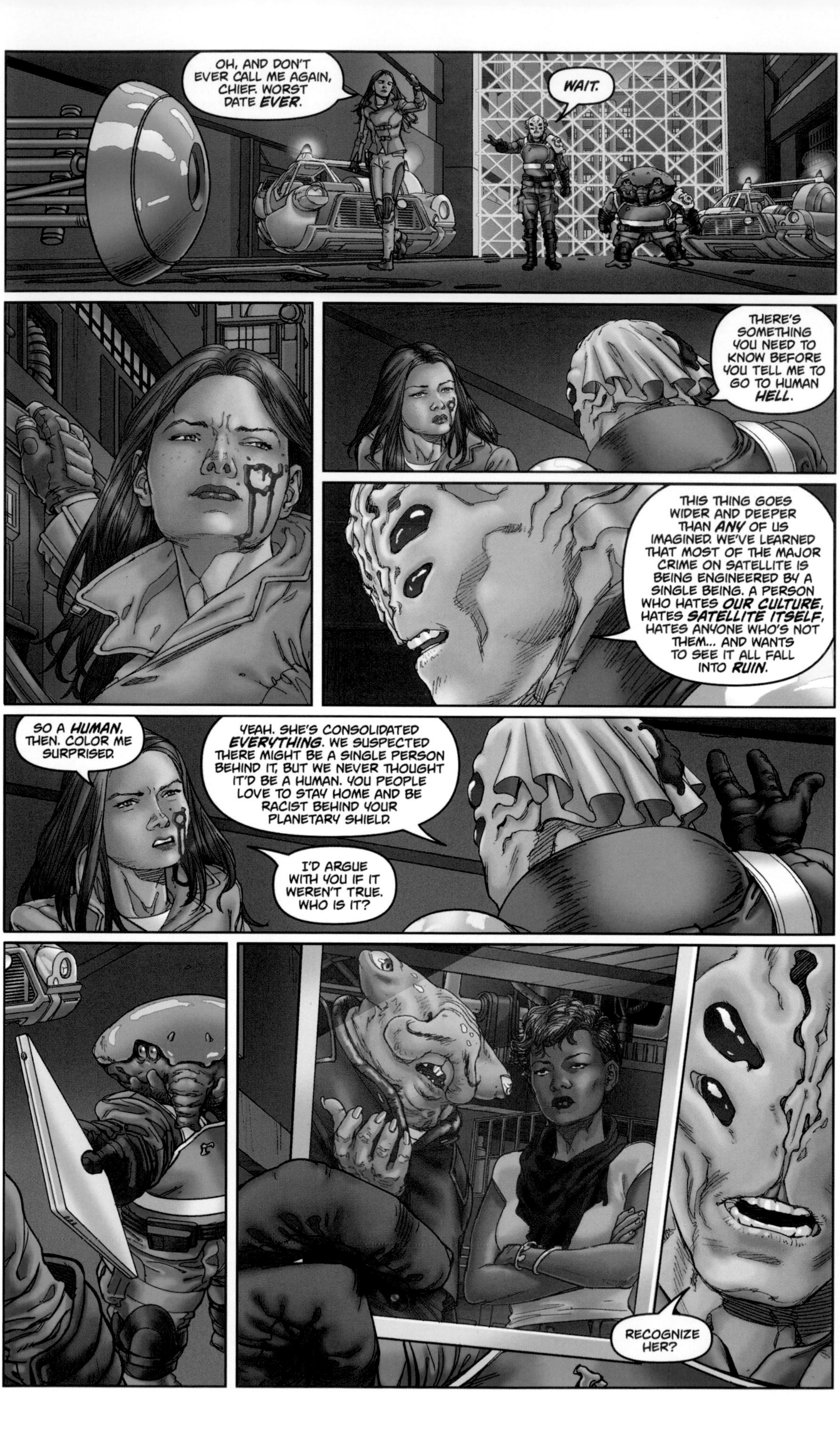
OH, AND DON'T EVER CALL ME AGAIN, CHIEF. WORST DATE EVER.
WAIT.
THERE'S SOMETHING YOU NEED TO KNOW BEFORE YOU TELL ME TO GO TO HUMAN HELL.
THIS THING GOES WIDER AND DEEPER THAN ANY OF US IMAGINED. WE'VE LEARNED THAT MOST OF THE MAJOR CRIME ON SATELLITE IS BEING ENGINEERED BY A SINGLE BEING. A PERSON WHO HATES OUR CULTURE, HATES SATELLITE ITSELF, HATES ANYONE WHO'S NOT THEM... AND WANTS TO SEE IT ALL FALL INTO RUIN.
SO A HUMAN, THEN. COLOR ME SURPRISED.
YEAH. SHE'S CONSOLIDATED EVERYTHING. WE SUSPECTED THERE MIGHT BE A SINGLE PERSON BEHIND IT, BUT WE NEVER THOUGHT IT'D BE A HUMAN. YOU PEOPLE LOVE TO STAY HOME AND BE RACIST BEHIND YOUR PLANETARY SHIELD.
I'D ARGUE WITH YOU IF IT WEREN'T TRUE. WHO IS IT?
RECOGNIZE HER?

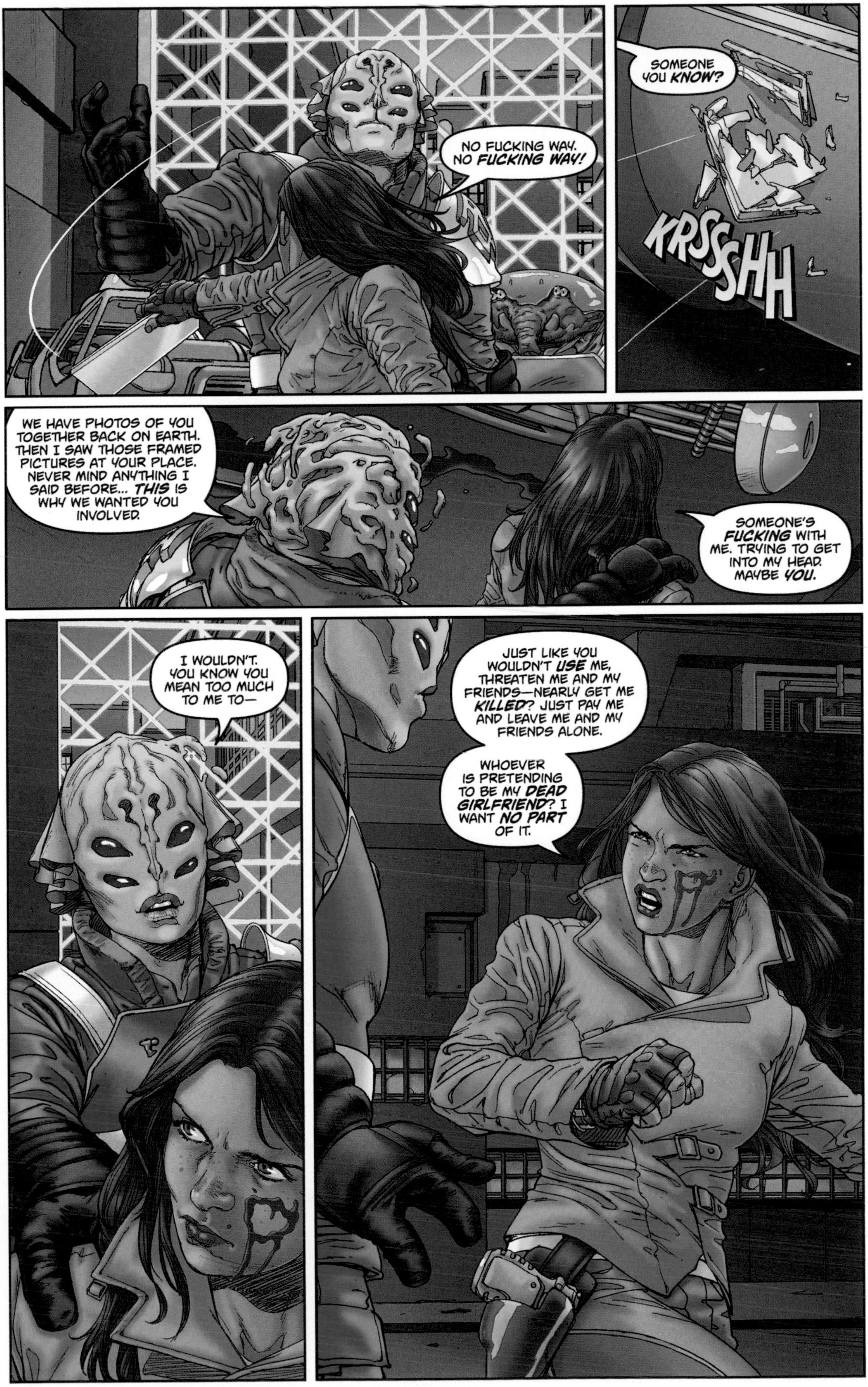
NO FUCKING WAY. NO FUCKING WAY!
SOMEONE YOU KNOW?
KRSSSHH
WE HAVE PHOTOS OF YOU TOGETHER BACK ON EARTH. THEN I SAW THOSE FRAMED PICTURES AT YOUR PLACE. NEVER MIND ANYTHING I SAID BEFORE... THIS IS WHY WE WANTED YOU INVOLVED.
SOMEONE'S FUCKING WITH ME. TRYING TO GET INTO MY HEAD. MAYBE YOU.
I WOULDN'T. YOU KNOW YOU MEAN TOO MUCH TO ME TO—
JUST LIKE YOU WOULDN'T USE ME, THREATEN ME AND MY FRIENDS—NEARLY GET ME KILLED? JUST PAY ME AND LEAVE ME AND MY FRIENDS ALONE.
WHOEVER IS PRETENDING TO BE MY DEAD GIRLFRIEND? I WANT NO PART OF IT.

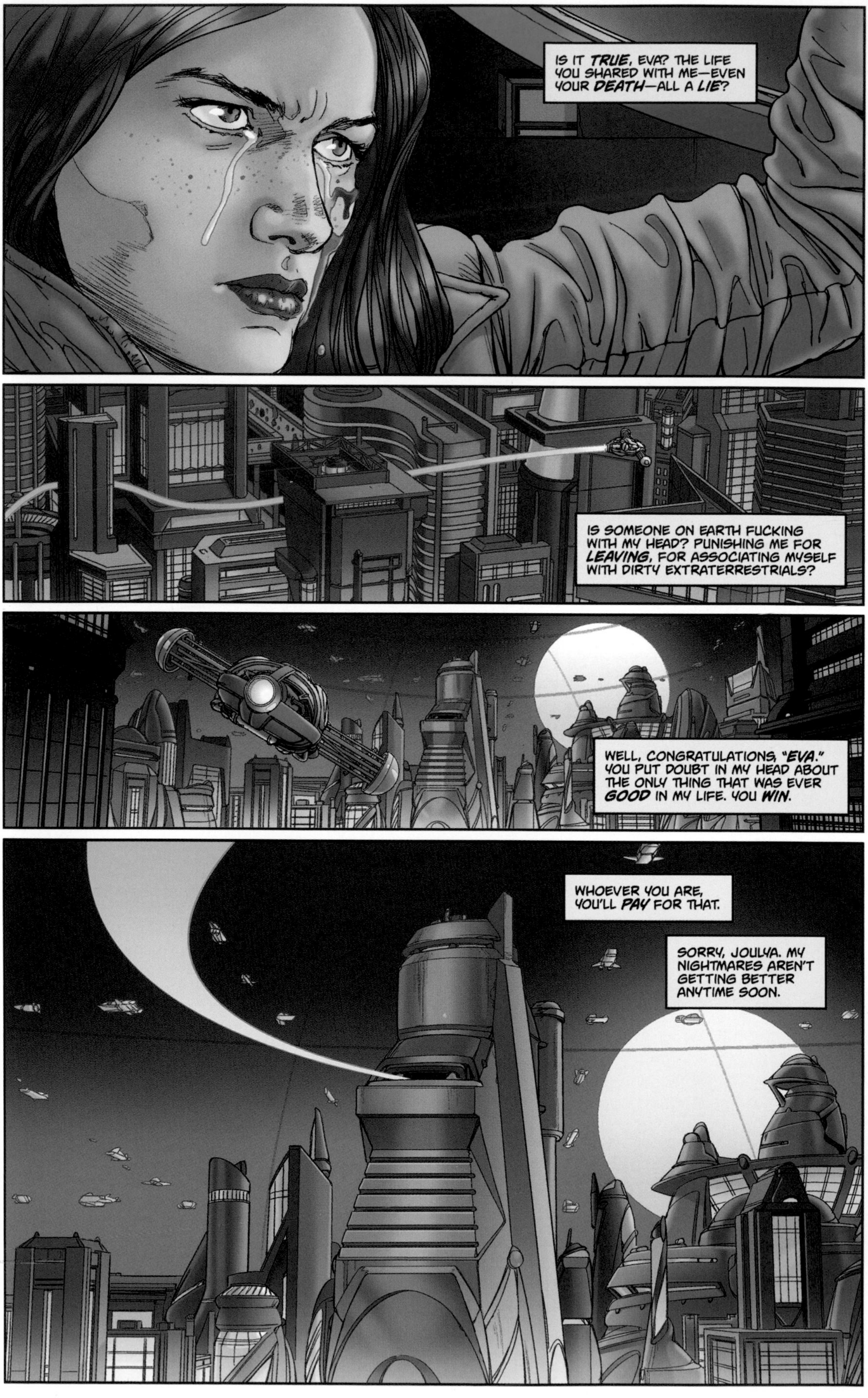
IS IT TRUE, EVA? THE LIFE YOU SHARED WITH ME—EVEN YOUR DEATH—ALL A LIE?
IS SOMEONE ON EARTH FUCKING WITH MY HEAD? PUNISHING ME FOR LEAVING, FOR ASSOCIATING MYSELF WITH DIRTY EXTRATERRESTRIALS?
WELL, CONGRATULATIONS, "EVA." YOU PUT DOUBT IN MY HEAD ABOUT THE ONLY THING THAT WAS EVER GOOD IN MY LIFE. YOU WIN.
WHOEVER YOU ARE, YOU'LL PAY FOR THAT.
SORRY, JOULYA. MY NIGHTMARES AREN'T GETTING BETTER ANYTIME SOON.

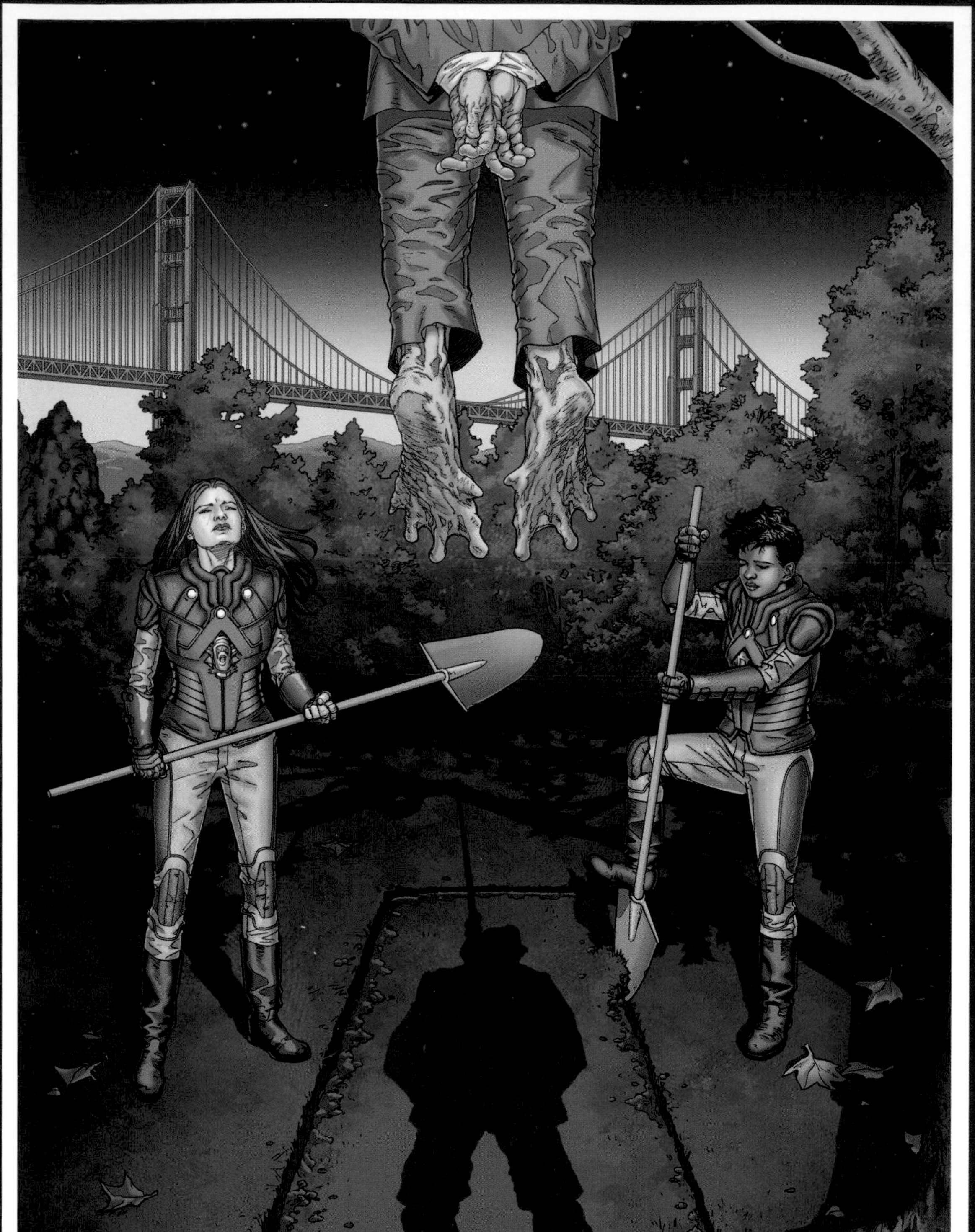

ART BY STEVEN THOMPSON • COLORS BY LISA JACKSON

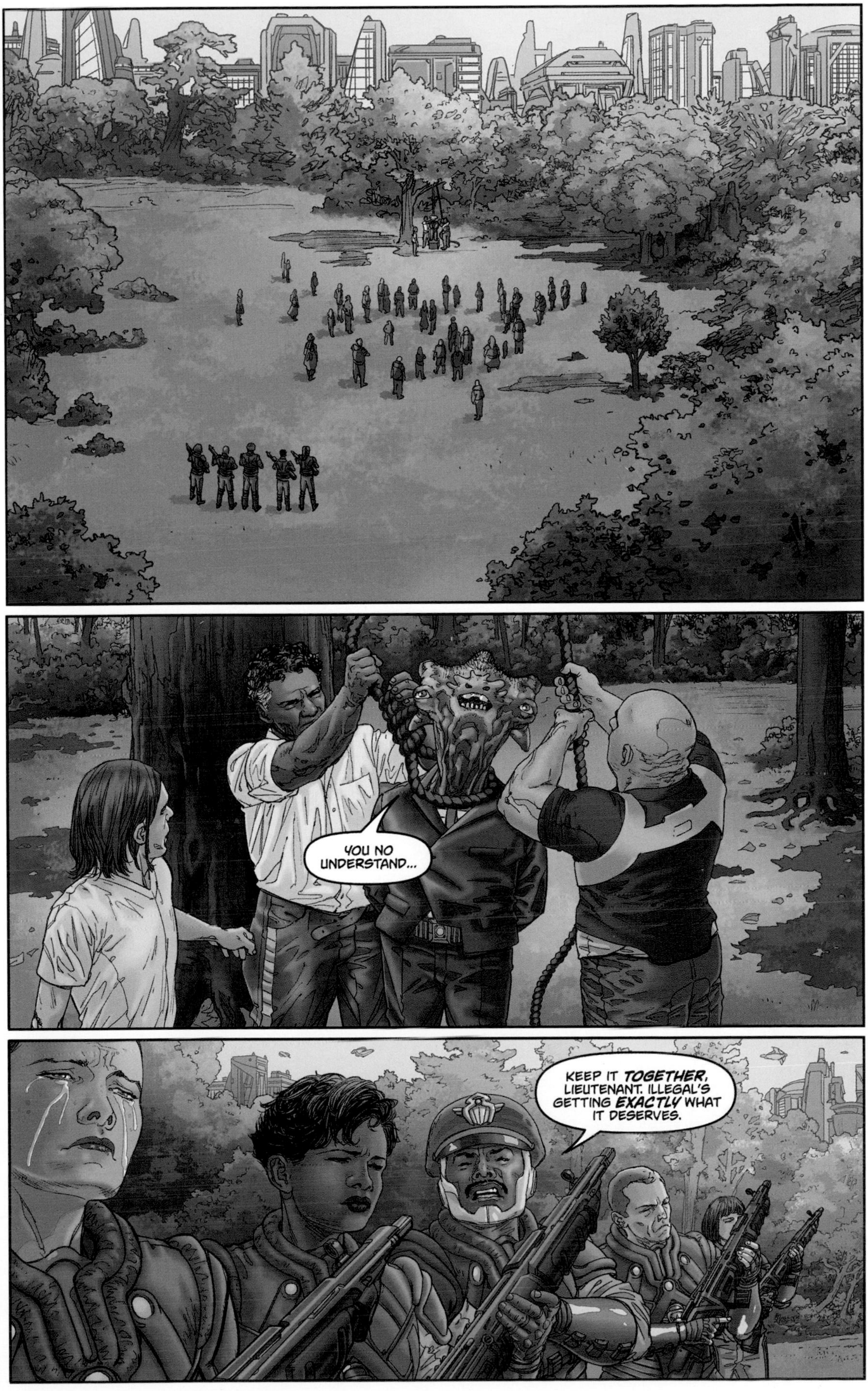
YOU NO UNDERSTAND...
KEEP IT TOGETHER, LIEUTENANT. ILLEGAL'S GETTING EXACTLY WHAT IT DESERVES.

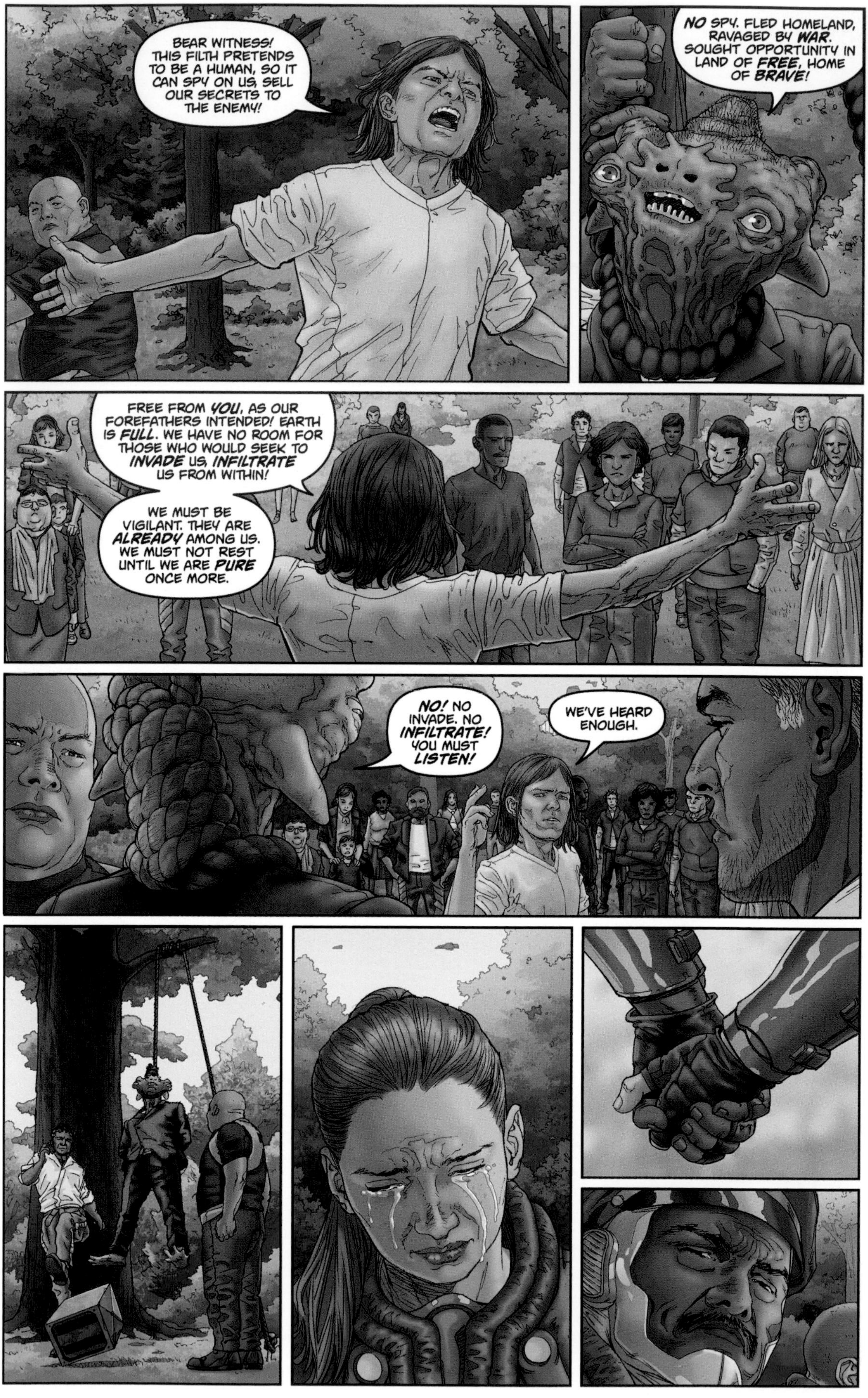
BEAR WITNESS! THIS FILTH PRETENDS TO BE A HUMAN, SO IT CAN SPY ON US, SELL OUR SECRETS TO THE ENEMY!
NO SPY. FLED HOMELAND, RAVAGED BY WAR. SOUGHT OPPORTUNITY IN LAND OF FREE, HOME OF BRAVE!
FREE FROM YOU, AS OUR FOREFATHERS INTENDED! EARTH IS FULL. WE HAVE NO ROOM FOR THOSE WHO WOULD SEEK TO INVADE US, INFILTRATE US FROM WITHIN!
WE MUST BE VIGILANT. THEY ARE ALREADY AMONG US. WE MUST NOT REST UNTIL WE ARE PURE ONCE MORE.
NO! NO INVADE. NO INFILTRATE! YOU MUST LISTEN!
WE'VE HEARD ENOUGH.

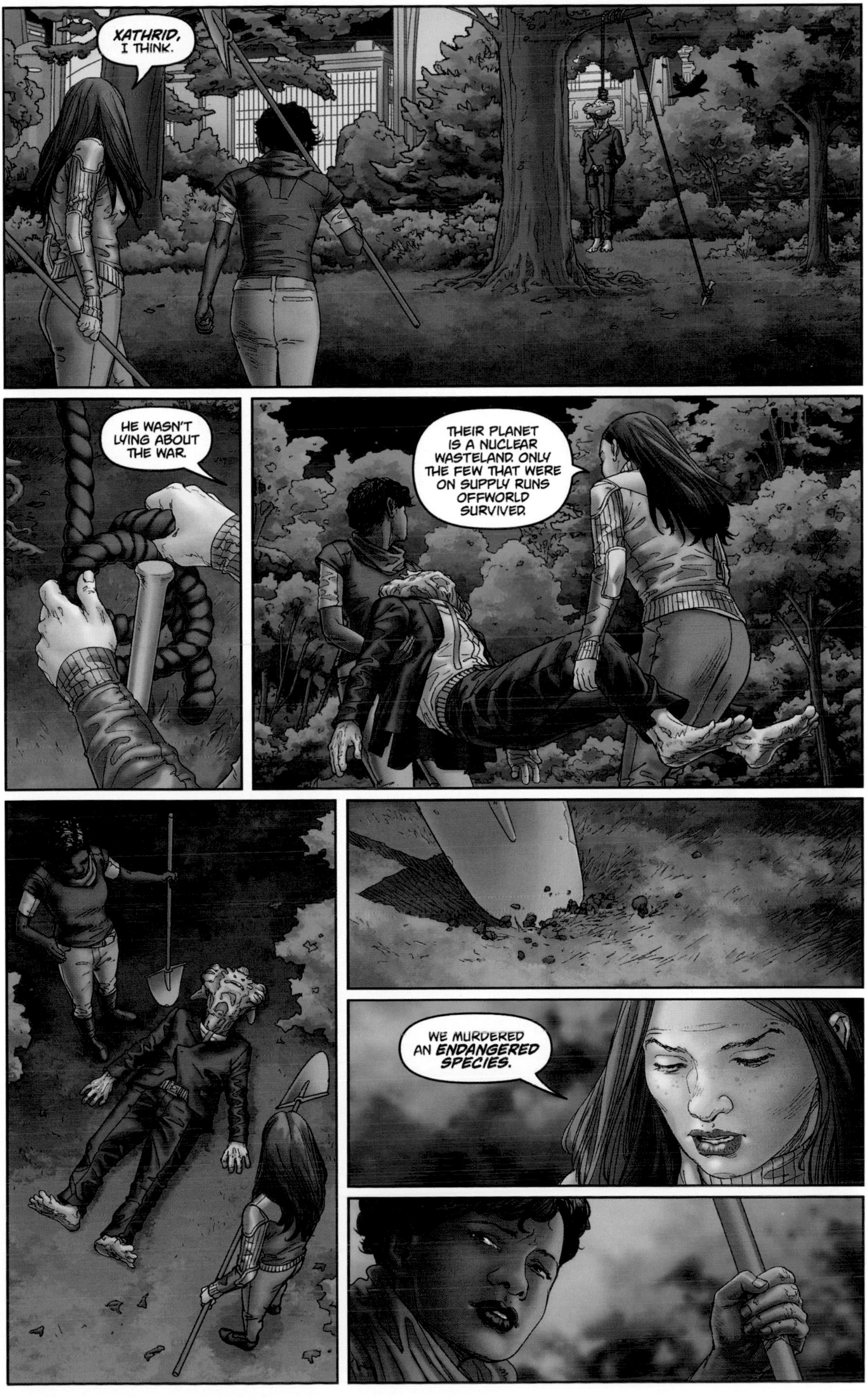
XATHRID, I THINK.
HE WASN'T LYING ABOUT THE WAR.
THEIR PLANET IS A NUCLEAR WASTELAND. ONLY THE FEW THAT WERE ON SUPPLY RUNS OFFWORLD SURVIVED.
WE MURDERED AN *ENDANGERED SPECIES.*

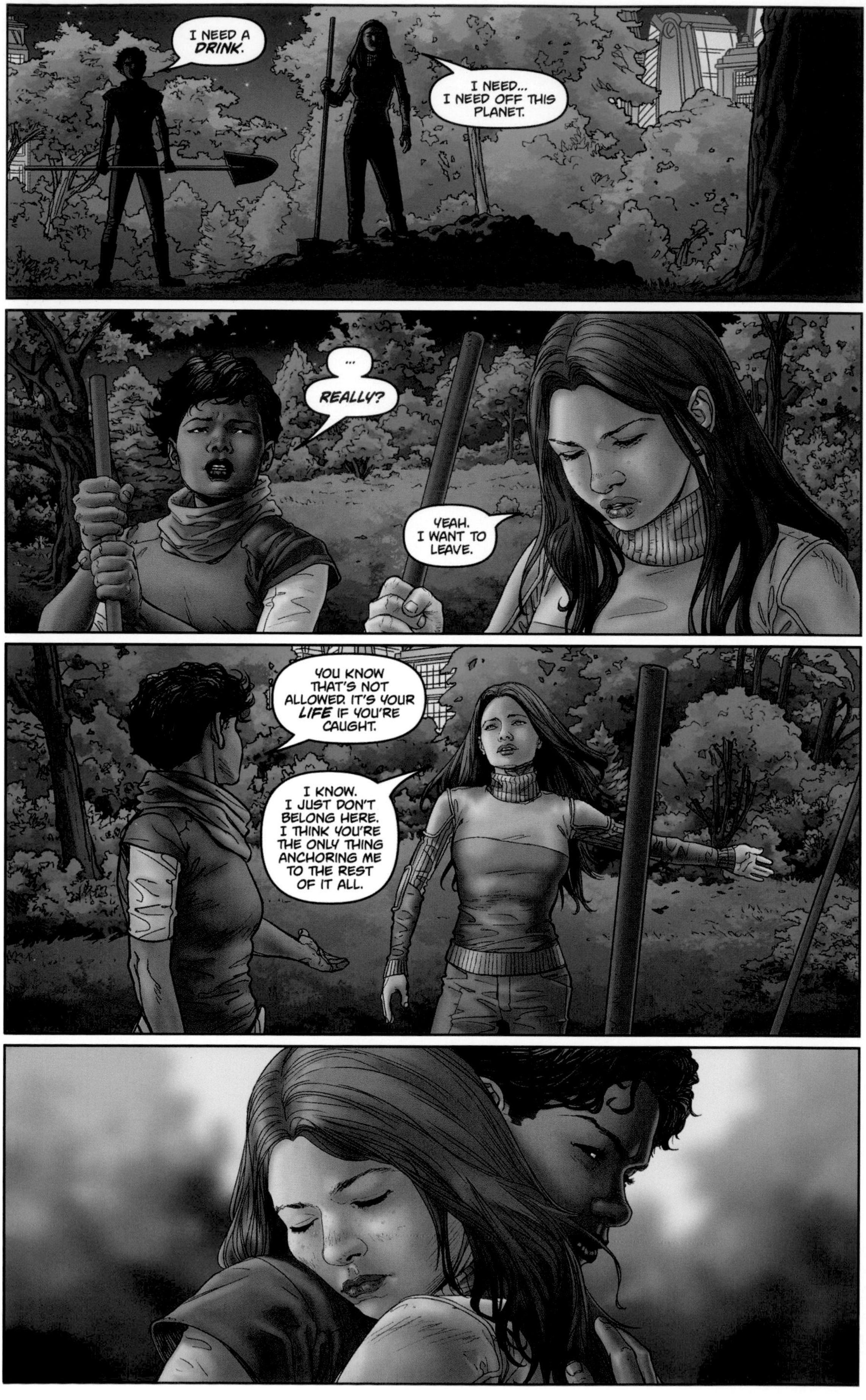
I NEED A DRINK.
I NEED... I NEED OFF THIS PLANET.
... REALLY?
YEAH. I WANT TO LEAVE.
YOU KNOW THAT'S NOT ALLOWED. IT'S YOUR LIFE IF YOU'RE CAUGHT.
I KNOW. I JUST DON'T BELONG HERE. I THINK YOU'RE THE ONLY THING ANCHORING ME TO THE REST OF IT ALL.

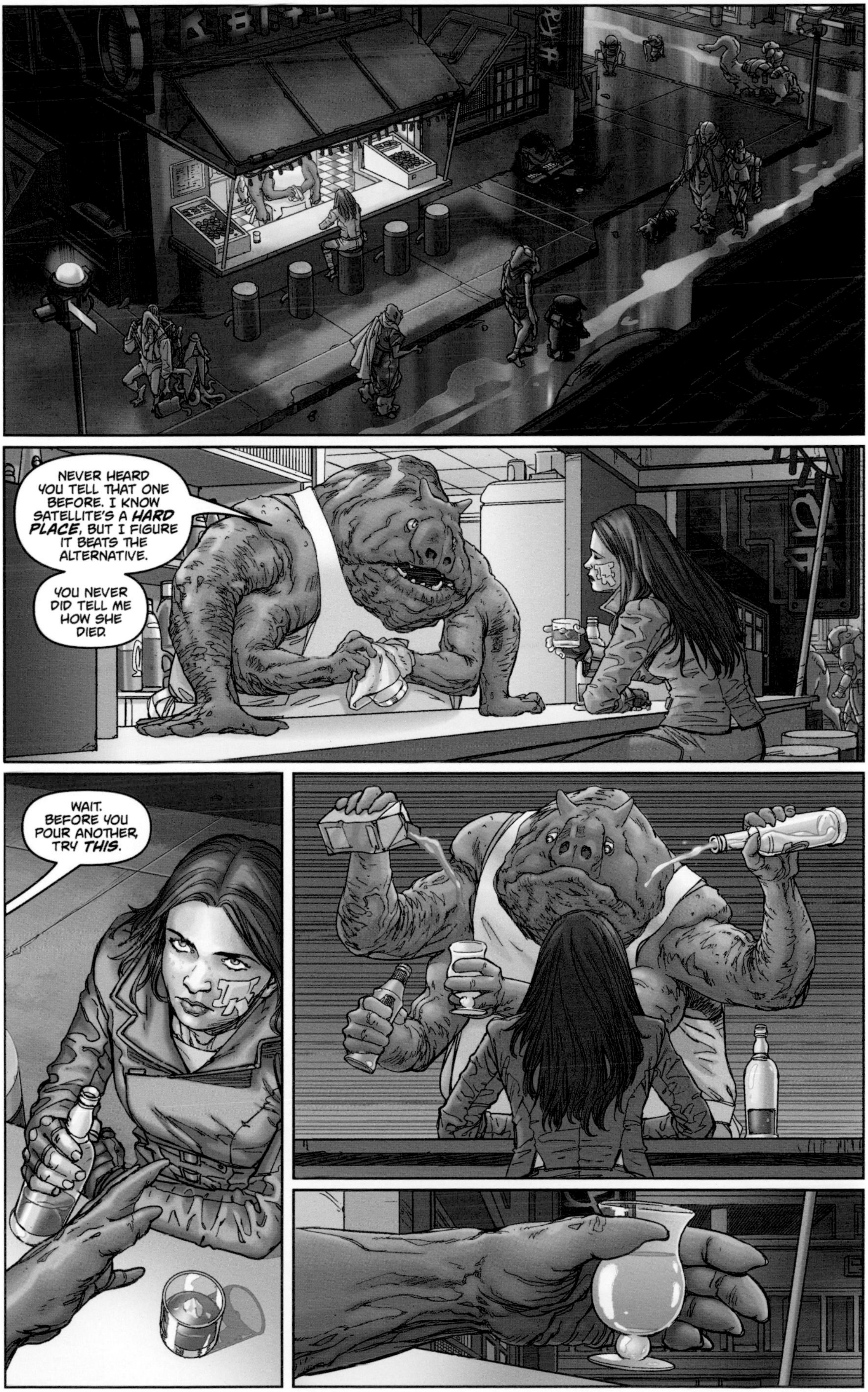
NEVER HEARD YOU TELL THAT ONE BEFORE. I KNOW SATELLITE'S A HARD PLACE, BUT I FIGURE IT BEATS THE ALTERNATIVE.
YOU NEVER DID TELL ME HOW SHE DIED.
WAIT. BEFORE YOU POUR ANOTHER, TRY THIS.

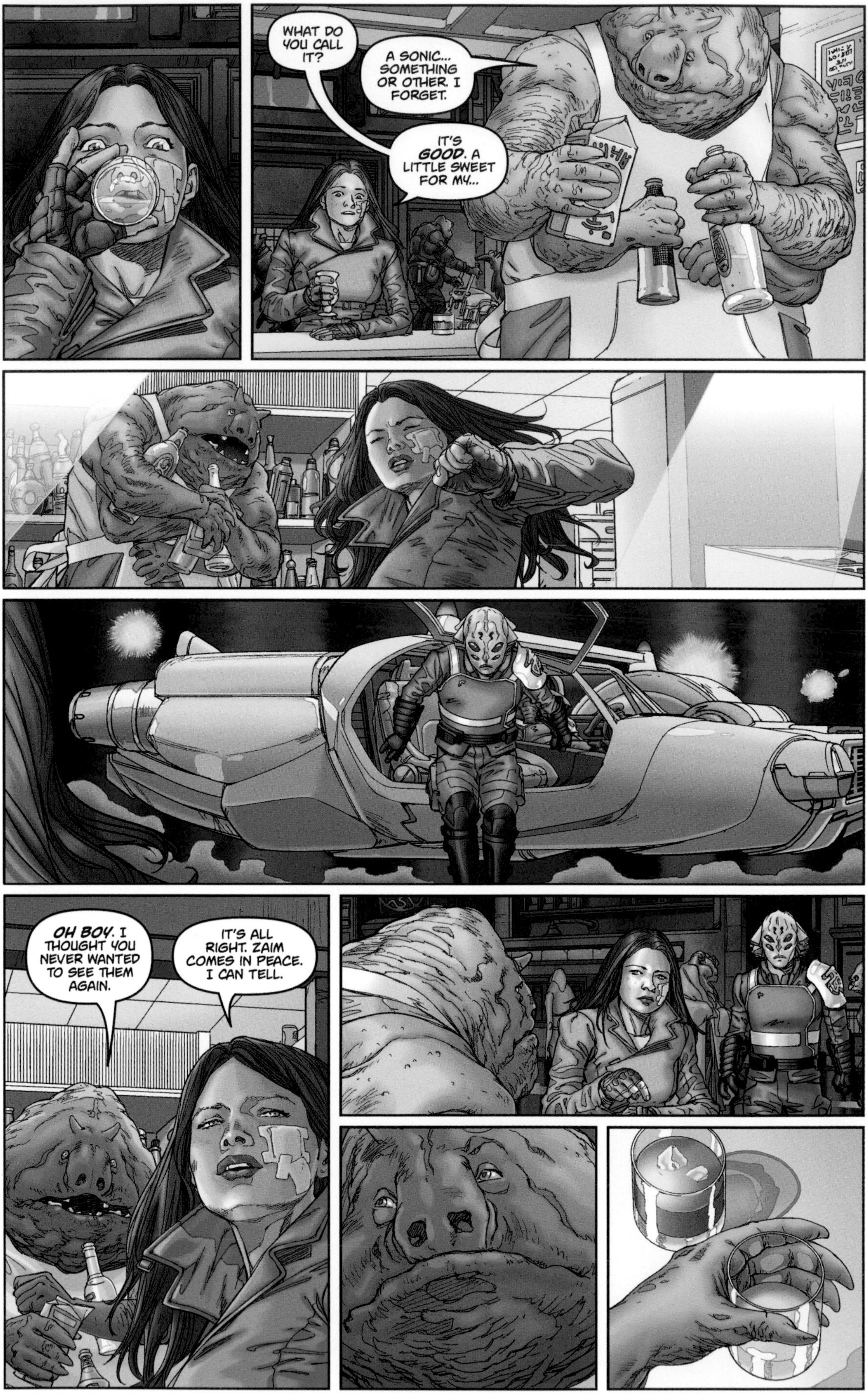
WHAT DO YOU CALL IT?
A SONIC... SOMETHING OR OTHER. I FORGET.
IT'S GOOD. A LITTLE SWEET FOR MY...
OH BOY. I THOUGHT YOU NEVER WANTED TO SEE THEM AGAIN.
IT'S ALL RIGHT. ZAIM COMES IN PEACE. I CAN TELL.

LILLY. WE NEED TO TALK. *NO STRINGS.* JUST WANT TO COMPARE NOTES ON THIS WHOLE EVA THING.

YOU'VE GOT FIVE MINUTES.

KARBIP.

CHIEF.

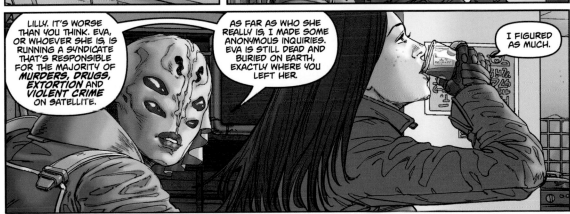

LILLY. IT'S WORSE THAN YOU THINK. EVA, OR WHOEVER SHE IS, IS RUNNING A SYNDICATE THAT'S RESPONSIBLE FOR THE MAJORITY OF *MURDERS, DRUGS, EXTORTION* AND *VIOLENT CRIME* ON SATELLITE.

AS FAR AS WHO SHE REALLY IS, I MADE SOME ANONYMOUS INQUIRIES. EVA IS STILL DEAD AND BURIED ON EARTH, EXACTLY WHERE YOU LEFT HER.

I FIGURED AS MUCH.

BUT WAIT, THERE'S *MORE.* WE'VE ANALYZED VIDEO, VOICE PRINTS, AUDIO, EVEN *HANDWRITING.* WHOEVER THIS IS, SHE'S A STARTLING COPY, FAR BEYOND ANY CLONE TECHNOLOGY KNOWN TO EXIST. SHE PASSES THE *TURING* TEST.

SHE WALKS, TALKS AND BELIEVES SHE IS EVA.

AND SHE'S ALSO IN A MASSIVE FREIGHTER ON THE FAR SIDE OF THAT GIANT SPINNING BALL OF *GAS* THAT WE ORBIT.

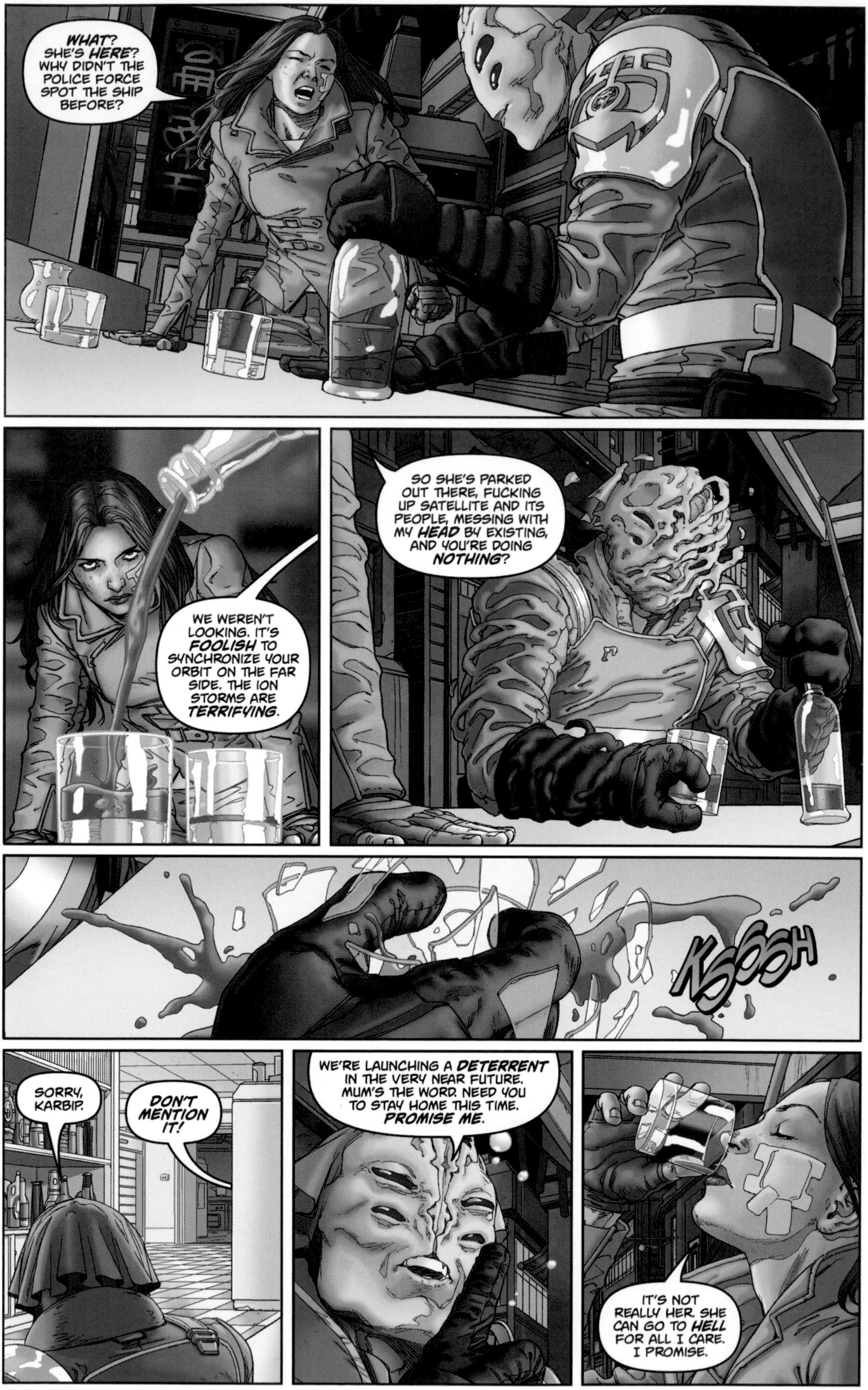
WHAT? SHE'S HERE? WHY DIDN'T THE POLICE FORCE SPOT THE SHIP BEFORE?
WE WEREN'T LOOKING. IT'S FOOLISH TO SYNCHRONIZE YOUR ORBIT ON THE FAR SIDE. THE ION STORMS ARE TERRIFYING.
SO SHE'S PARKED OUT THERE, FUCKING UP SATELLITE AND ITS PEOPLE, MESSING WITH MY HEAD BY EXISTING, AND YOU'RE DOING NOTHING?
KSSSH
SORRY, KARBIP.
DON'T MENTION IT!
WE'RE LAUNCHING A DETERRENT IN THE VERY NEAR FUTURE. MUM'S THE WORD. NEED YOU TO STAY HOME THIS TIME. PROMISE ME.
IT'S NOT REALLY HER. SHE CAN GO TO HELL FOR ALL I CARE. I PROMISE.

I'VE GOT YOUR **WORD**!

LIEUTENANT, YOU DRIVE.

OW!

YOU'RE NOT REALLY GOING TO STAY **AWAY**, ARE YOU?

YOU KIDDING? I HAVE TO **KNOW**.

I SUPPOSE YOU NEED MY HELP, THEN.

WOULDN'T **HURT**. YOU DO **OWE** ME, REMEMBER THE IXBA JOB?

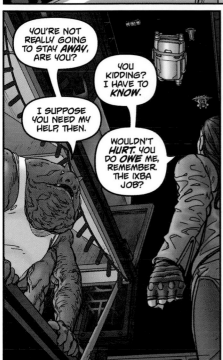

"HAD ONE TOO MANY. COME BACK LATER."

NICE.

IT'D BE FUNNIER IF IT WASN'T TRUE. **COME ON.** I GOT SOME PEOPLE I WANT TO INTRODUCE TO YOU.

YOU'LL HAVE TO **PAY THEM**, THOUGH. THEY DON'T TRADE FAVORS.

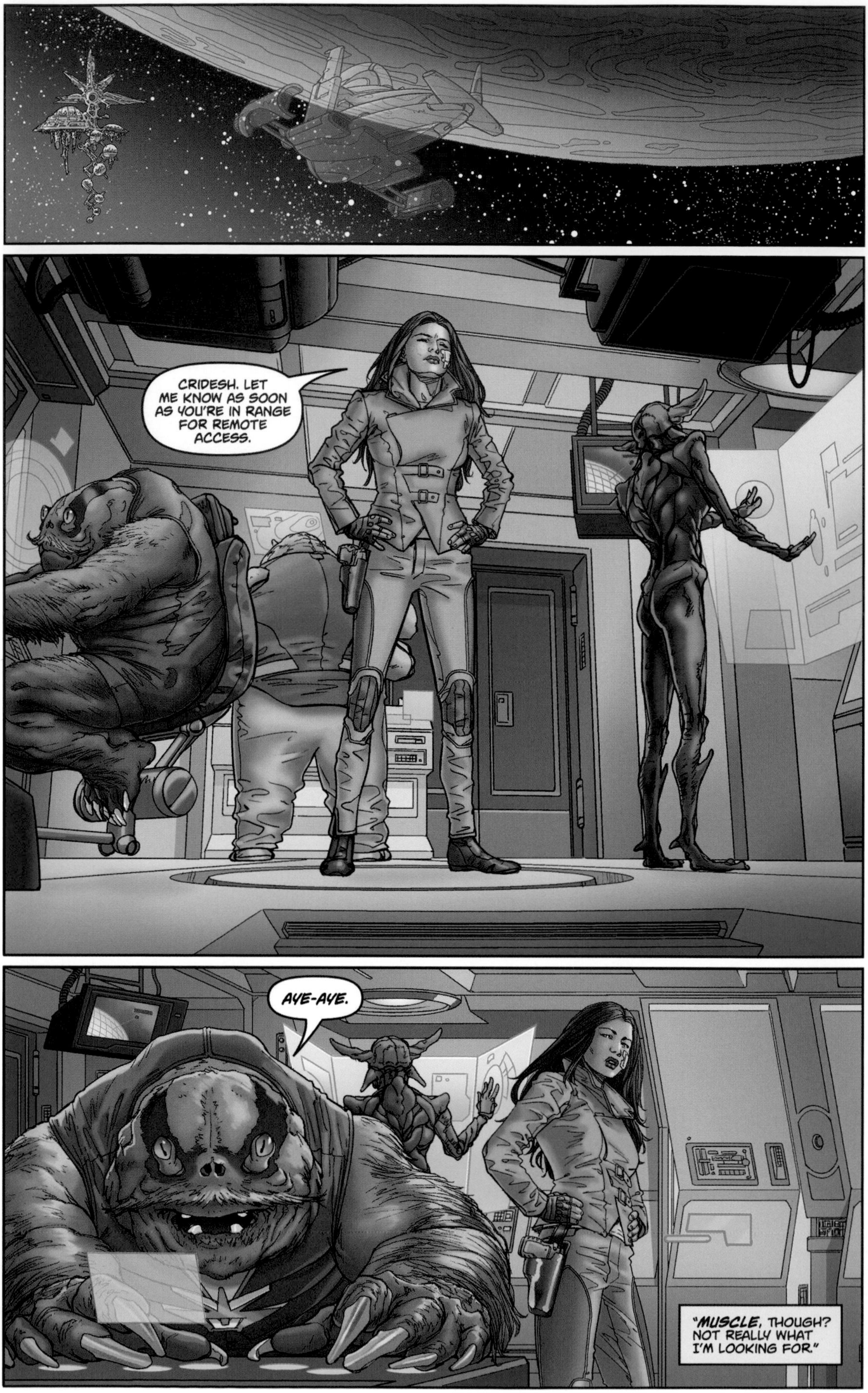
CRIDESH. LET ME KNOW AS SOON AS YOU'RE IN RANGE FOR REMOTE ACCESS.
AYE-AYE.
"MUSCLE, THOUGH? NOT REALLY WHAT I'M LOOKING FOR."

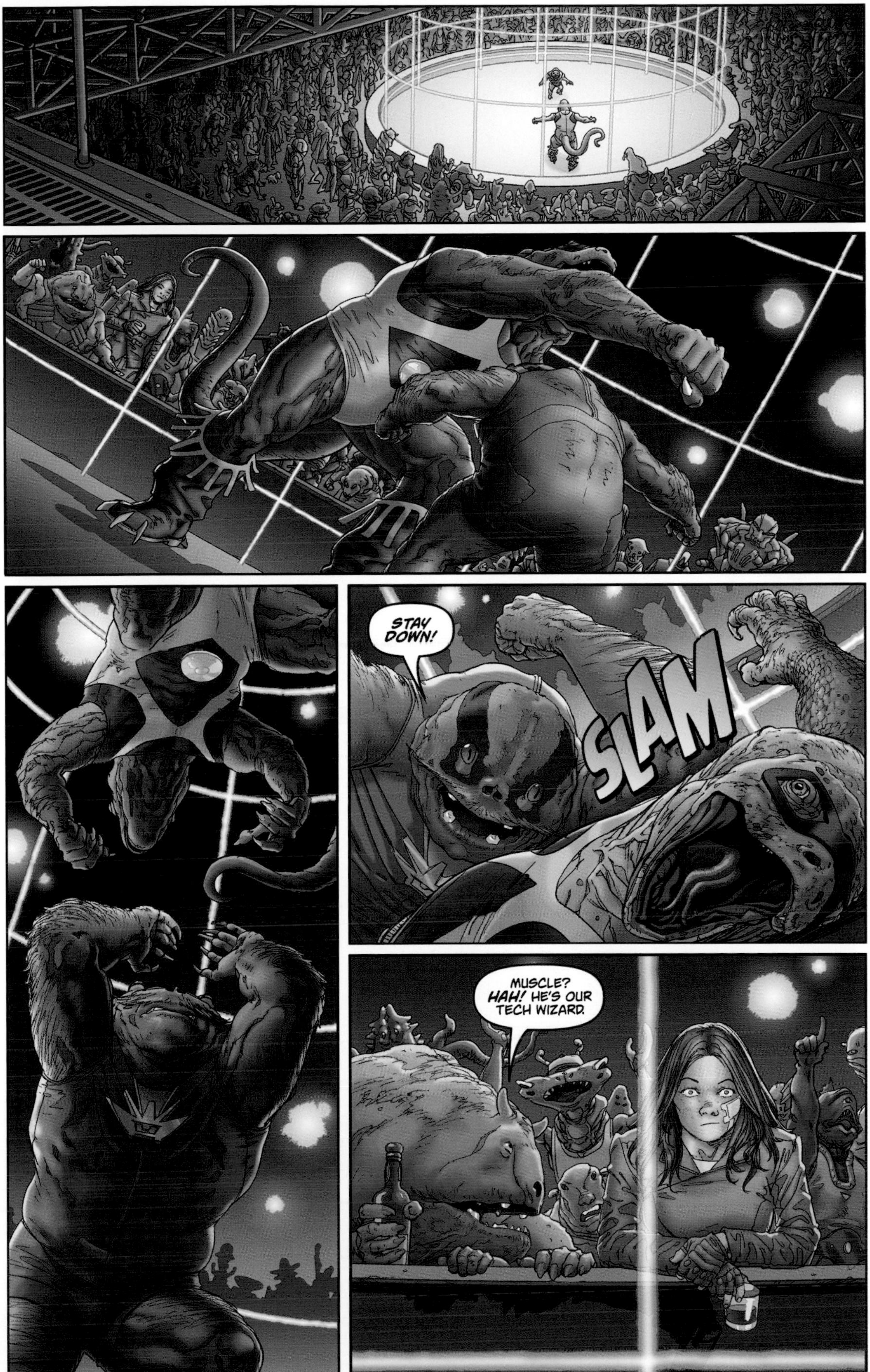
STAY DOWN!
SLAM
MUSCLE? HAH! HE'S OUR TECH WIZARD.

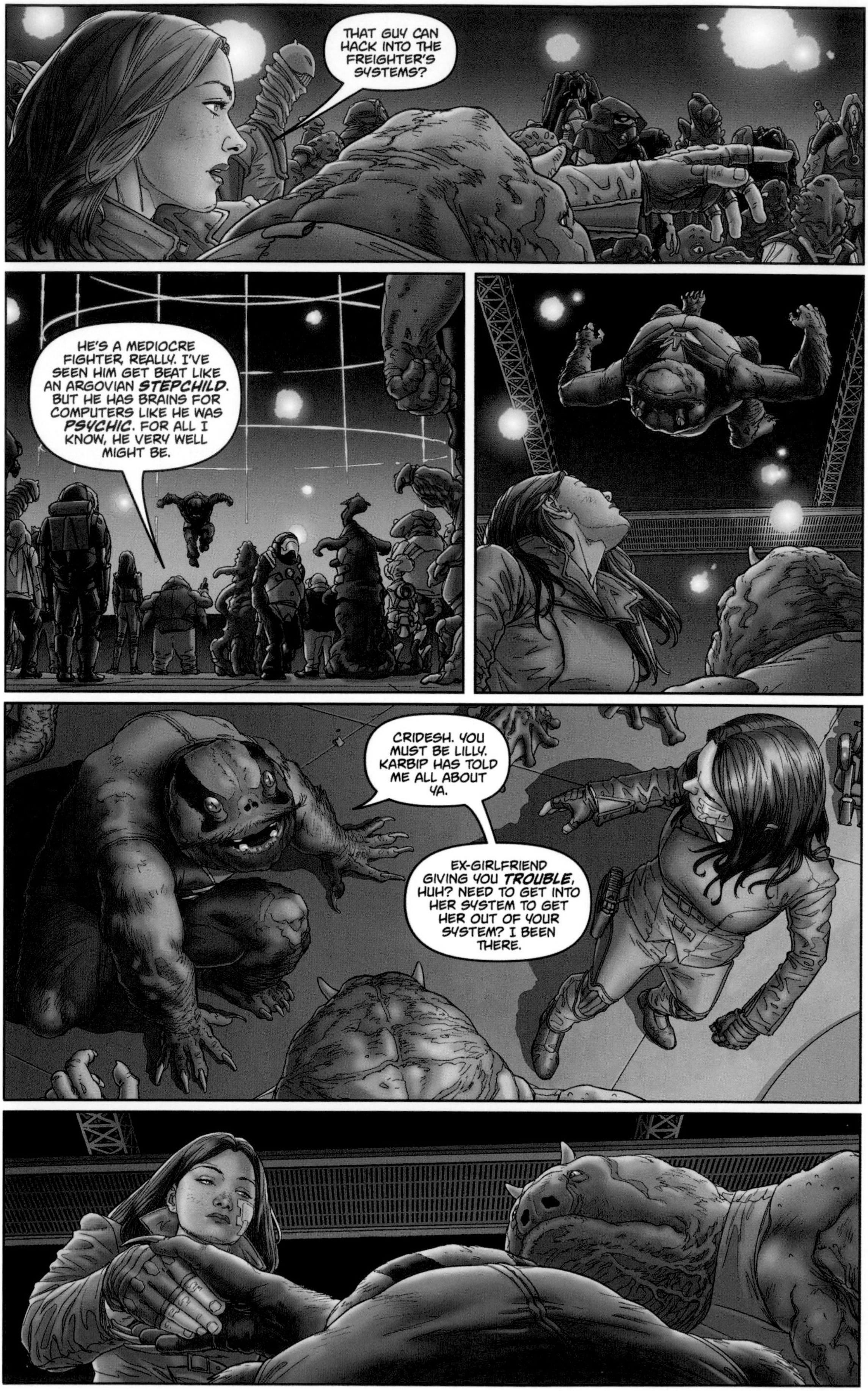
THAT GUY CAN HACK INTO THE FREIGHTER'S SYSTEMS?
HE'S A MEDIOCRE FIGHTER, REALLY. I'VE SEEN HIM GET BEAT LIKE AN ARGOVIAN STEPCHILD. BUT HE HAS BRAINS FOR COMPUTERS LIKE HE WAS PSYCHIC. FOR ALL I KNOW, HE VERY WELL MIGHT BE.
CRIDESH. YOU MUST BE LILLY. KARBIP HAS TOLD ME ALL ABOUT YA.
EX-GIRLFRIEND GIVING YOU TROUBLE, HUH? NEED TO GET INTO HER SYSTEM TO GET HER OUT OF YOUR SYSTEM? I BEEN THERE.

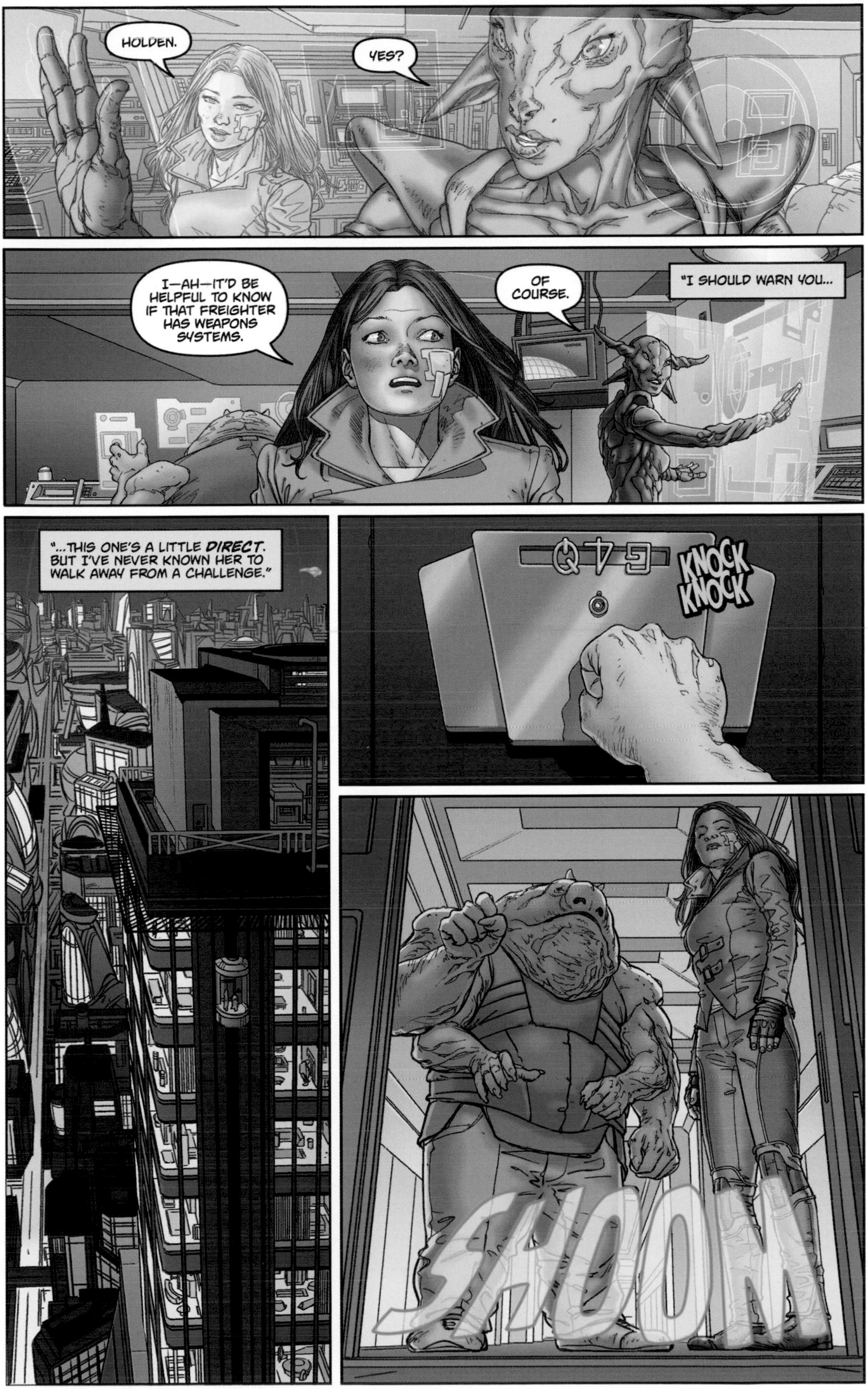
HOLDEN.
YES?
I—AH—IT'D BE HELPFUL TO KNOW IF THAT FREIGHTER HAS WEAPONS SYSTEMS.
OF COURSE.
"I SHOULD WARN YOU...
"...THIS ONE'S A LITTLE *DIRECT*. BUT I'VE NEVER KNOWN HER TO WALK AWAY FROM A CHALLENGE."
KNOCK KNOCK
SHOOM

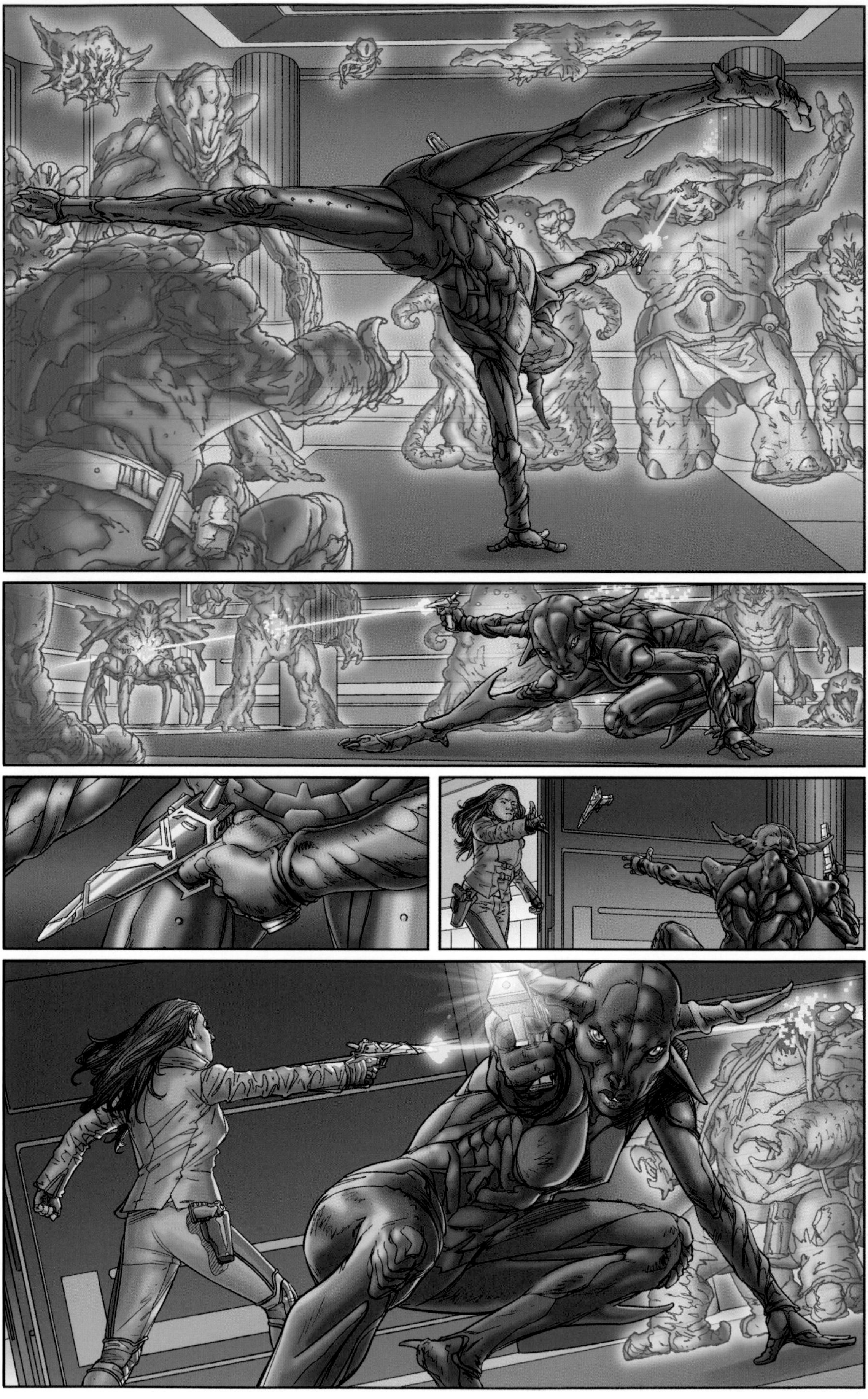

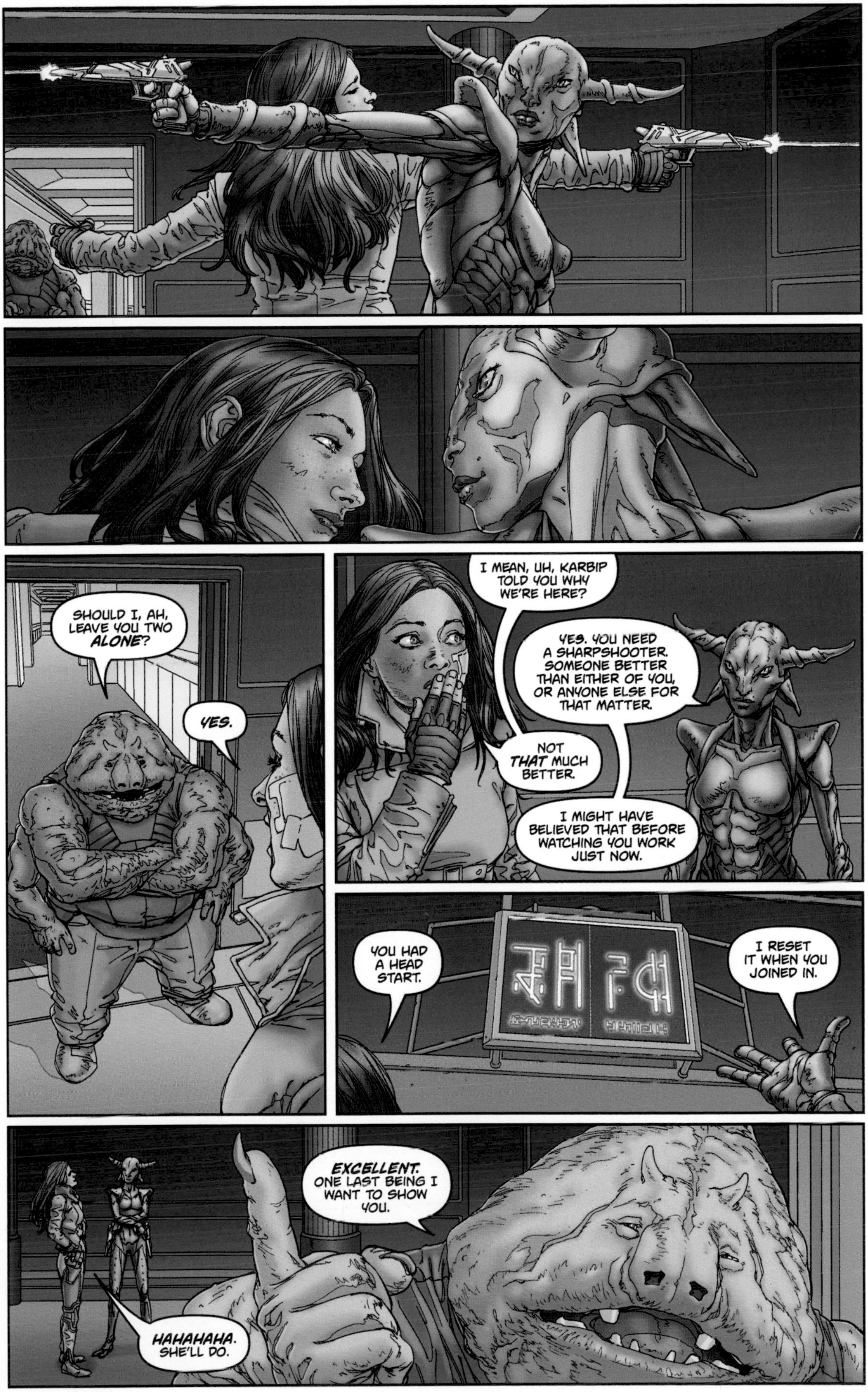
SHOULD I, AH, LEAVE YOU TWO ALONE?
YES.
I MEAN, UH, KARBIP TOLD YOU WHY WE'RE HERE?
YES. YOU NEED A SHARPSHOOTER. SOMEONE BETTER THAN EITHER OF YOU, OR ANYONE ELSE FOR THAT MATTER.
NOT THAT MUCH BETTER.
I MIGHT HAVE BELIEVED THAT BEFORE WATCHING YOU WORK JUST NOW.
YOU HAD A HEAD START.
I RESET IT WHEN YOU JOINED IN.
EXCELLENT. ONE LAST BEING I WANT TO SHOW YOU.
HAHAHAHA. SHE'LL DO.

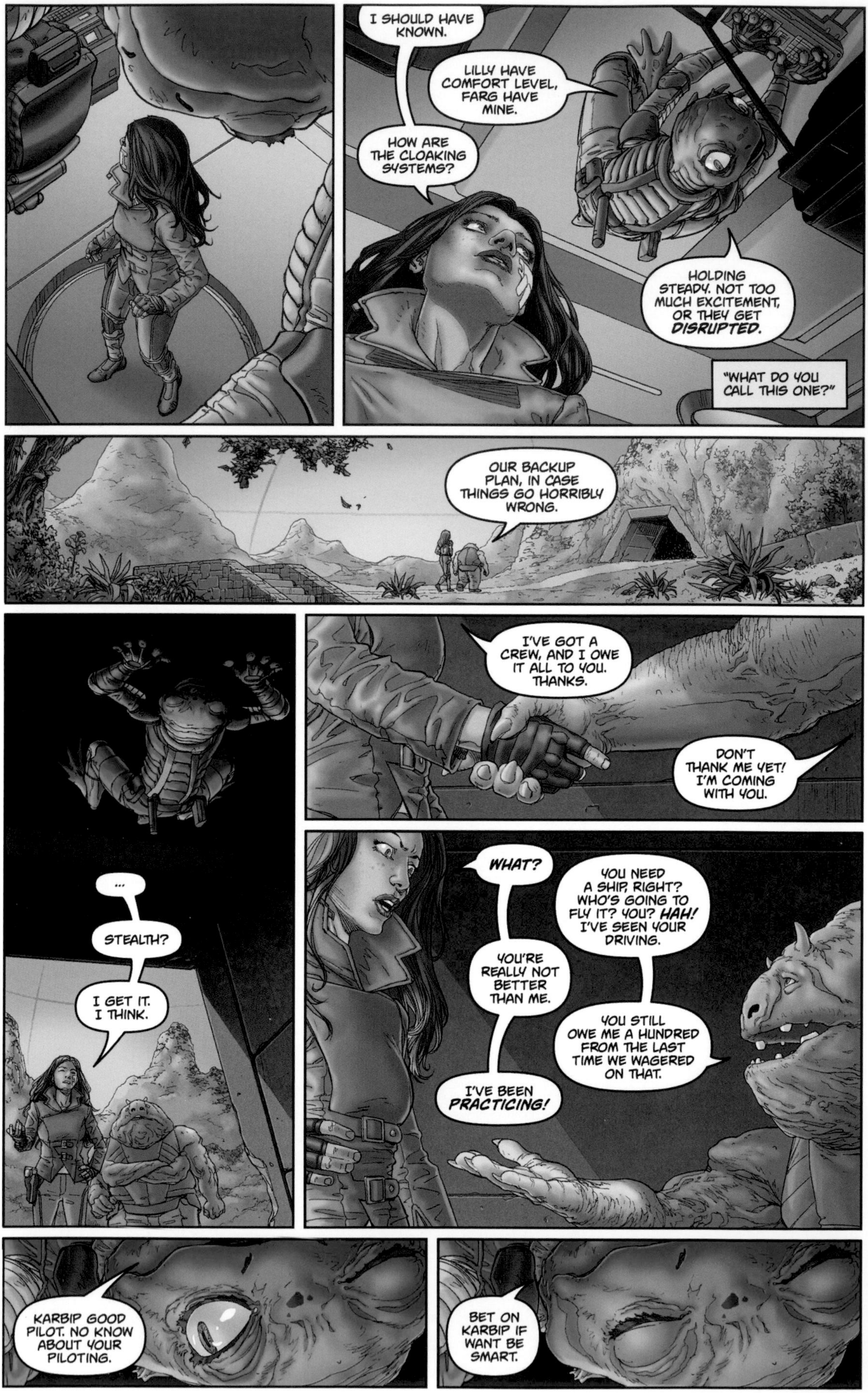
I SHOULD HAVE KNOWN.
LILLY HAVE COMFORT LEVEL, FARG HAVE MINE.
HOW ARE THE CLOAKING SYSTEMS?
HOLDING STEADY. NOT TOO MUCH EXCITEMENT, OR THEY GET DISRUPTED.
"WHAT DO YOU CALL THIS ONE?"
OUR BACKUP PLAN, IN CASE THINGS GO HORRIBLY WRONG.
...
STEALTH?
I GET IT. I THINK.
I'VE GOT A CREW, AND I OWE IT ALL TO YOU. THANKS.
DON'T THANK ME YET! I'M COMING WITH YOU.
WHAT?
YOU NEED A SHIP, RIGHT? WHO'S GOING TO FLY IT? YOU? HAH! I'VE SEEN YOUR DRIVING.
YOU'RE REALLY NOT BETTER THAN ME.
YOU STILL OWE ME A HUNDRED FROM THE LAST TIME WE WAGERED ON THAT.
I'VE BEEN PRACTICING!
KARBIP GOOD PILOT. NO KNOW ABOUT YOUR PILOTING.
BET ON KARBIP IF WANT BE SMART.

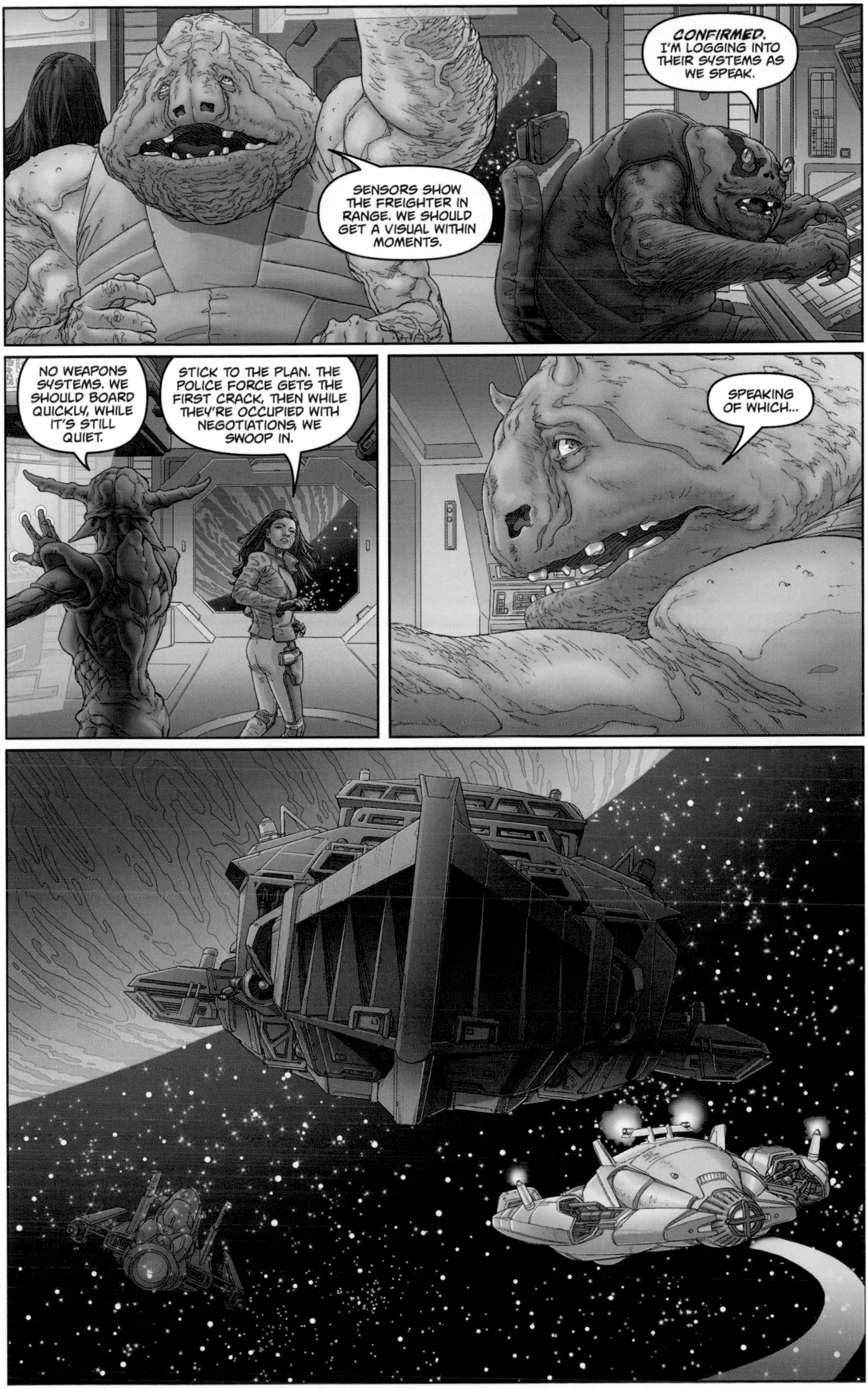
CONFIRMED. I'M LOGGING INTO THEIR SYSTEMS AS WE SPEAK.
SENSORS SHOW THE FREIGHTER IN RANGE. WE SHOULD GET A VISUAL WITHIN MOMENTS.
NO WEAPONS SYSTEMS. WE SHOULD BOARD QUICKLY, WHILE IT'S STILL QUIET.
STICK TO THE PLAN. THE POLICE FORCE GETS THE FIRST CRACK, THEN WHILE THEY'RE OCCUPIED WITH NEGOTIATIONS, WE SWOOP IN.
SPEAKING OF WHICH...

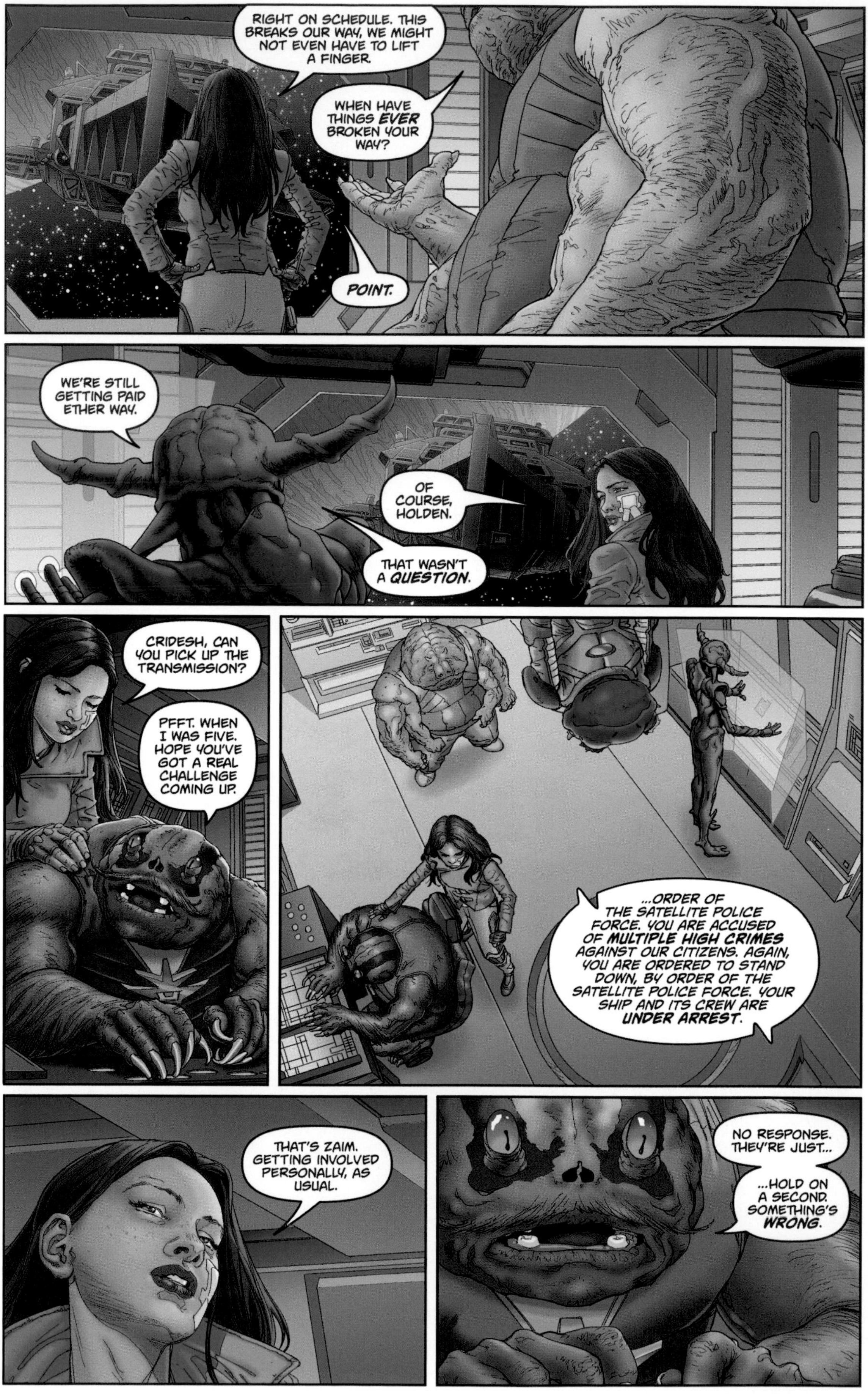

RIGHT ON SCHEDULE. THIS BREAKS OUR WAY, WE MIGHT NOT EVEN HAVE TO LIFT A FINGER.
WHEN HAVE THINGS EVER BROKEN YOUR WAY?
POINT.
WE'RE STILL GETTING PAID ETHER WAY.
OF COURSE, HOLDEN.
THAT WASN'T A QUESTION.
CRIDESH, CAN YOU PICK UP THE TRANSMISSION?
PFFT. WHEN I WAS FIVE. HOPE YOU'VE GOT A REAL CHALLENGE COMING UP.
...ORDER OF THE SATELLITE POLICE FORCE. YOU ARE ACCUSED OF MULTIPLE HIGH CRIMES AGAINST OUR CITIZENS. AGAIN, YOU ARE ORDERED TO STAND DOWN, BY ORDER OF THE SATELLITE POLICE FORCE. YOUR SHIP AND ITS CREW ARE UNDER ARREST.
THAT'S ZAIM. GETTING INVOLVED PERSONALLY, AS USUAL.
NO RESPONSE. THEY'RE JUST...
...HOLD ON A SECOND. SOMETHING'S WRONG.

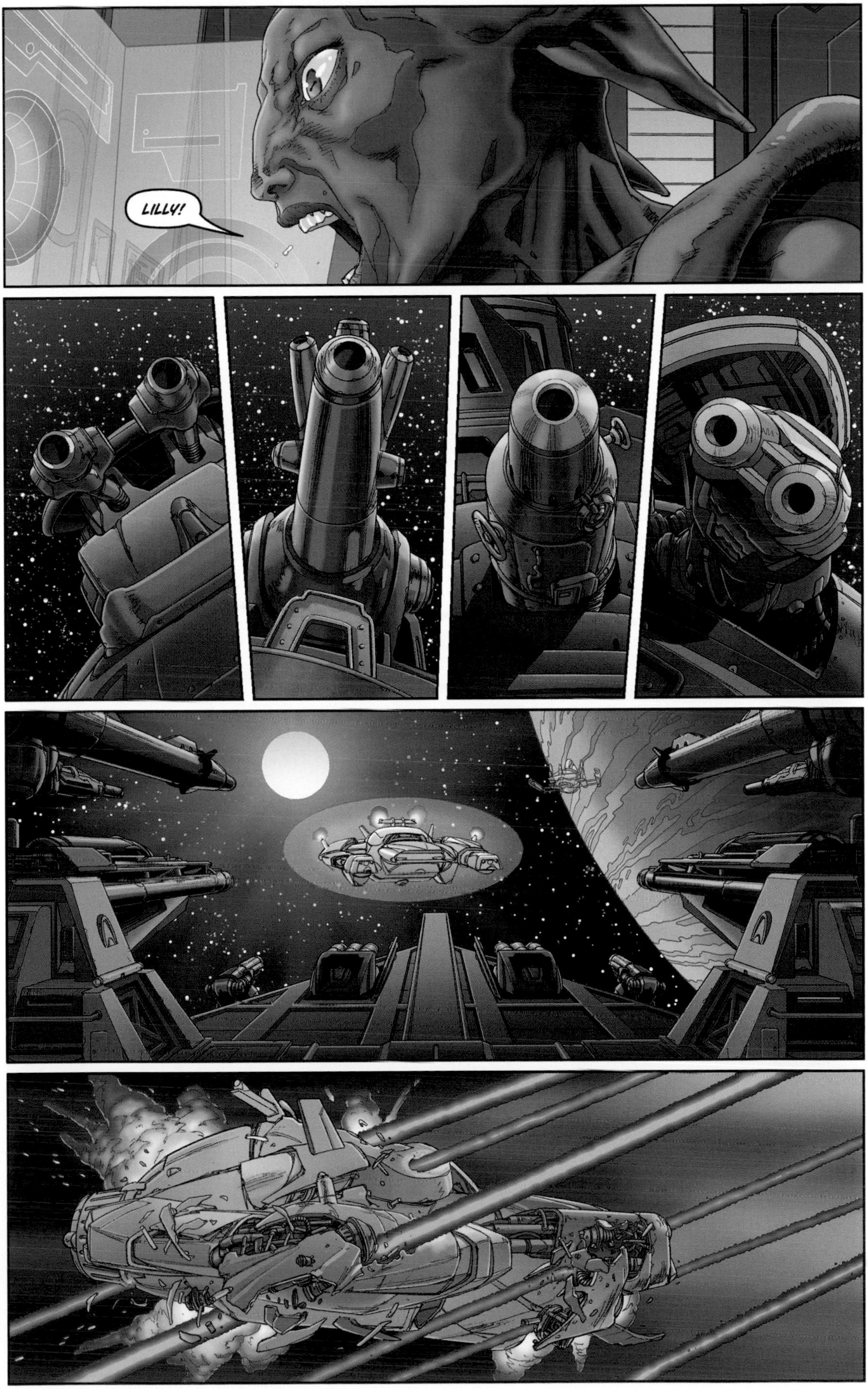
LILLY!

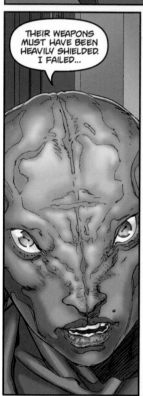

THEIR WEAPONS MUST HAVE BEEN HEAVILY SHIELDED. I FAILED...

I DIDN'T SEE THEM IN MY INITIAL SYSTEM SCAN. SPOTTED THEM RUNNING HOT AT THE LAST SECOND.

THEY WENT TO A LOT OF TROUBLE TO KEEP THE WEAPONS A SECRET. REAL BLACK-MARKET STUFF.

NO WAY CHIEF COULD HAVE KNOWN.

NOW THEY'RE DUSTED. NOBODY DESERVES THAT.

ZAIM...

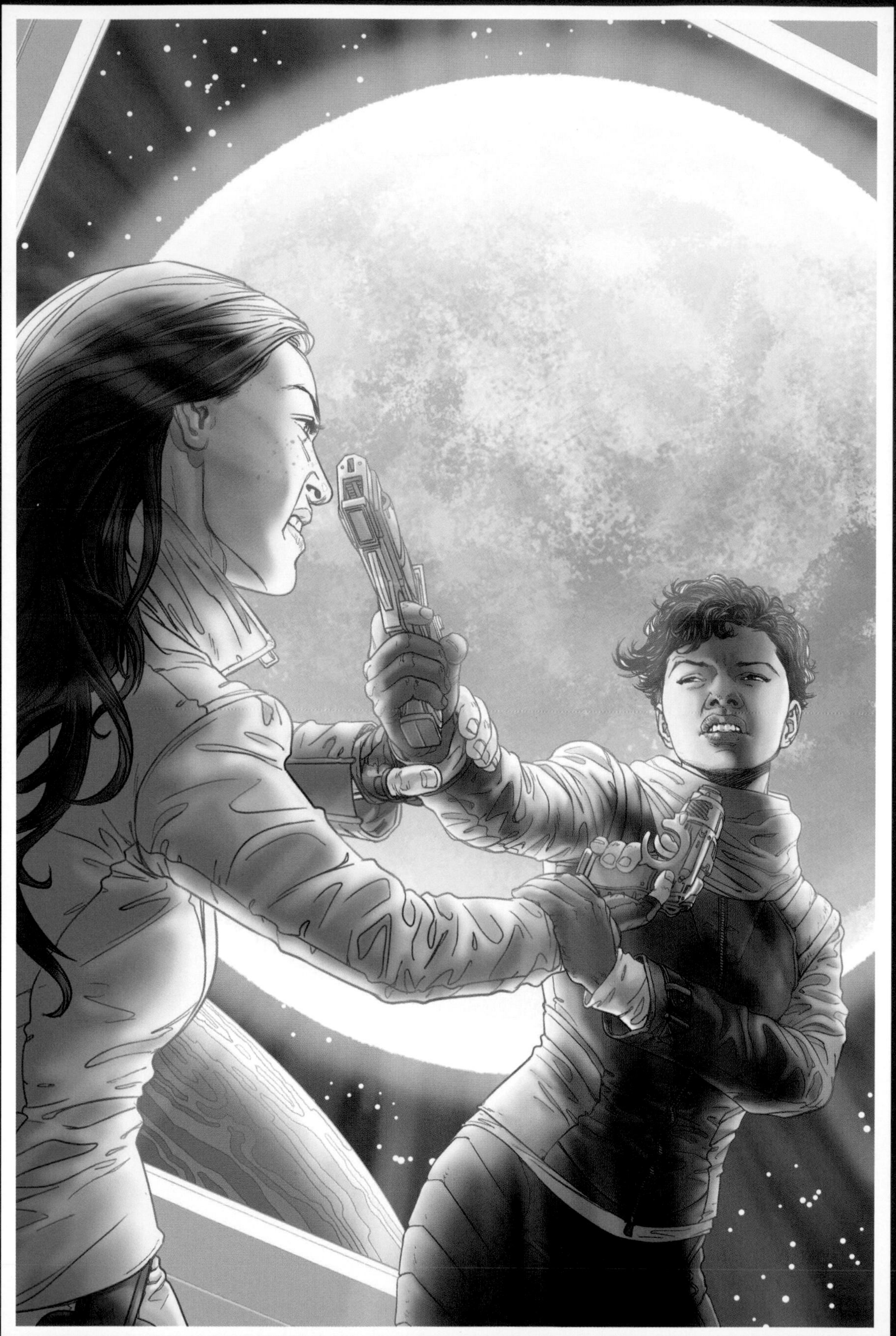

ART BY STEVEN THOMPSON • COLORS BY LISA JACKSON

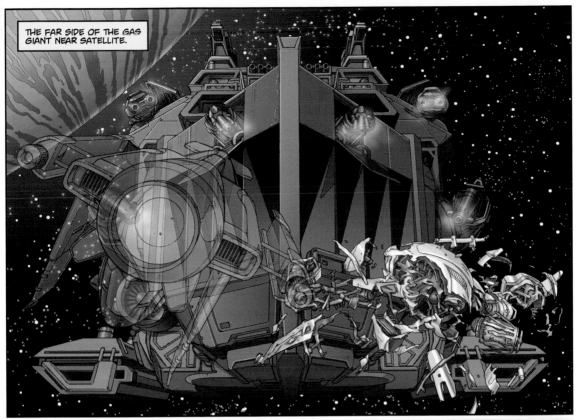

THE FAR SIDE OF THE GAS GIANT NEAR SATELLITE.

EVERYONE ACCOUNTED FOR? *REPORT!*

WEAPONS ARE POWERING DOWN AND BEGINNING TO RECEDE. CONFIRMED *NO SURVIVORS.*

ZAIM IS DEAD.

I'M IN THEIR SUBSYSTEMS, FINALLY. THAT FIREPOWER WAS ENOUGH TO PULVERIZE A *FLEET* OF CRUISERS. I SHOULD HAVE DETECTED IT SOONER...

DON'T BEAT YOURSELF UP. THEY WERE SHIELDED WELL.

BELIEVE OUR STEALTH *HOLDING,* LILLY.

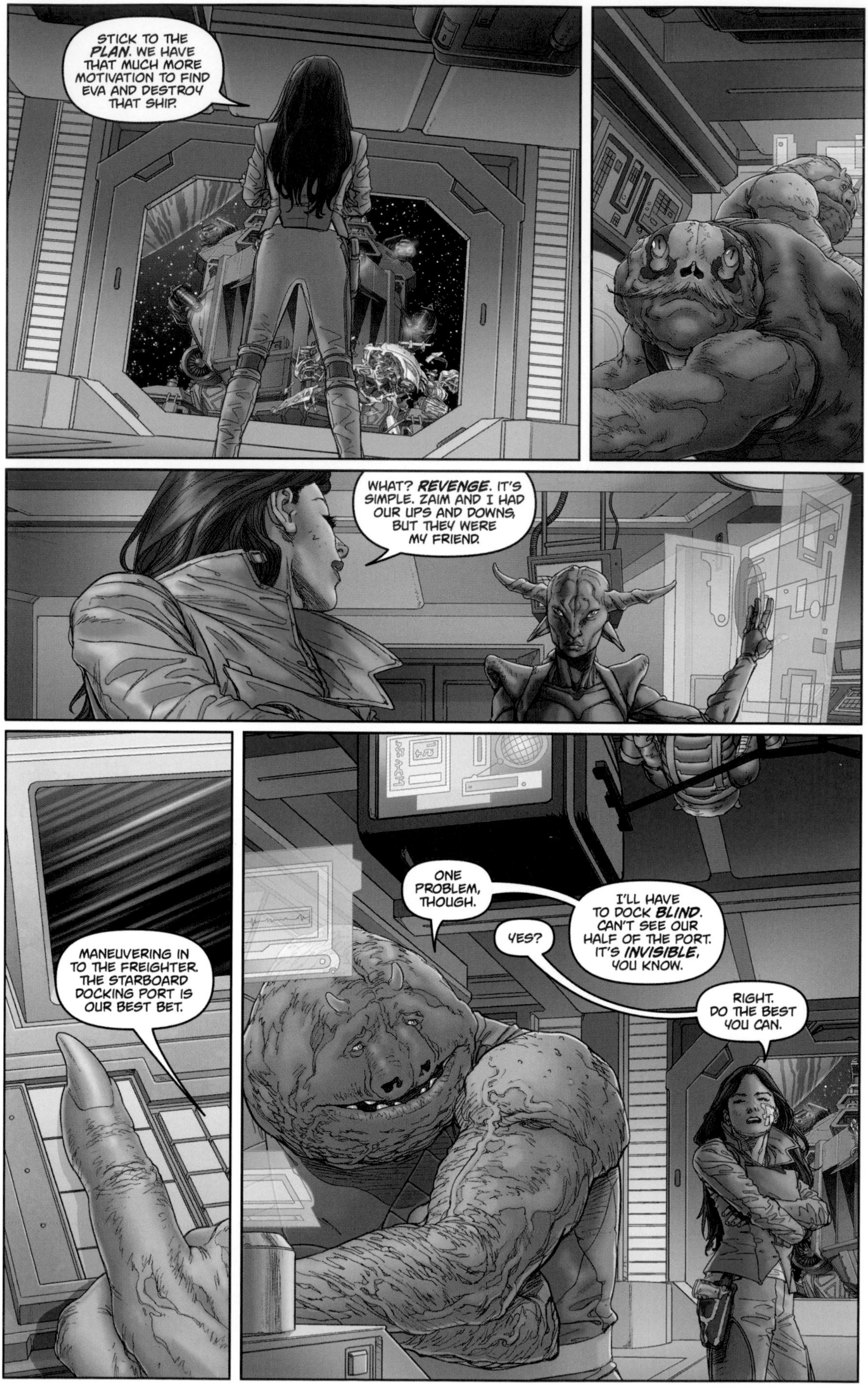
STICK TO THE PLAN. WE HAVE THAT MUCH MORE MOTIVATION TO FIND EVA AND DESTROY THAT SHIP.
WHAT? REVENGE. IT'S SIMPLE. ZAIM AND I HAD OUR UPS AND DOWNS, BUT THEY WERE MY FRIEND.
MANEUVERING IN TO THE FREIGHTER. THE STARBOARD DOCKING PORT IS OUR BEST BET.
ONE PROBLEM, THOUGH.
YES?
I'LL HAVE TO DOCK BLIND. CAN'T SEE OUR HALF OF THE PORT. IT'S INVISIBLE, YOU KNOW.
RIGHT. DO THE BEST YOU CAN.

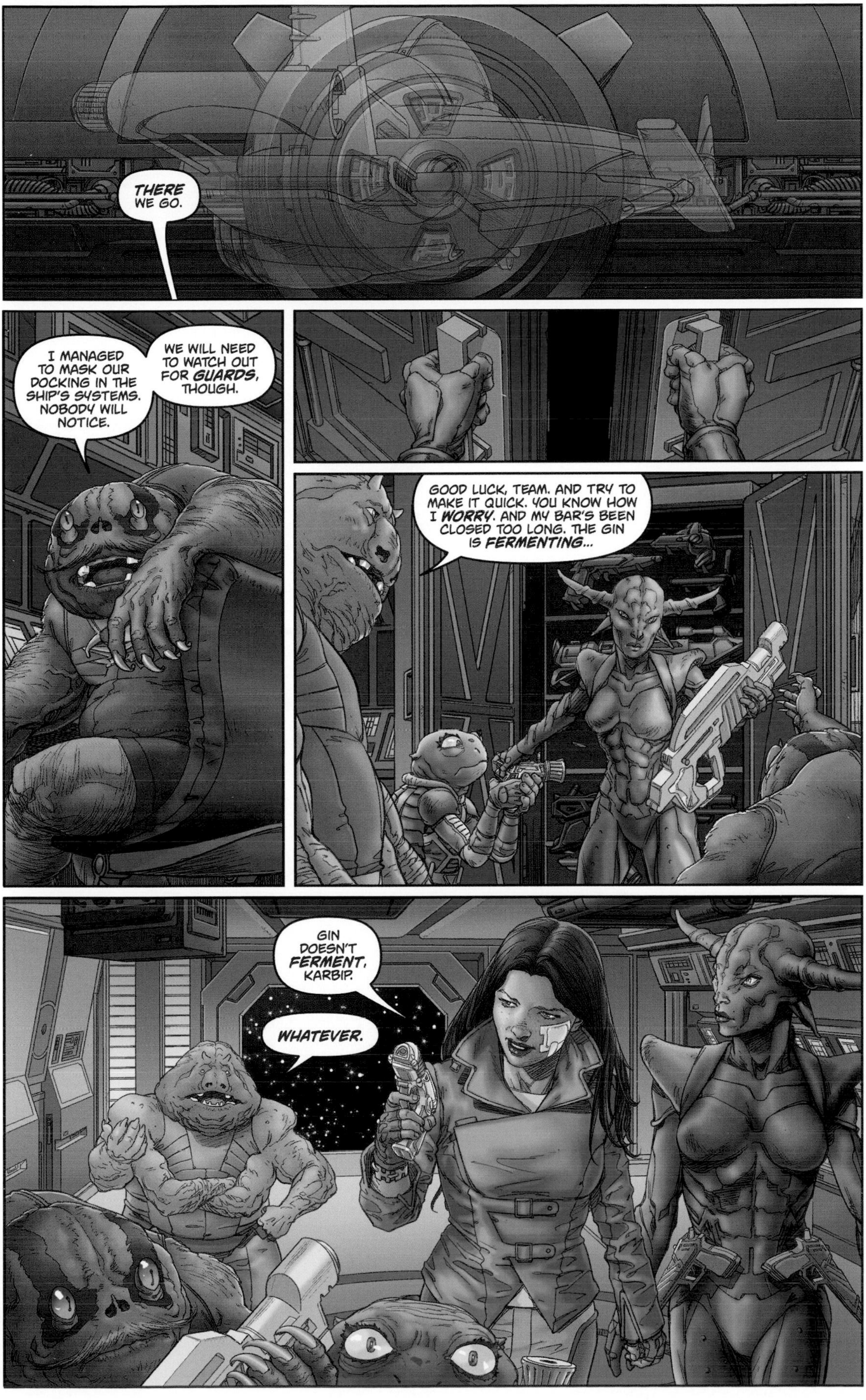
THERE WE GO.
I MANAGED TO MASK OUR DOCKING IN THE SHIP'S SYSTEMS. NOBODY WILL NOTICE.
WE WILL NEED TO WATCH OUT FOR GUARDS, THOUGH.
GOOD LUCK, TEAM. AND TRY TO MAKE IT QUICK. YOU KNOW HOW I WORRY. AND MY BAR'S BEEN CLOSED TOO LONG. THE GIN IS FERMENTING...
GIN DOESN'T FERMENT, KARBIP.
WHATEVER.

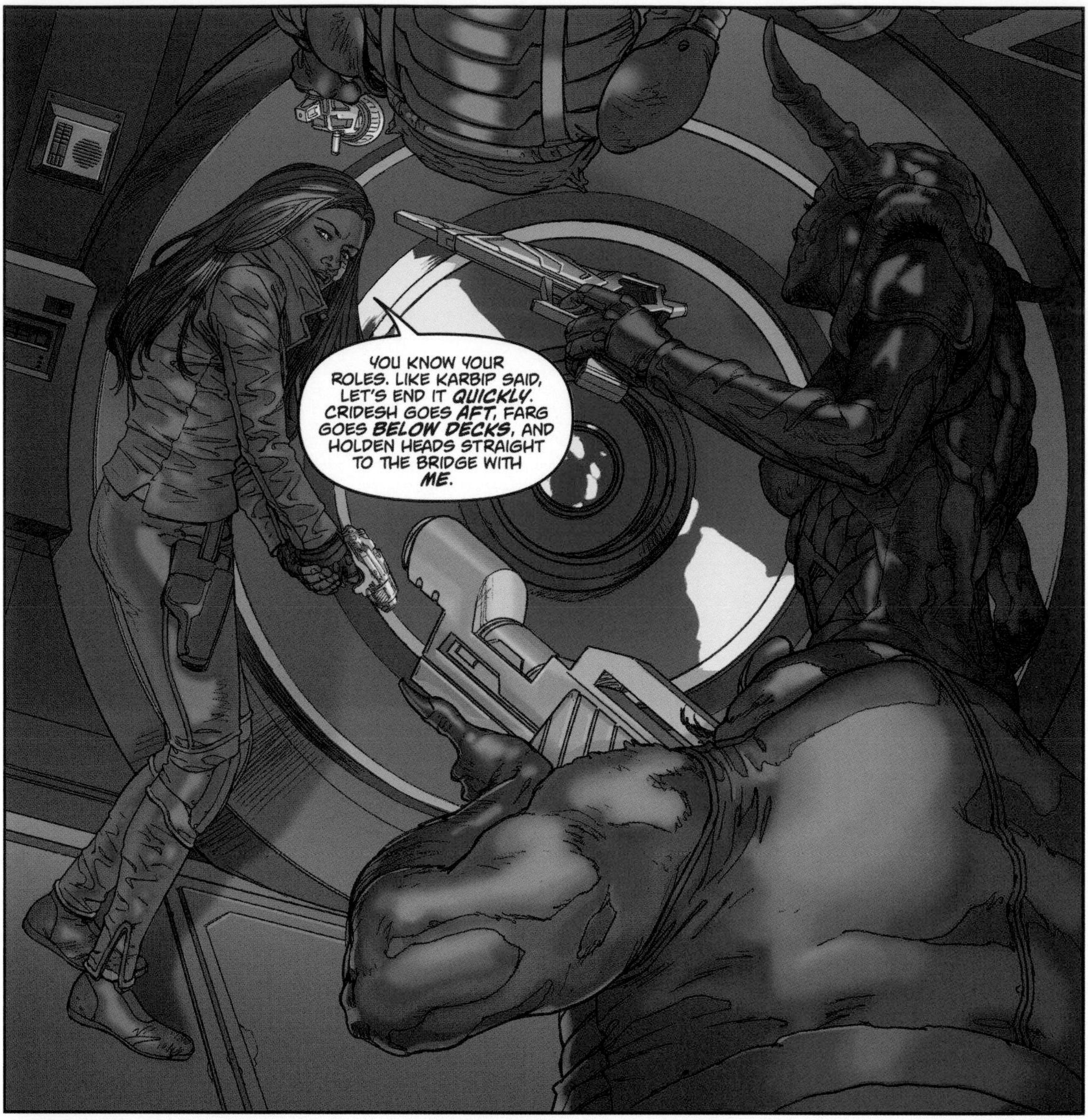
YOU KNOW YOUR ROLES. LIKE KARBIP SAID, LET'S END IT QUICKLY. CRIDESH GOES AFT, FARG GOES BELOW DECKS, AND HOLDEN HEADS STRAIGHT TO THE BRIDGE WITH ME.

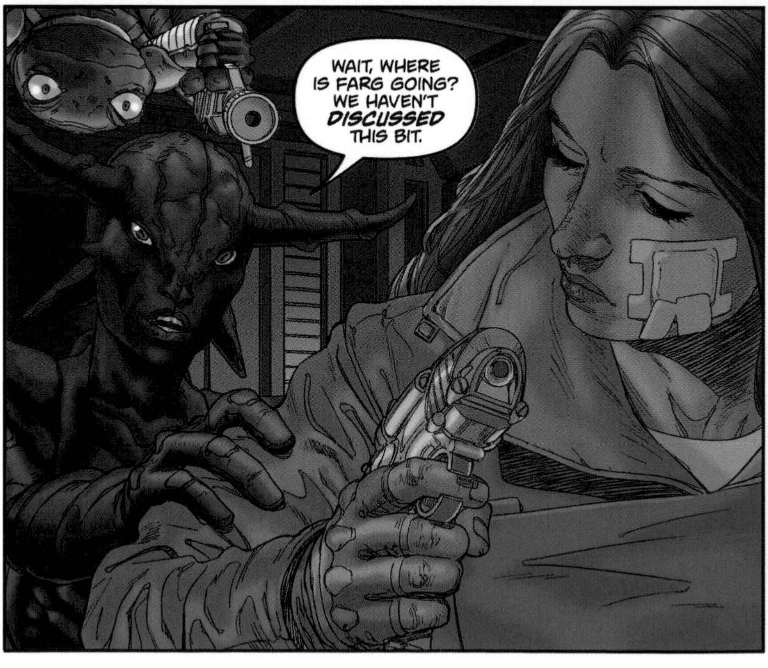
WAIT, WHERE IS FARG GOING? WE HAVEN'T DISCUSSED THIS BIT.

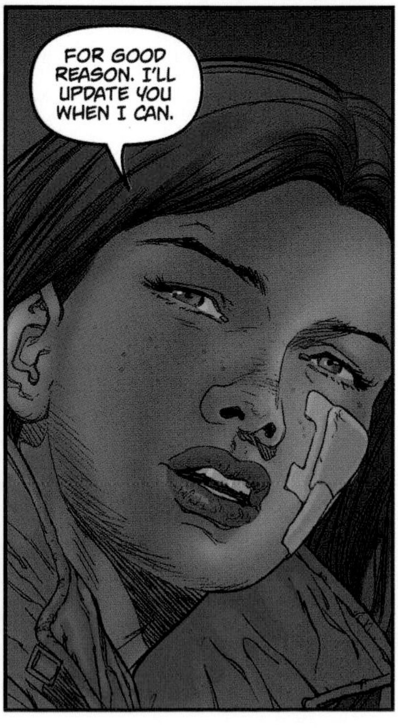
FOR GOOD REASON. I'LL UPDATE YOU WHEN I CAN.

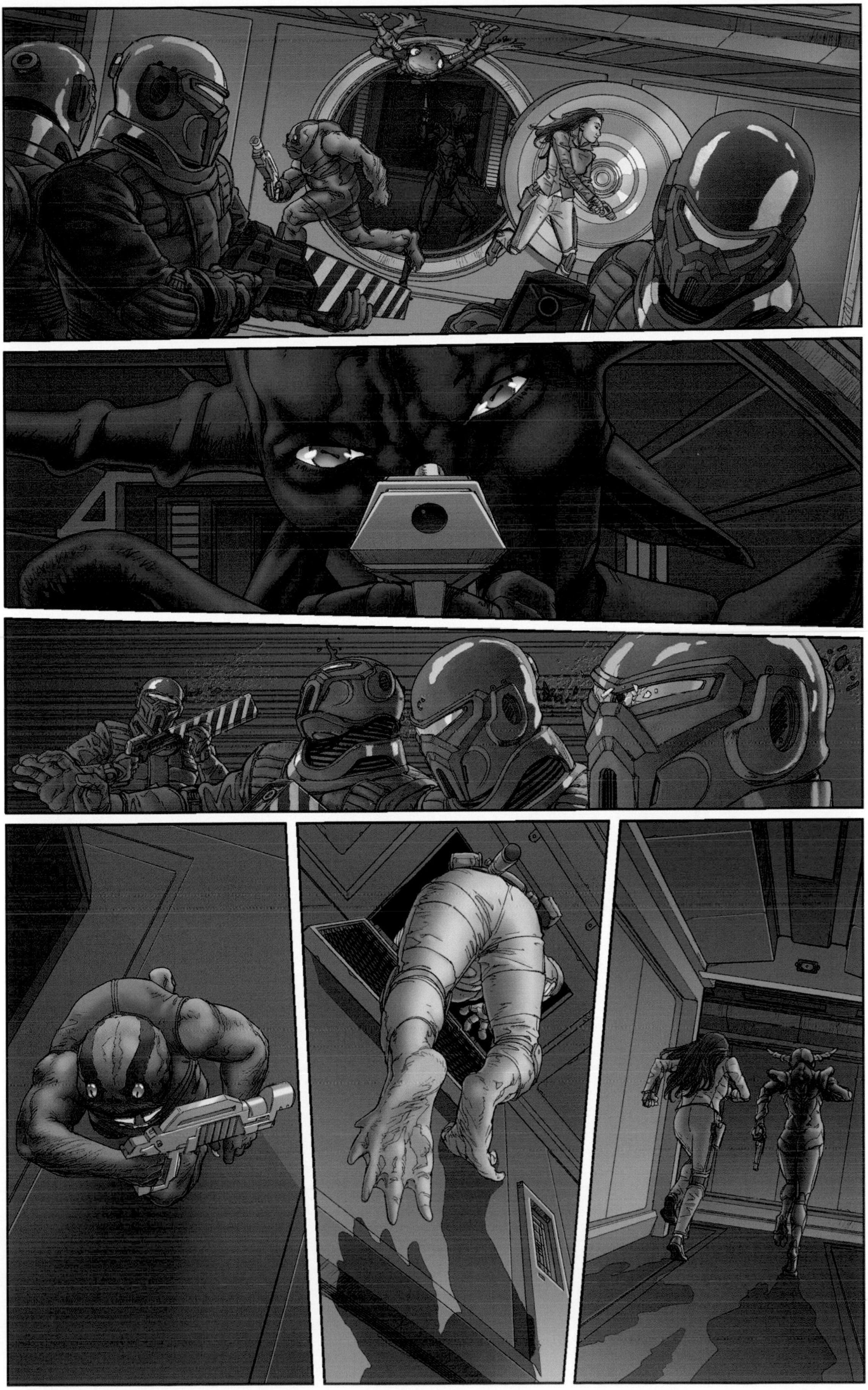

YOU DON'T *TRUST* ME? I'VE SAVED YOUR LIFE *TWELVE TIMES* IN THE SHORT TIME WE'VE KNOWN EACH OTHER.

IT'S NOT THAT. IN CASE WE'RE CAPTURED, I WANT FARG TO SUCCEED IN WHAT HE'S DOING. YOU COULD BE TORTURED. THEY COULD EXTRACT IT FROM YOUR MIND...

...PAINFULLY.

THAT'S A PLEASANT THOUGHT.

CRIDESH! ARE YOU PLUGGED IN?

AFFIRMATIVE. JUST READ OFF THE DOOR TAGS AS YOU GO.

X-23!

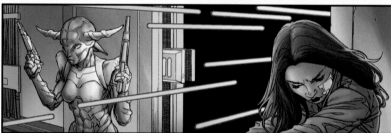

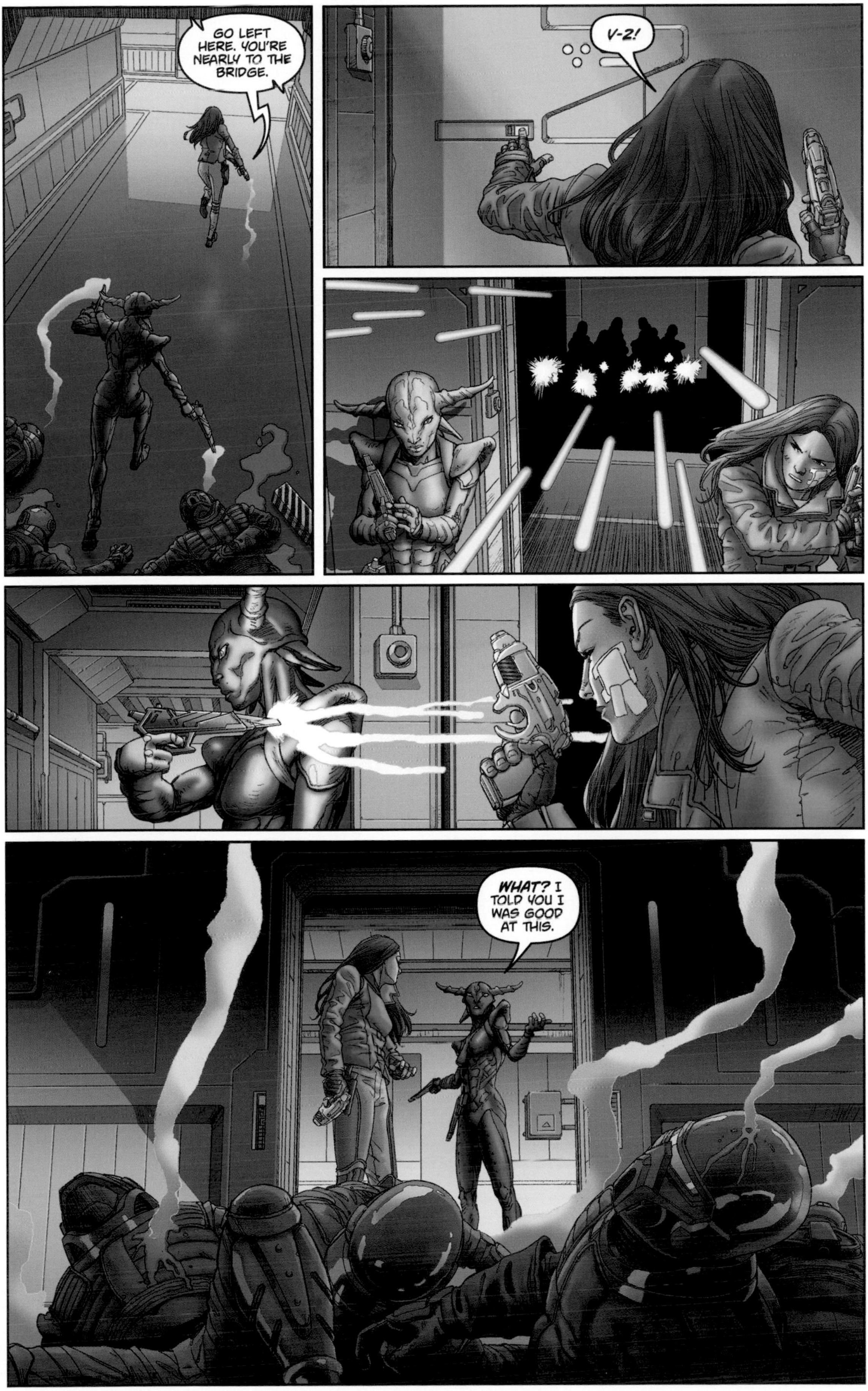
GO LEFT HERE. YOU'RE NEARLY TO THE BRIDGE.
V-2!
WHAT? I TOLD YOU I WAS GOOD AT THIS.

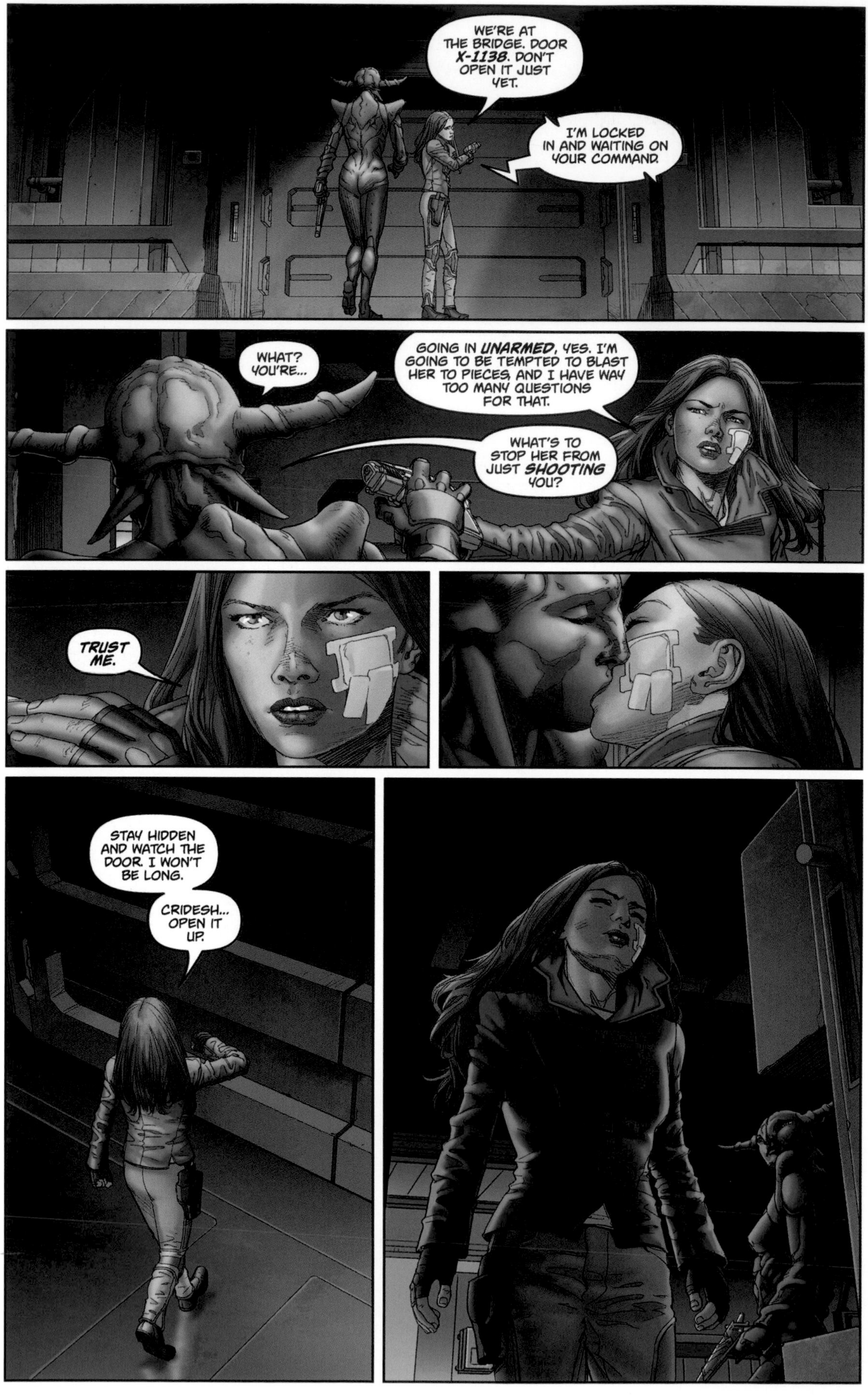
WE'RE AT THE BRIDGE. DOOR X-1138. DON'T OPEN IT JUST YET.
I'M LOCKED IN AND WAITING ON YOUR COMMAND.
WHAT? YOU'RE...
GOING IN UNARMED, YES. I'M GOING TO BE TEMPTED TO BLAST HER TO PIECES, AND I HAVE WAY TOO MANY QUESTIONS FOR THAT.
WHAT'S TO STOP HER FROM JUST SHOOTING YOU?
TRUST ME.
STAY HIDDEN AND WATCH THE DOOR. I WON'T BE LONG.
CRIDESH... OPEN IT UP.

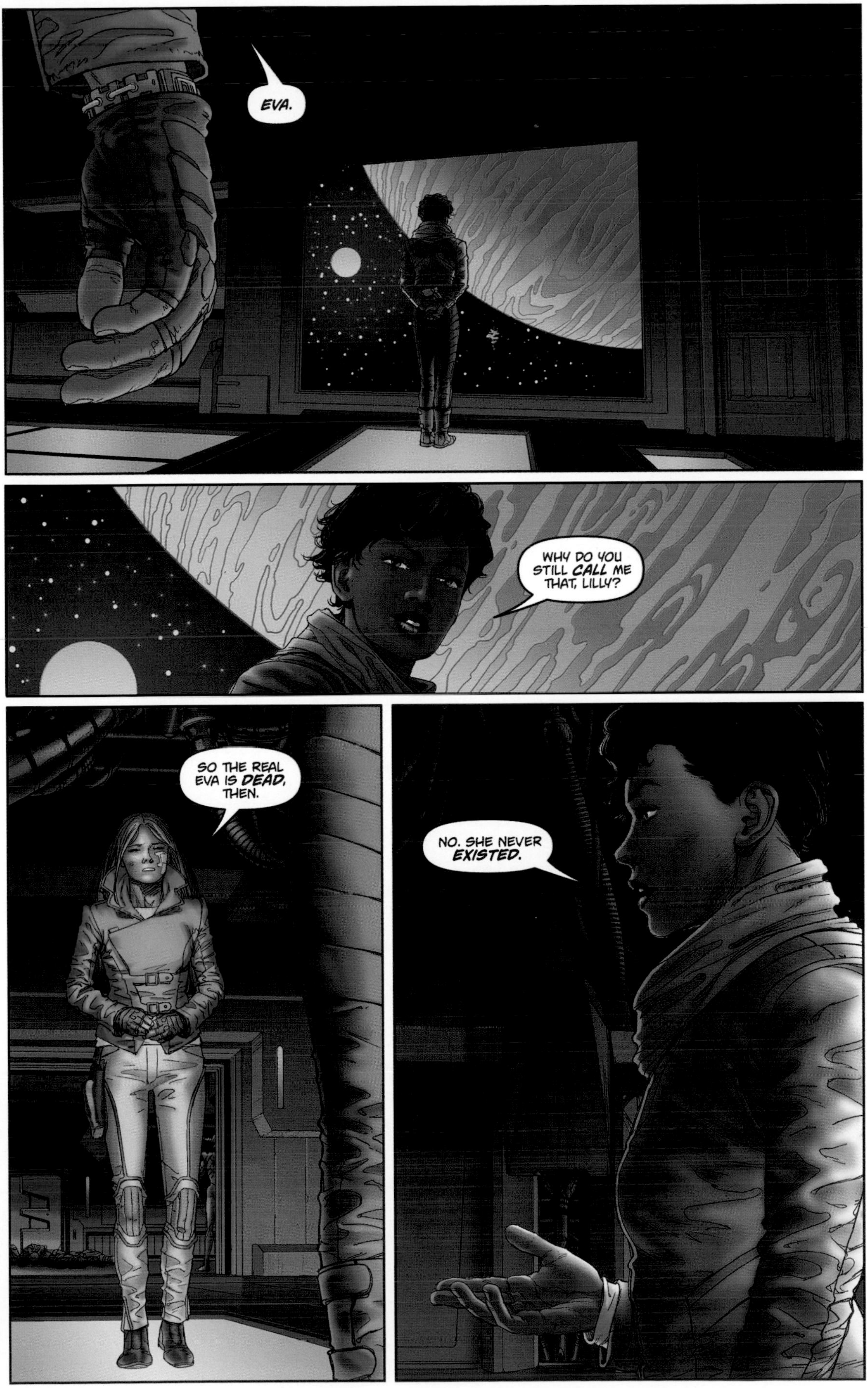
EVA.
WHY DO YOU STILL CALL ME THAT, LILLY?
SO THE REAL EVA IS DEAD, THEN.
NO. SHE NEVER EXISTED.

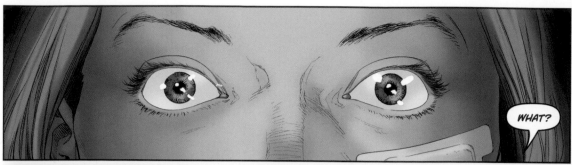

WHAT?

EVA WAS A *CONSTRUCT.* EARTHGOV STANDARD ISSUE *ALTER* OF A HUMAN VOLUNTEER...

...DESIGNED TO SEDUCE, SUPPRESS, AND ULTIMATELY *DRIVE AWAY* DISSIDENTS WITHOUT COSTING PRECIOUS HUMAN LIVES.

YOU WERE A *CATFISH.*

YOU KNOW YOUR ANCIENT EARTH EXPRESSIONS.

WE FIND THAT CREATING A RELATIONSHIP, THEN FAKING DEATH, HAS *ASTONISHING EFFECTS* ON THE PSYCHE OF ALIEN SYMPATHIZERS.

NEVER HAD ONE ESCAPE EARTH ALTOGETHER, THOUGH. YOU WARRANTED FURTHER STUDY.

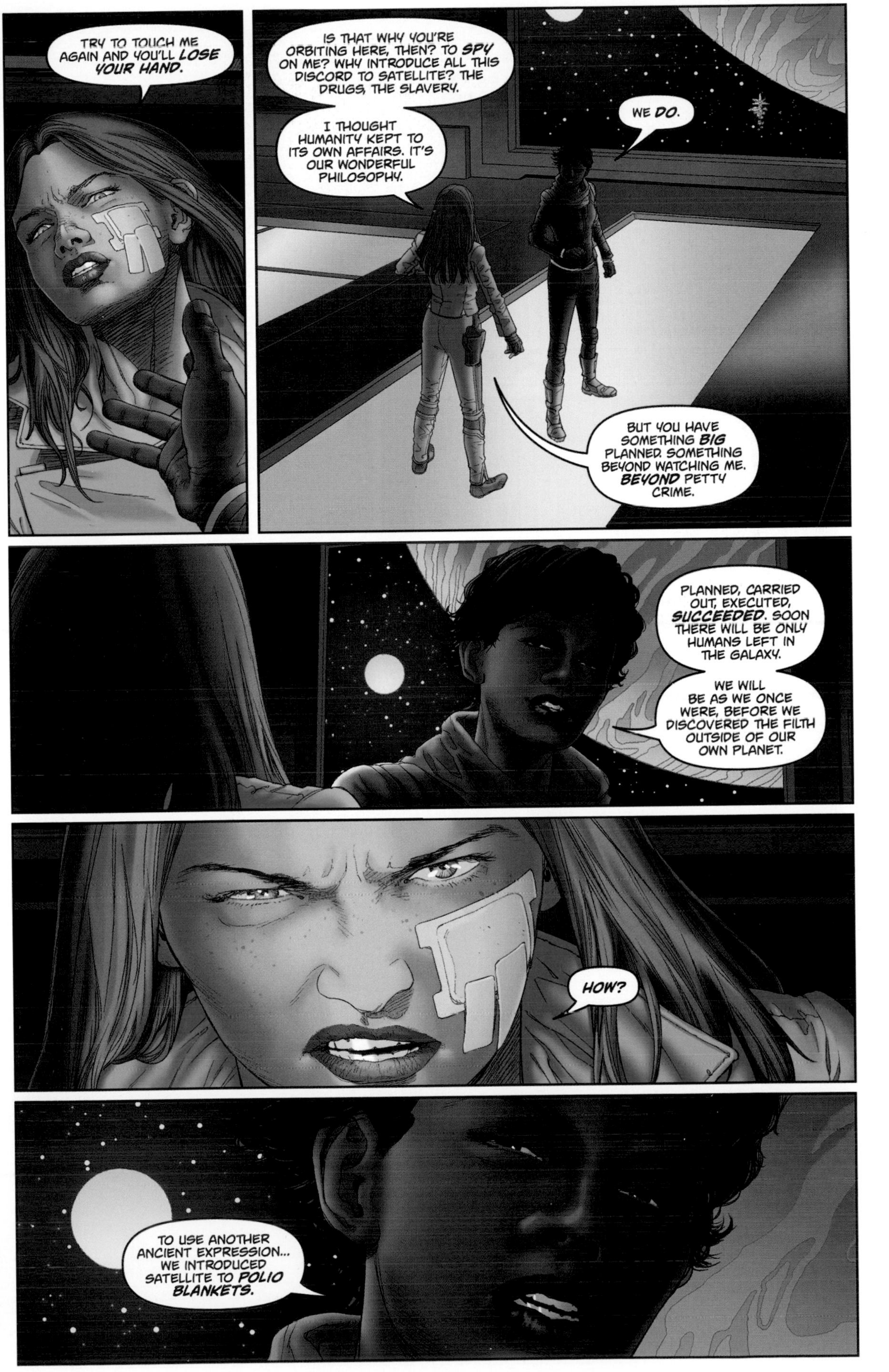
TRY TO TOUCH ME AGAIN AND YOU'LL LOSE YOUR HAND.
IS THAT WHY YOU'RE ORBITING HERE, THEN? TO SPY ON ME? WHY INTRODUCE ALL THIS DISCORD TO SATELLITE? THE DRUGS, THE SLAVERY.
I THOUGHT HUMANITY KEPT TO ITS OWN AFFAIRS. IT'S OUR WONDERFUL PHILOSOPHY.
WE DO.
BUT YOU HAVE SOMETHING BIG PLANNED. SOMETHING BEYOND WATCHING ME. BEYOND PETTY CRIME.
PLANNED, CARRIED OUT, EXECUTED, SUCCEEDED. SOON THERE WILL BE ONLY HUMANS LEFT IN THE GALAXY.
WE WILL BE AS WE ONCE WERE, BEFORE WE DISCOVERED THE FILTH OUTSIDE OF OUR OWN PLANET.
HOW?
TO USE ANOTHER ANCIENT EXPRESSION... WE INTRODUCED SATELLITE TO POLIO BLANKETS.

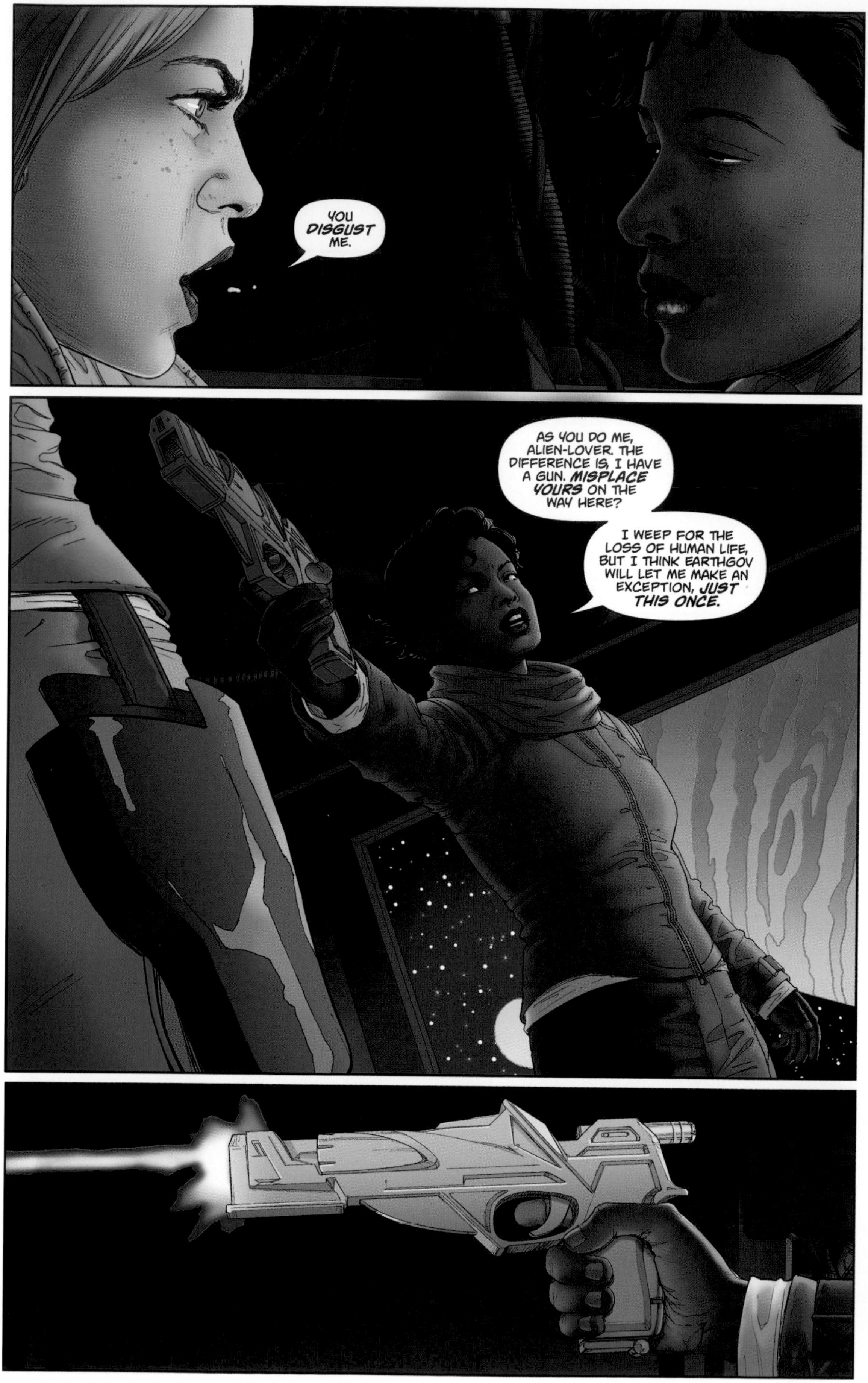
YOU DISGUST ME.
AS YOU DO ME, ALIEN-LOVER. THE DIFFERENCE IS, I HAVE A GUN. MISPLACE YOURS ON THE WAY HERE?
I WEEP FOR THE LOSS OF HUMAN LIFE, BUT I THINK EARTHGOV WILL LET ME MAKE AN EXCEPTION, JUST THIS ONCE.

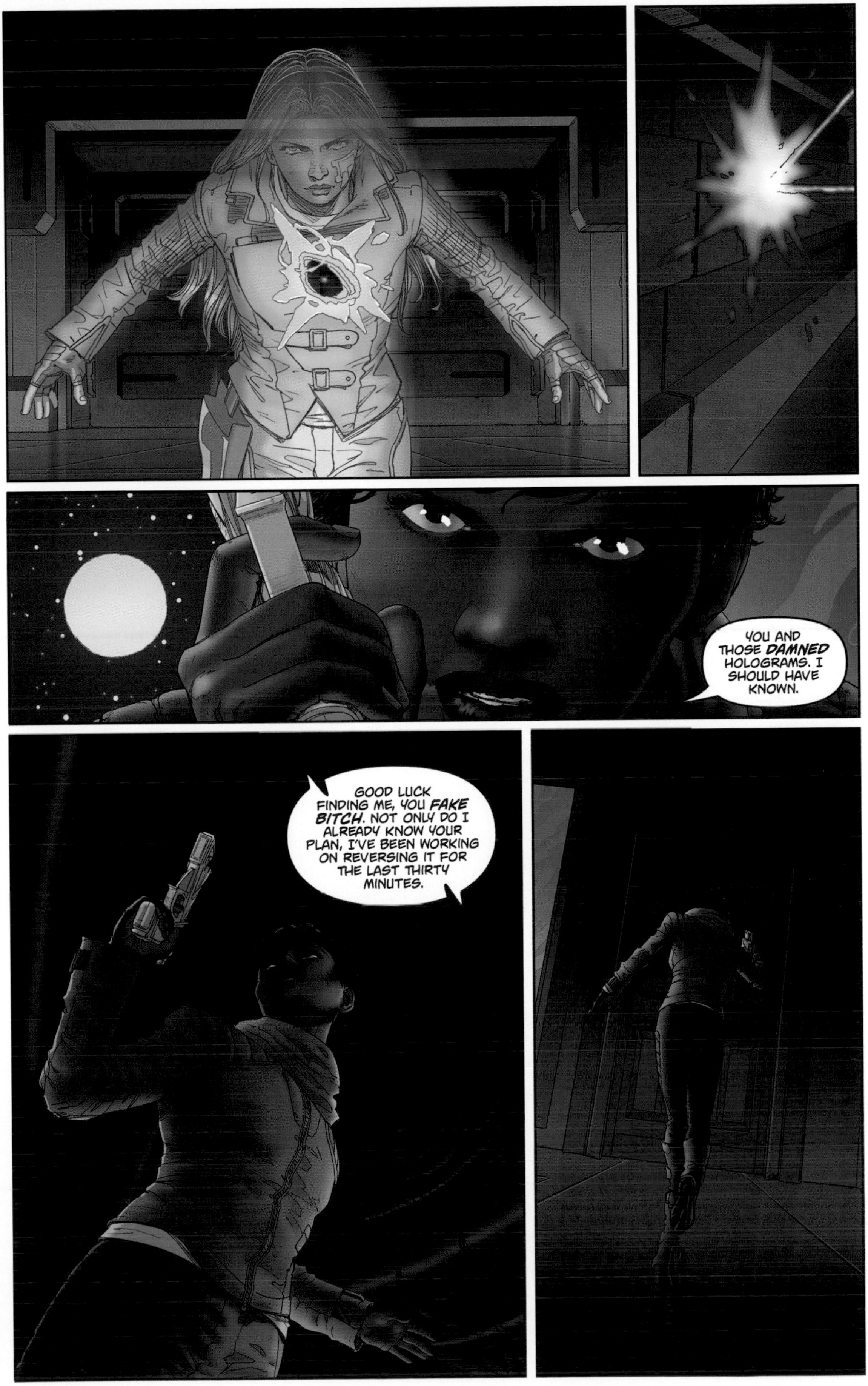
YOU AND THOSE DAMNED HOLOGRAMS. I SHOULD HAVE KNOWN.
GOOD LUCK FINDING ME, YOU FAKE BITCH. NOT ONLY DO I ALREADY KNOW YOUR PLAN, I'VE BEEN WORKING ON REVERSING IT FOR THE LAST THIRTY MINUTES.

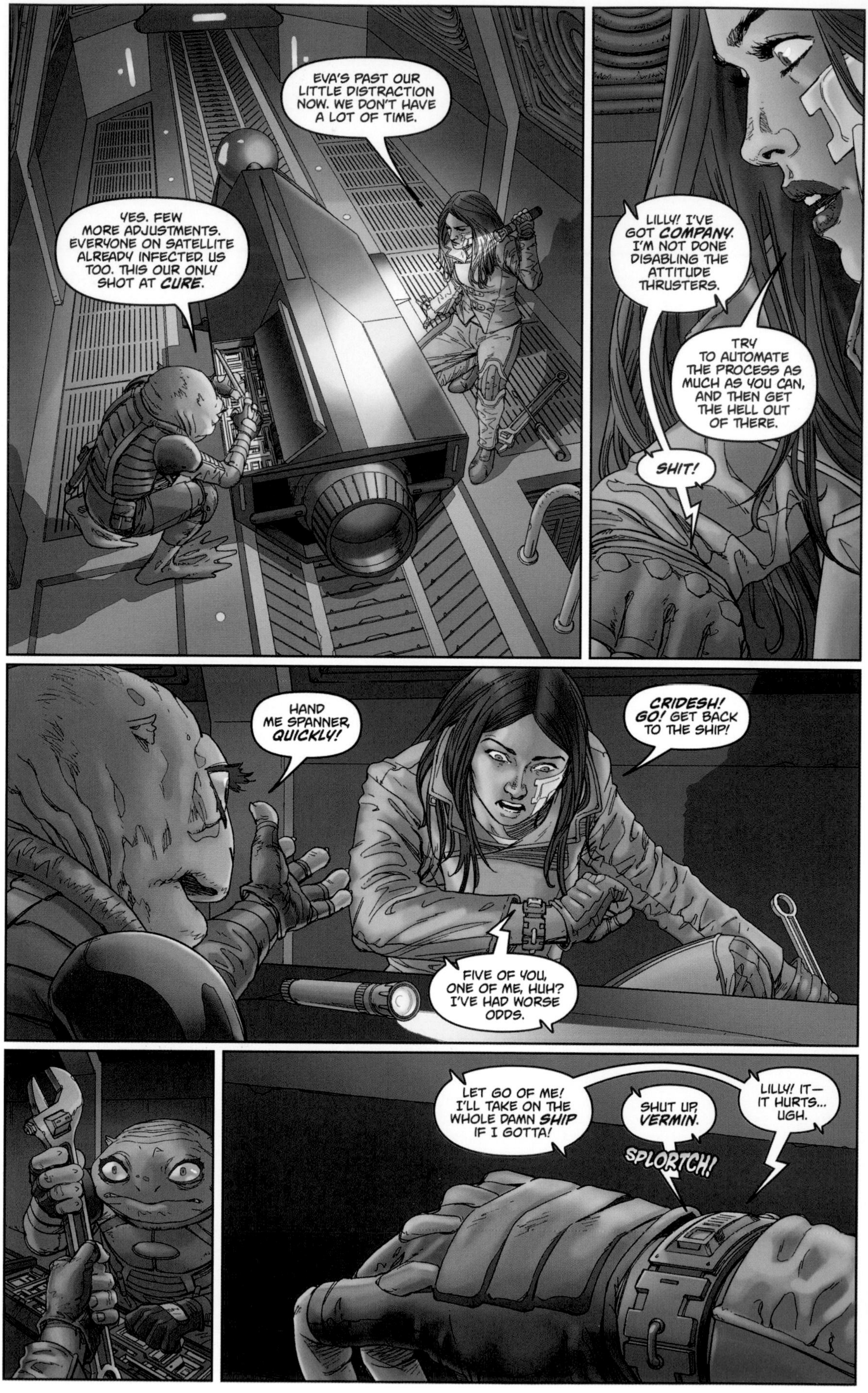

EVA'S PAST OUR LITTLE DISTRACTION NOW. WE DON'T HAVE A LOT OF TIME.
YES. FEW MORE ADJUSTMENTS. EVERYONE ON SATELLITE ALREADY INFECTED. US TOO. THIS OUR ONLY SHOT AT CURE.
LILLY! I'VE GOT COMPANY. I'M NOT DONE DISABLING THE ATTITUDE THRUSTERS.
TRY TO AUTOMATE THE PROCESS AS MUCH AS YOU CAN, AND THEN GET THE HELL OUT OF THERE.
SHIT!
HAND ME SPANNER, QUICKLY!
CRIDESH! GO! GET BACK TO THE SHIP!
FIVE OF YOU, ONE OF ME, HUH? I'VE HAD WORSE ODDS.
LET GO OF ME! I'LL TAKE ON THE WHOLE DAMN SHIP IF I GOTTA!
SHUT UP, VERMIN.
LILLY! IT— IT HURTS... UGH.
SPLORTCH!

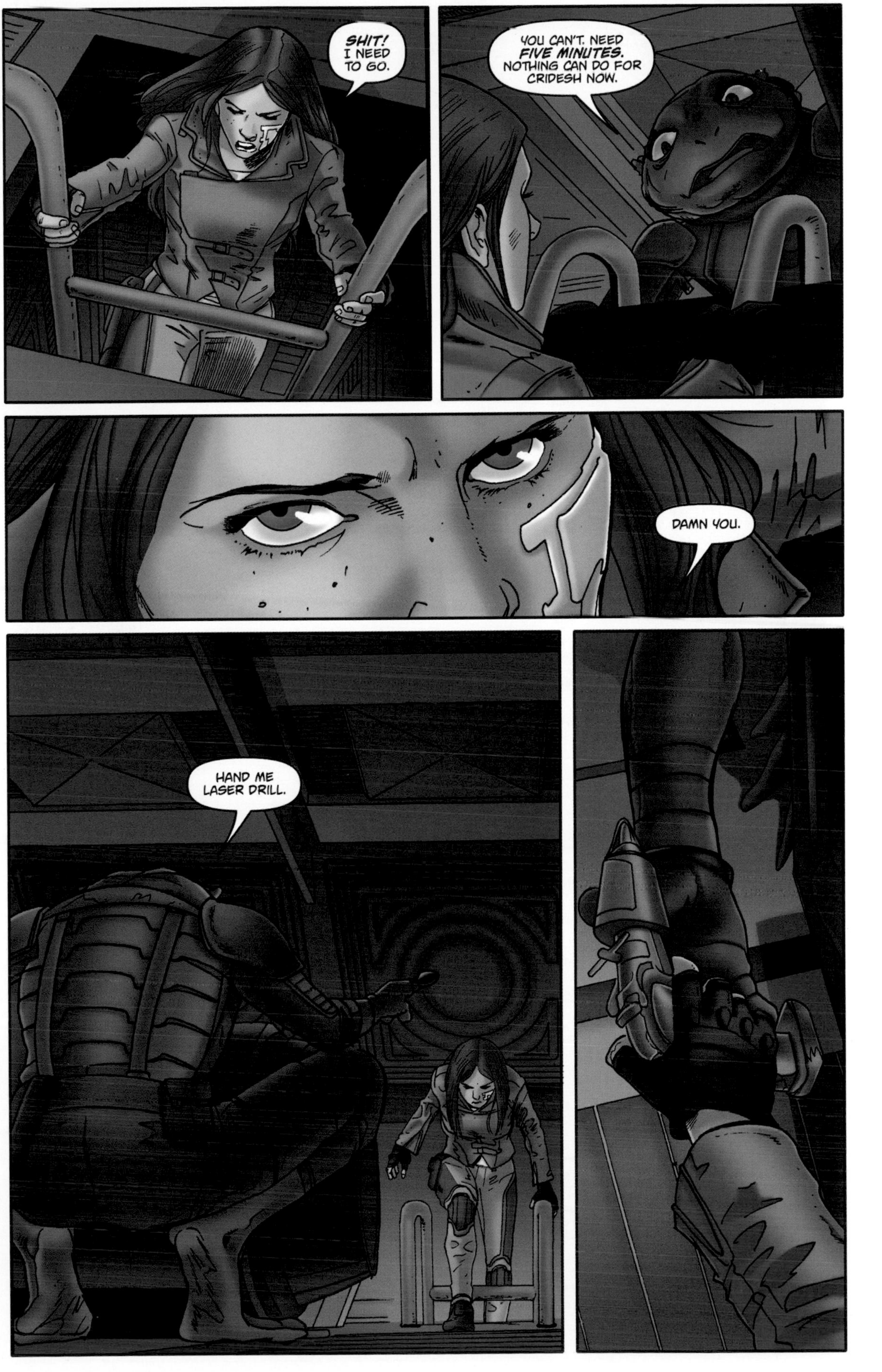
SHIT! I NEED TO GO.
YOU CAN'T. NEED FIVE MINUTES. NOTHING CAN DO FOR CRIDESH NOW.
DAMN YOU.
HAND ME LASER DRILL.

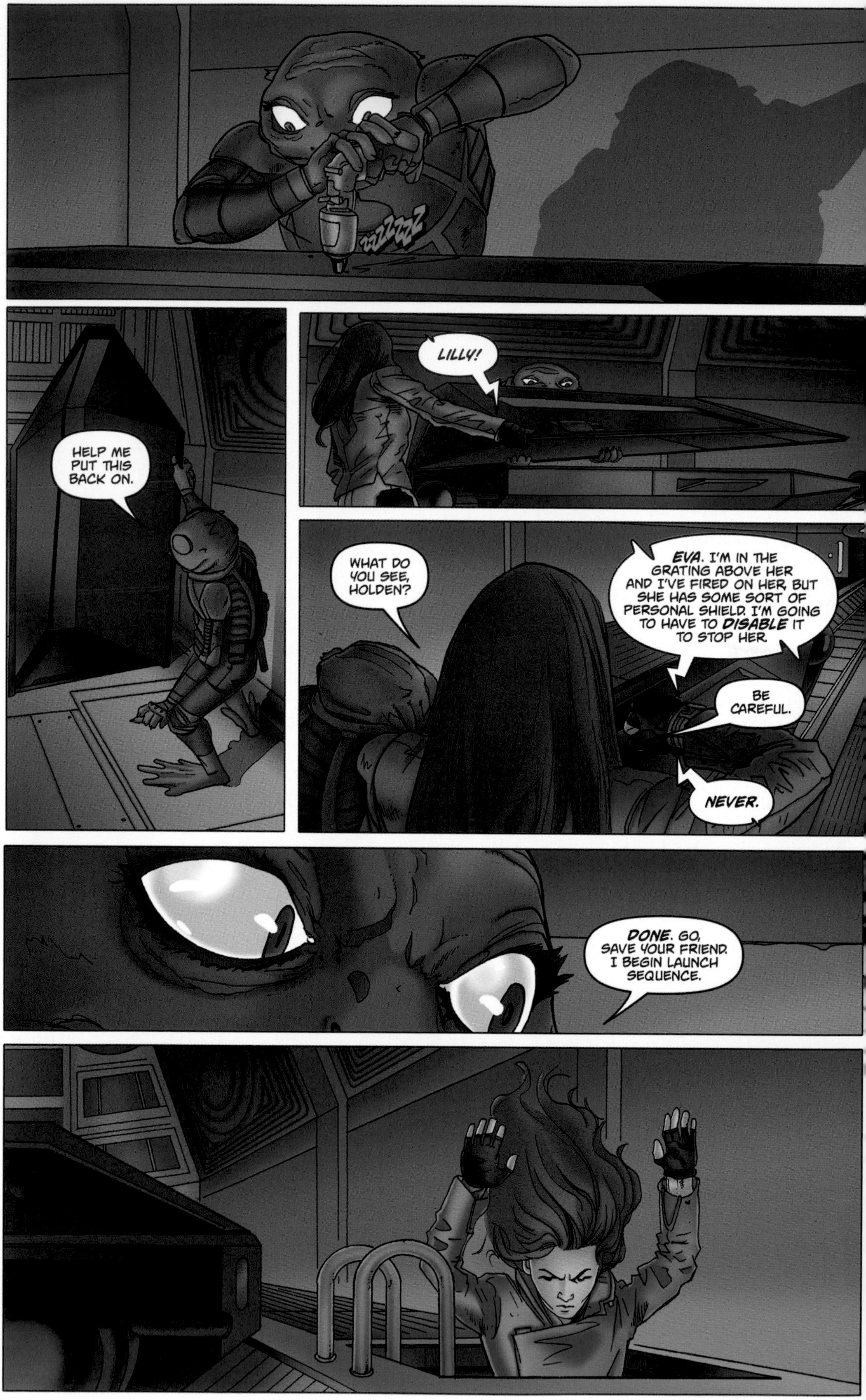
ZZZZZZZ
HELP ME PUT THIS BACK ON.
LILLY!
WHAT DO YOU SEE, HOLDEN?
EVA. I'M IN THE GRATING ABOVE HER AND I'VE FIRED ON HER, BUT SHE HAS SOME SORT OF PERSONAL SHIELD. I'M GOING TO HAVE TO DISABLE IT TO STOP HER.
BE CAREFUL.
NEVER.
DONE. GO, SAVE YOUR FRIEND. I BEGIN LAUNCH SEQUENCE.

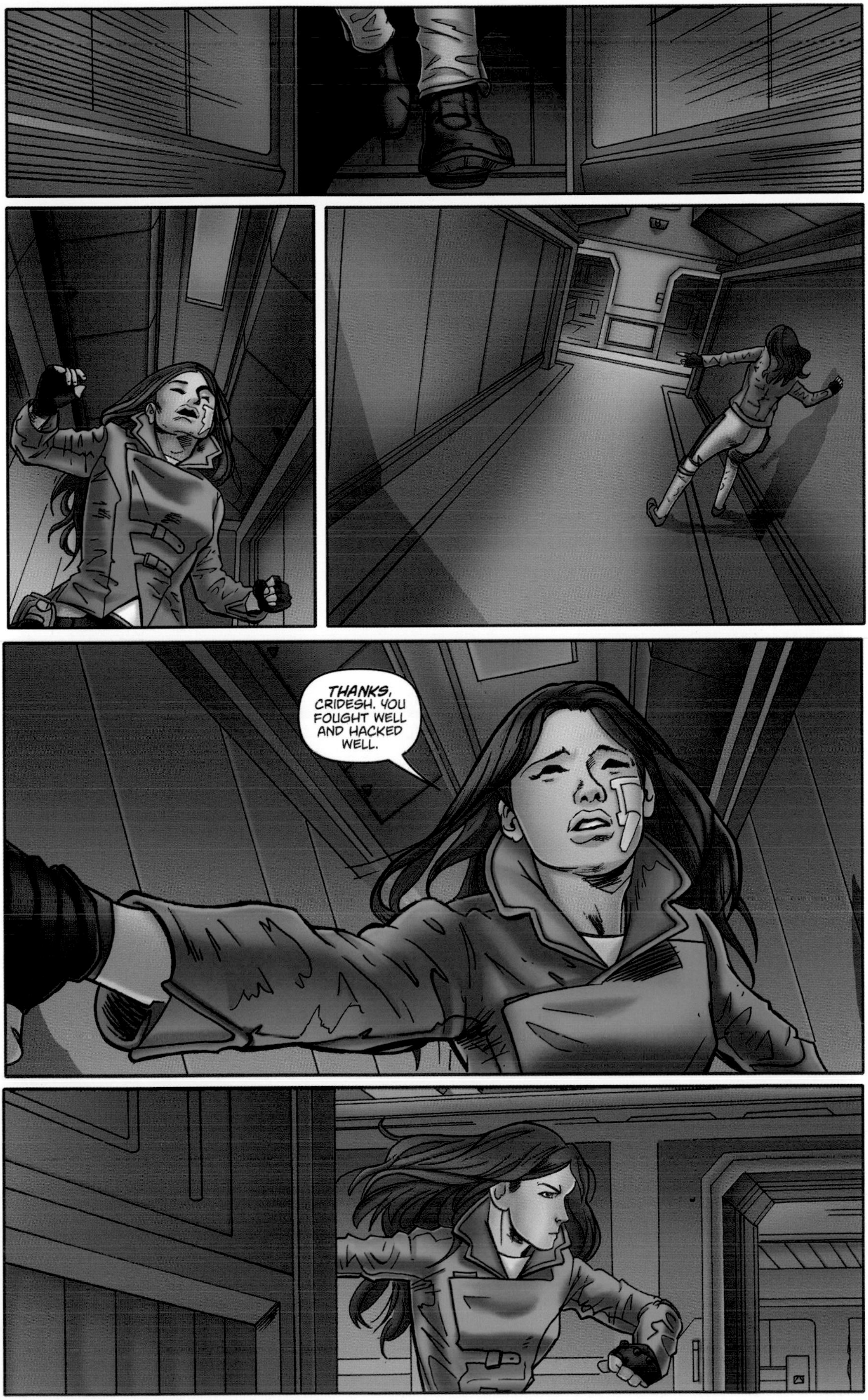
THANKS, CRIDESH. YOU FOUGHT WELL AND HACKED WELL.

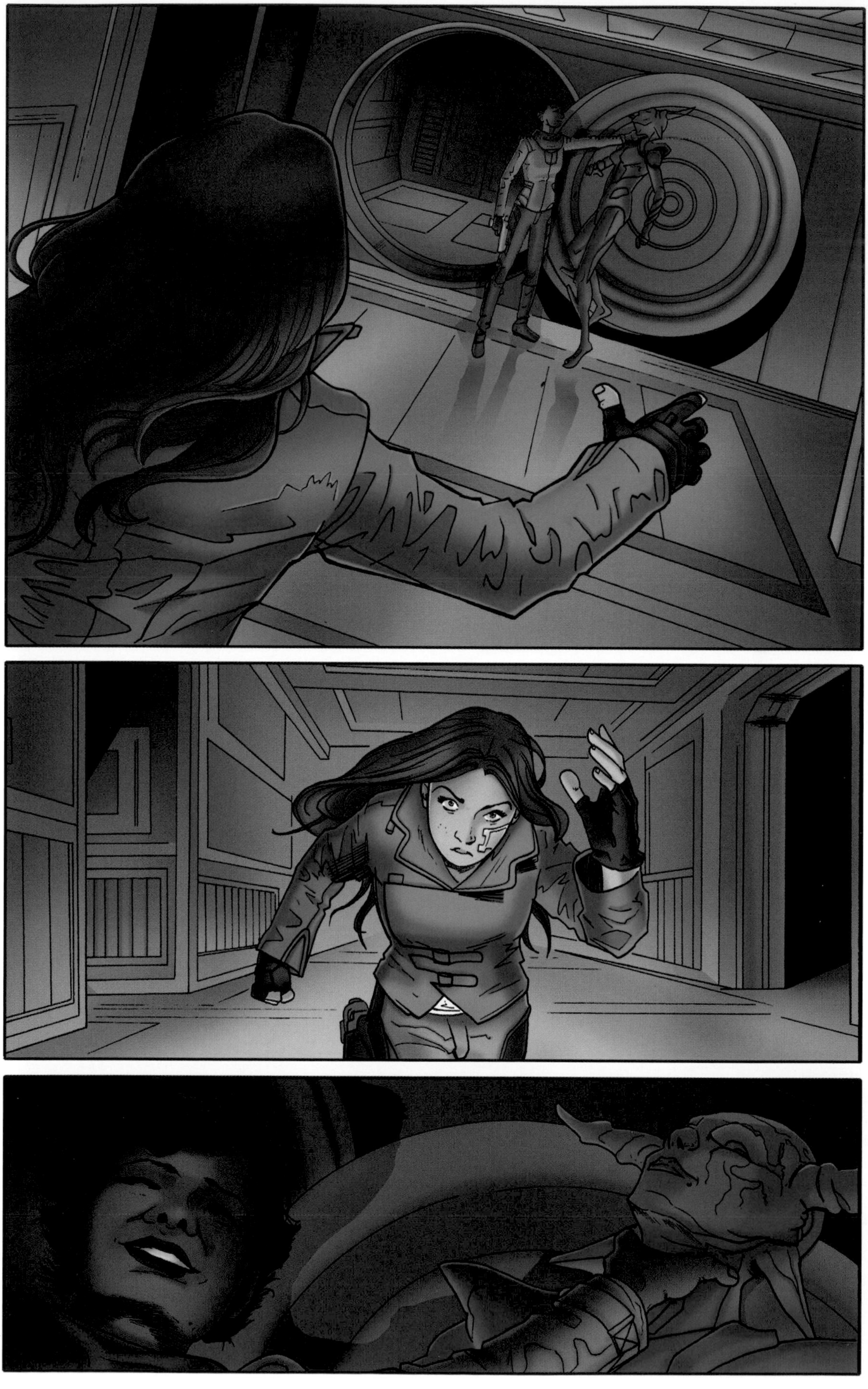

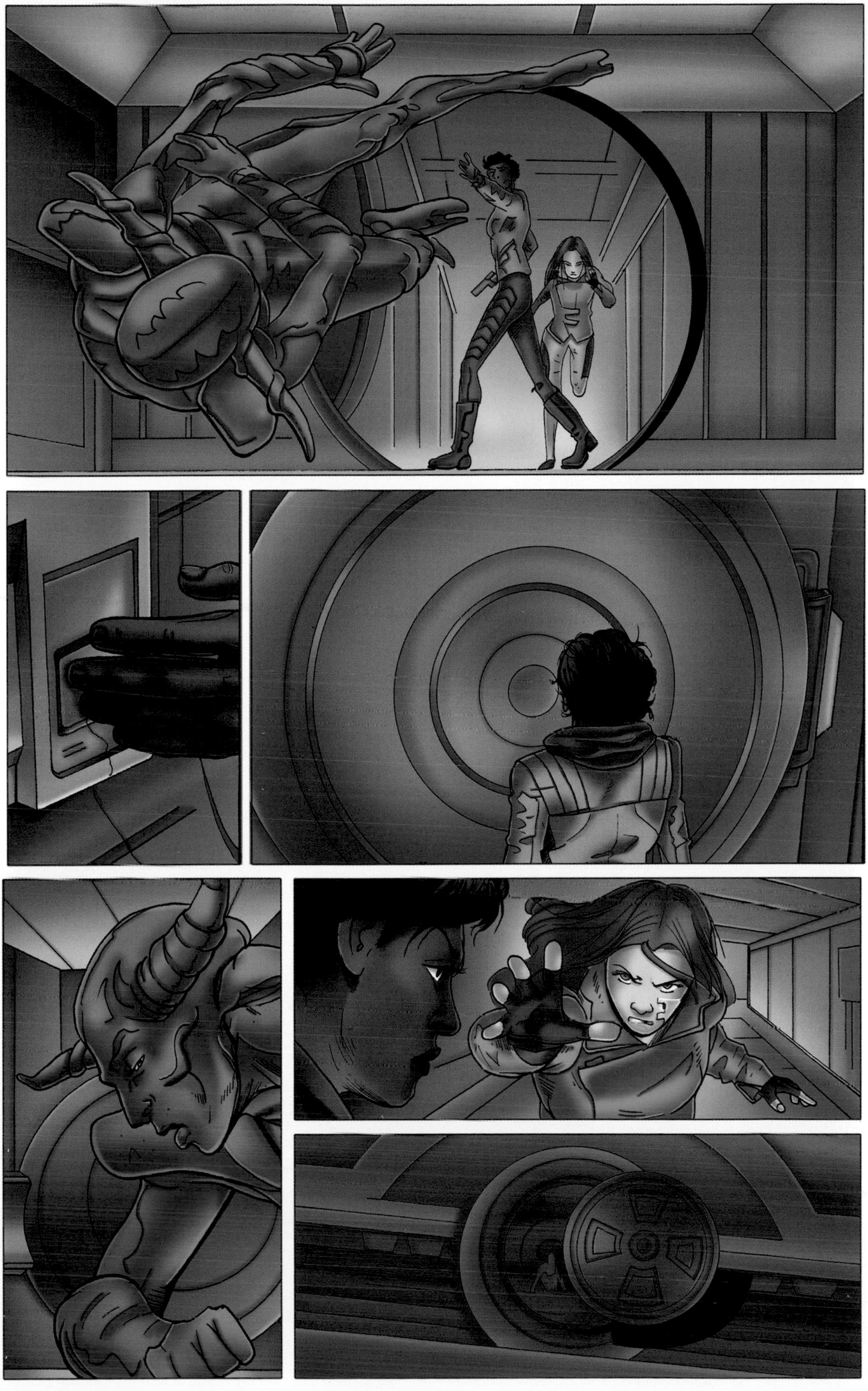

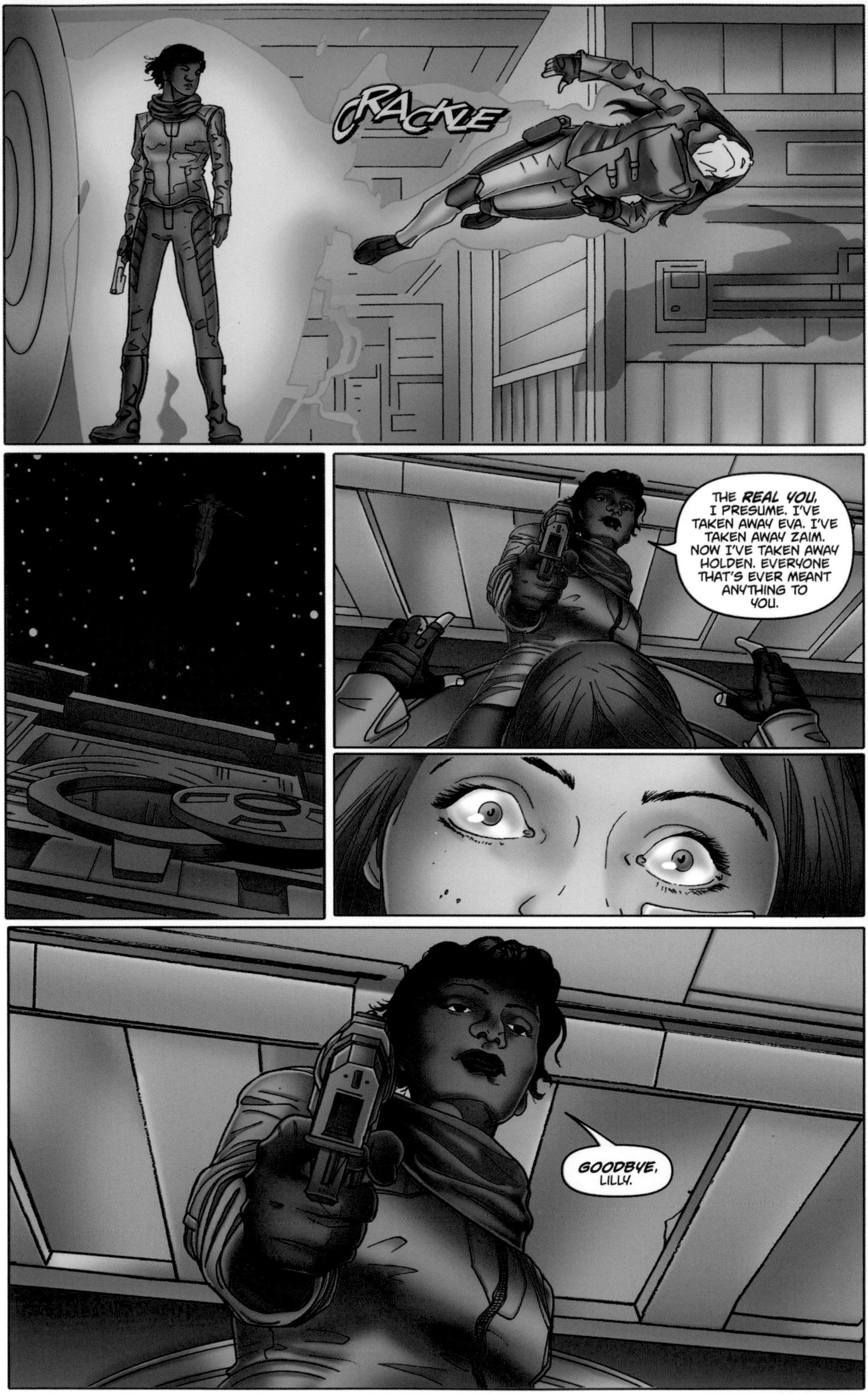
CRACKLE
THE REAL YOU, I PRESUME. I'VE TAKEN AWAY EVA. I'VE TAKEN AWAY ZAIM. NOW I'VE TAKEN AWAY HOLDEN. EVERYONE THAT'S EVER MEANT ANYTHING TO YOU.
GOODBYE, LILLY.

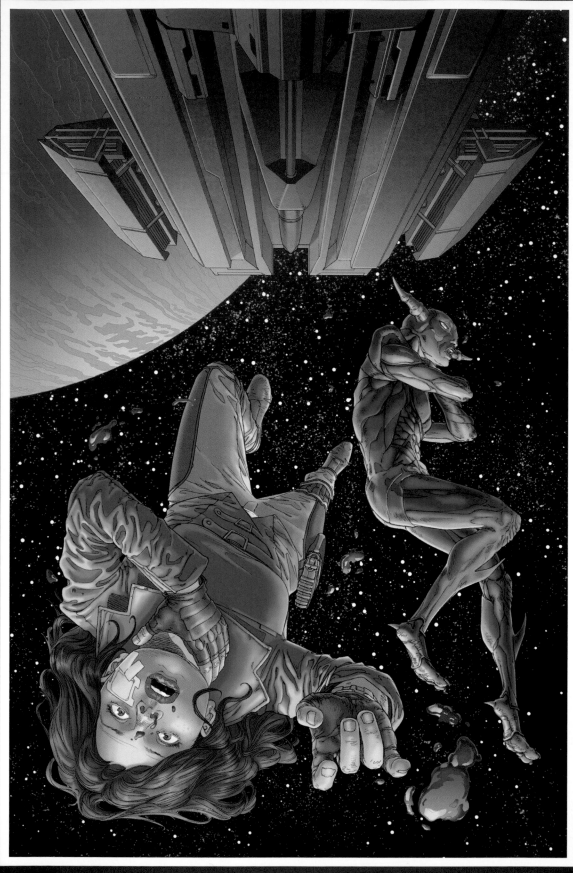

ART BY **STEVEN THOMPSON** • COLORS BY **LISA JACKSON**

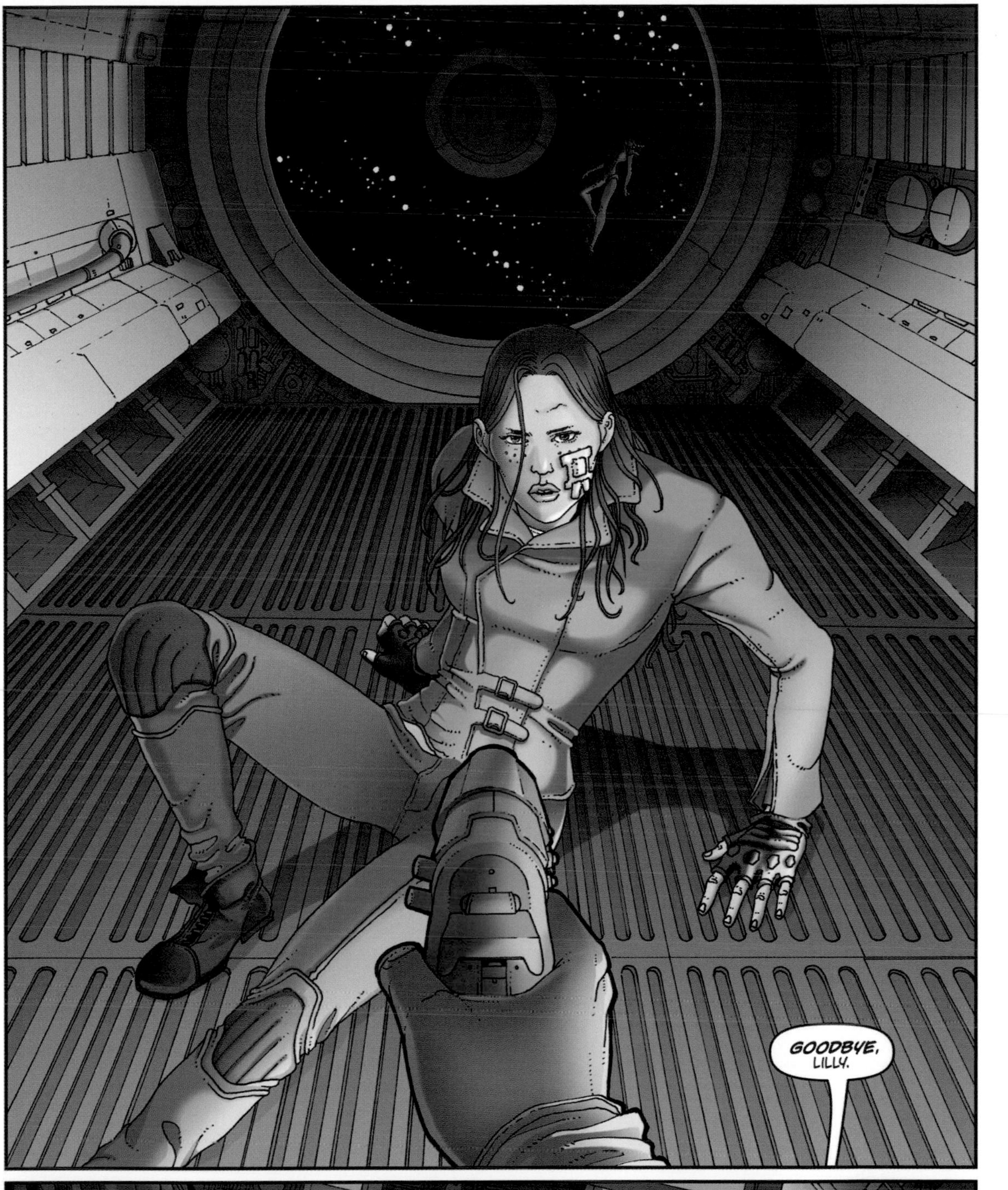
GOODBYE, LILLY.
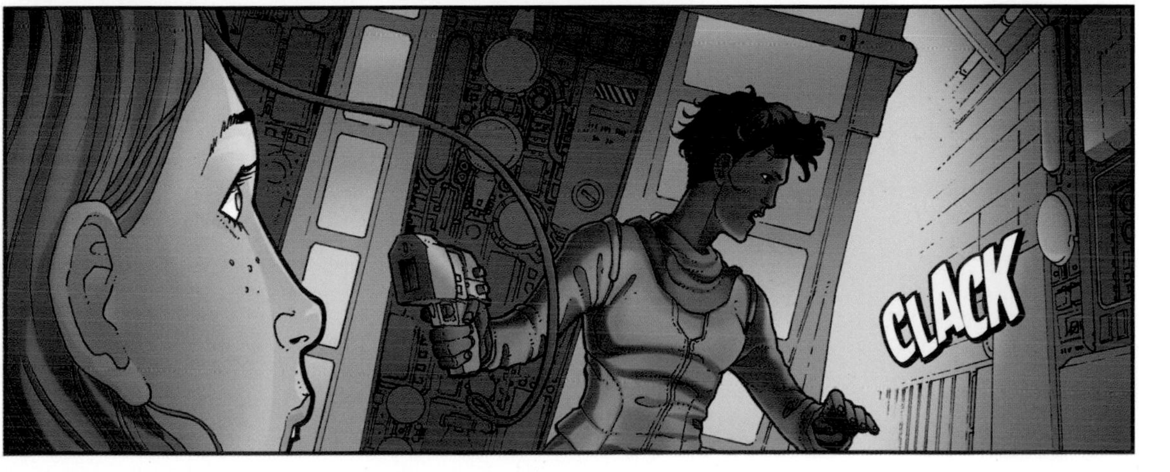
CLACK

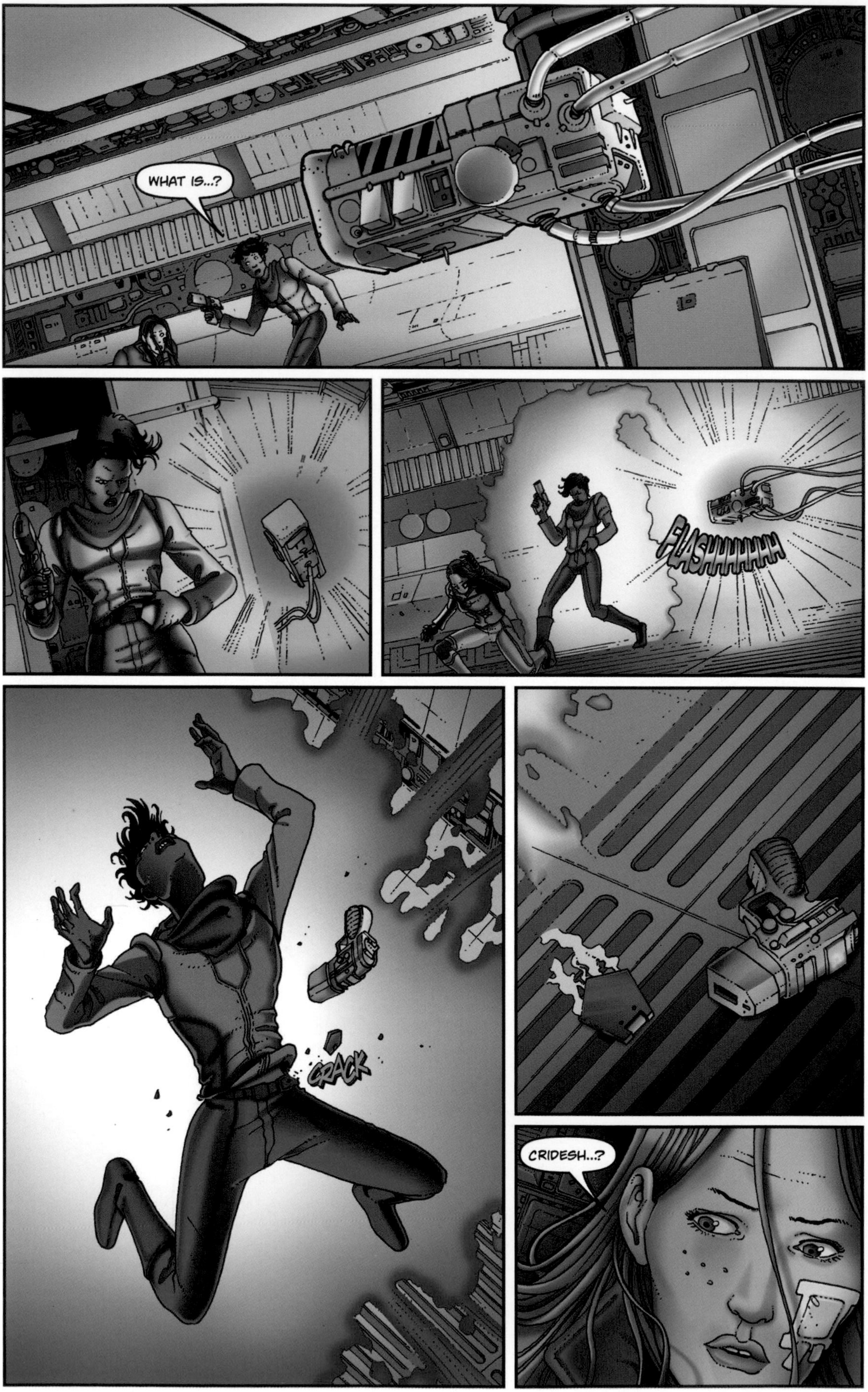
WHAT IS...?
FLASHHHHHHH
CRACK
CRIDESH...?

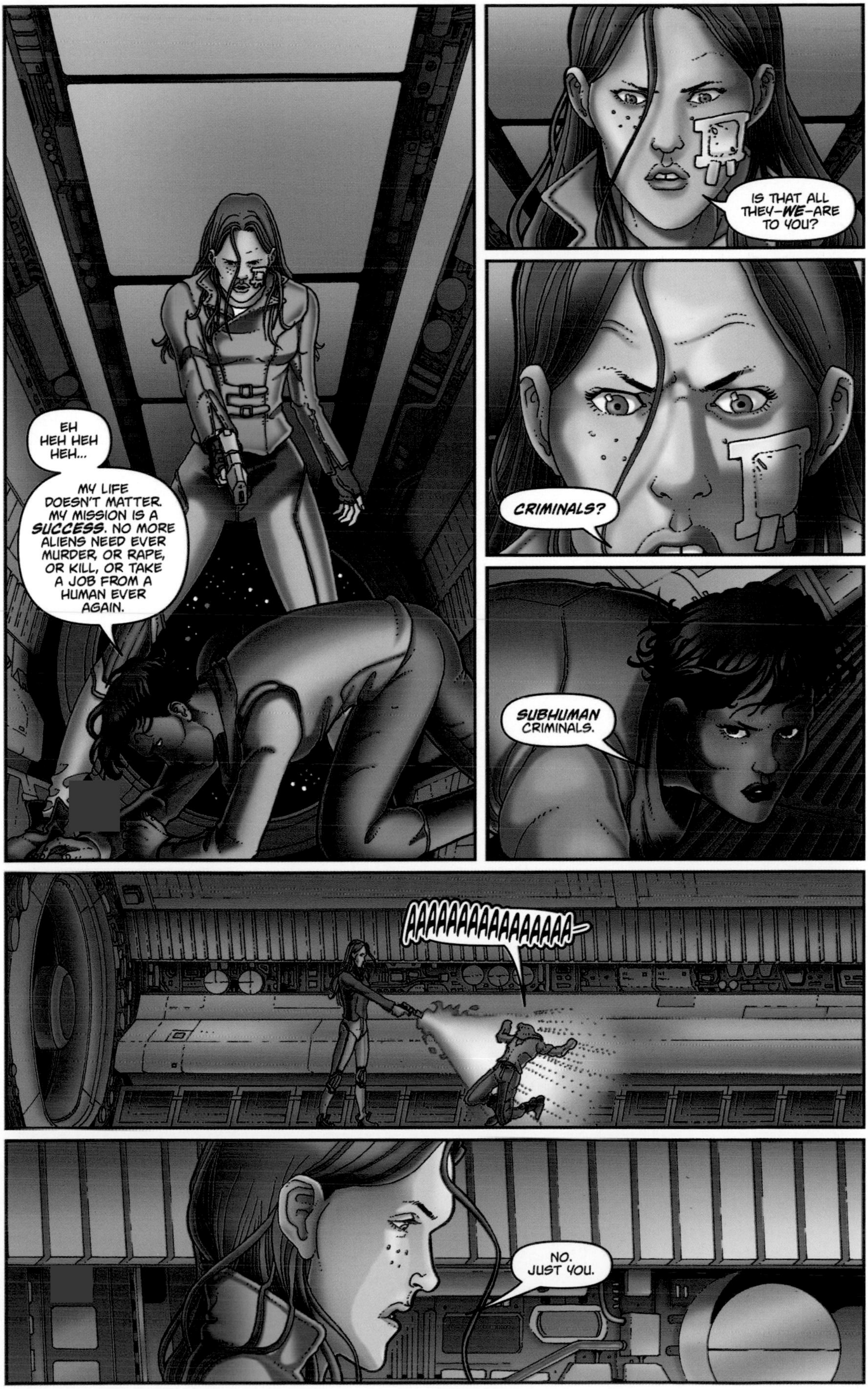
EH HEH HEH HEH...
MY LIFE DOESN'T MATTER. MY MISSION IS A *SUCCESS*. NO MORE ALIENS NEED EVER MURDER, OR RAPE, OR KILL, OR TAKE A JOB FROM A HUMAN EVER AGAIN.
IS THAT ALL THEY—*WE*—ARE TO YOU?
CRIMINALS?
SUBHUMAN CRIMINALS.
AAAAAAAAAAAAAAAA—
NO. JUST YOU.

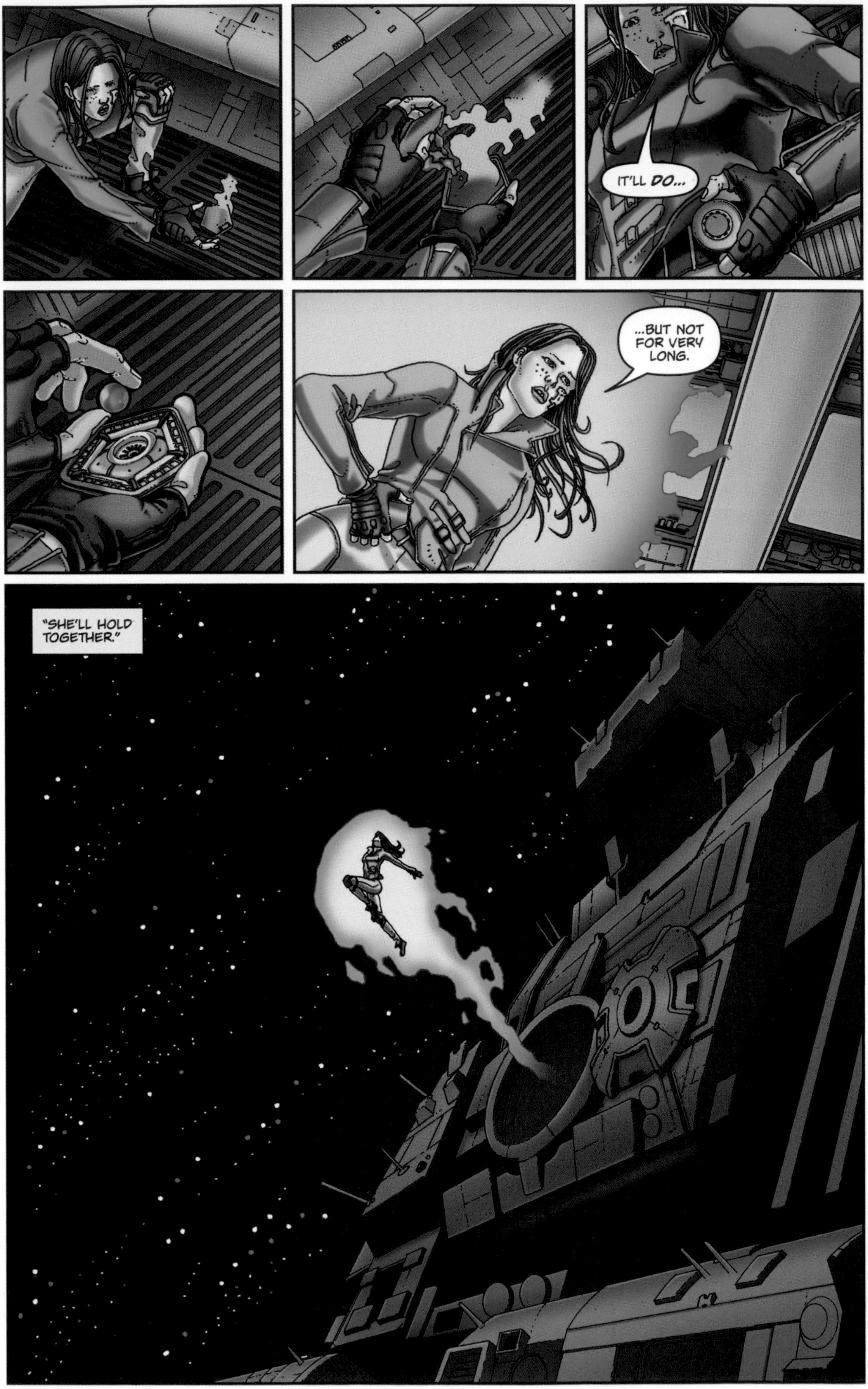
IT'LL DO...
...BUT NOT FOR VERY LONG.
"SHE'LL HOLD TOGETHER."

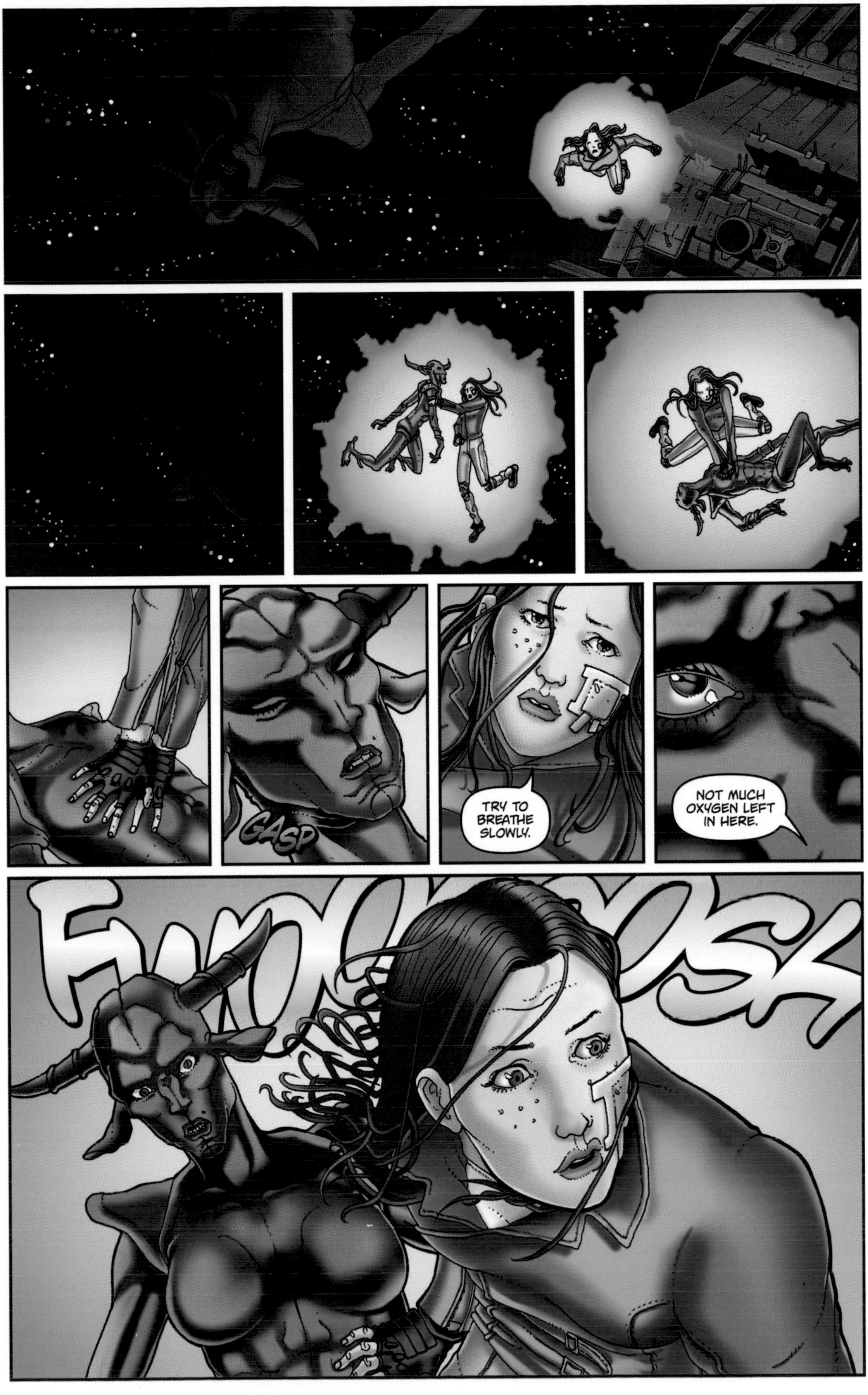
GASP
TRY TO BREATHE SLOWLY.
NOT MUCH OXYGEN LEFT IN HERE.

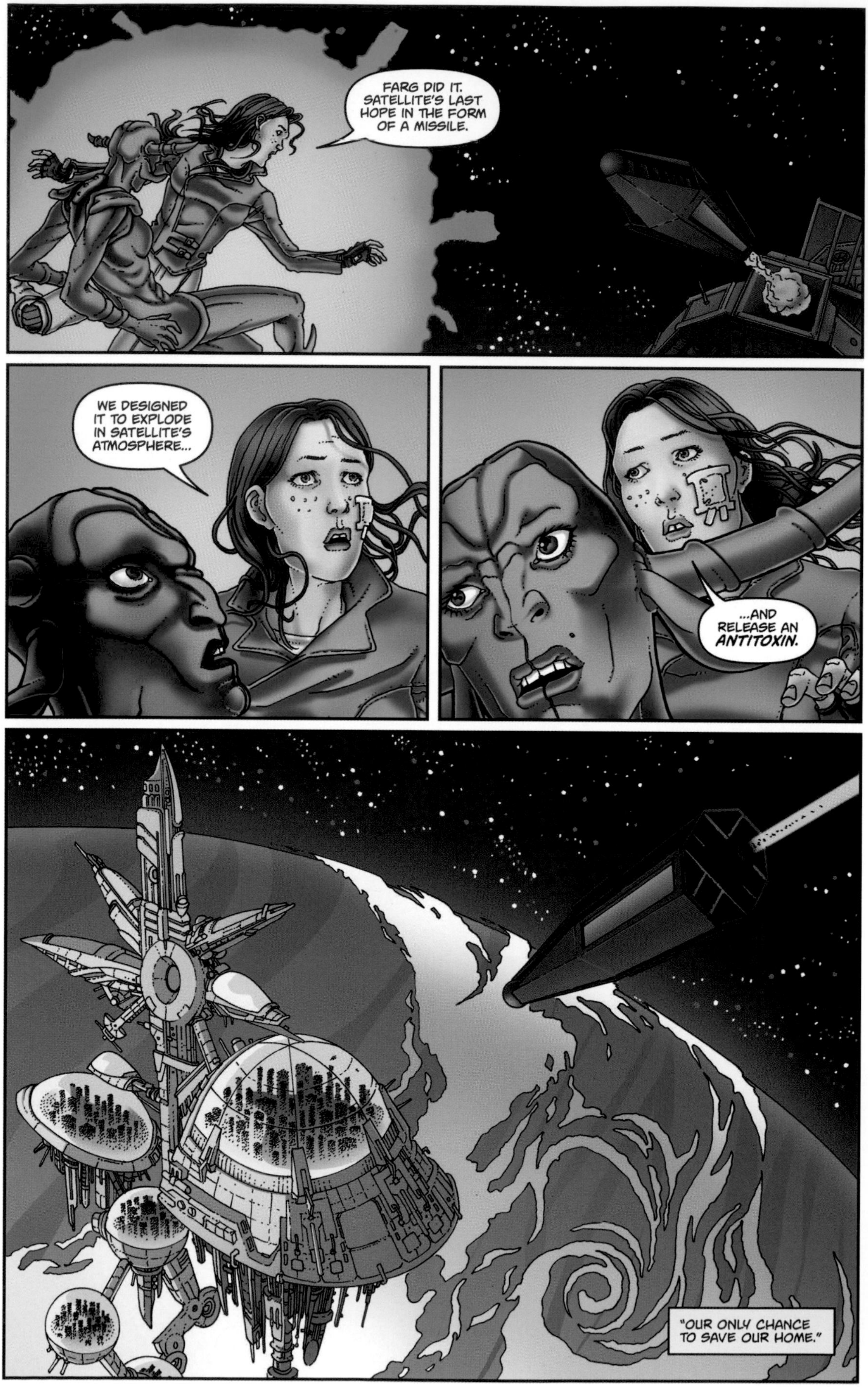
FARG DID IT. SATELLITE'S LAST HOPE IN THE FORM OF A MISSILE.
WE DESIGNED IT TO EXPLODE IN SATELLITE'S ATMOSPHERE...
...AND RELEASE AN *ANTITOXIN.*
"OUR ONLY CHANCE TO SAVE OUR HOME."

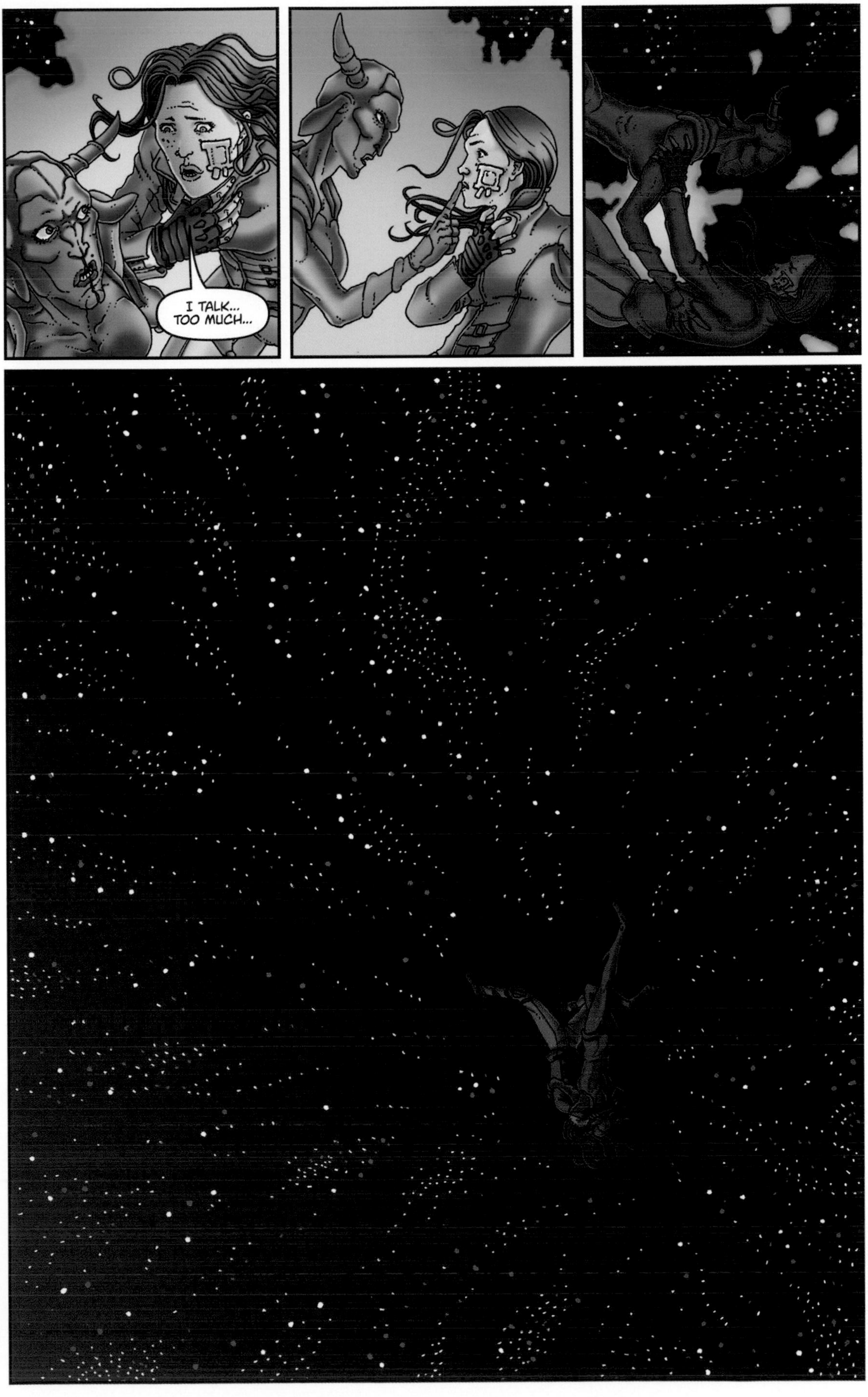
I TALK... TOO MUCH...

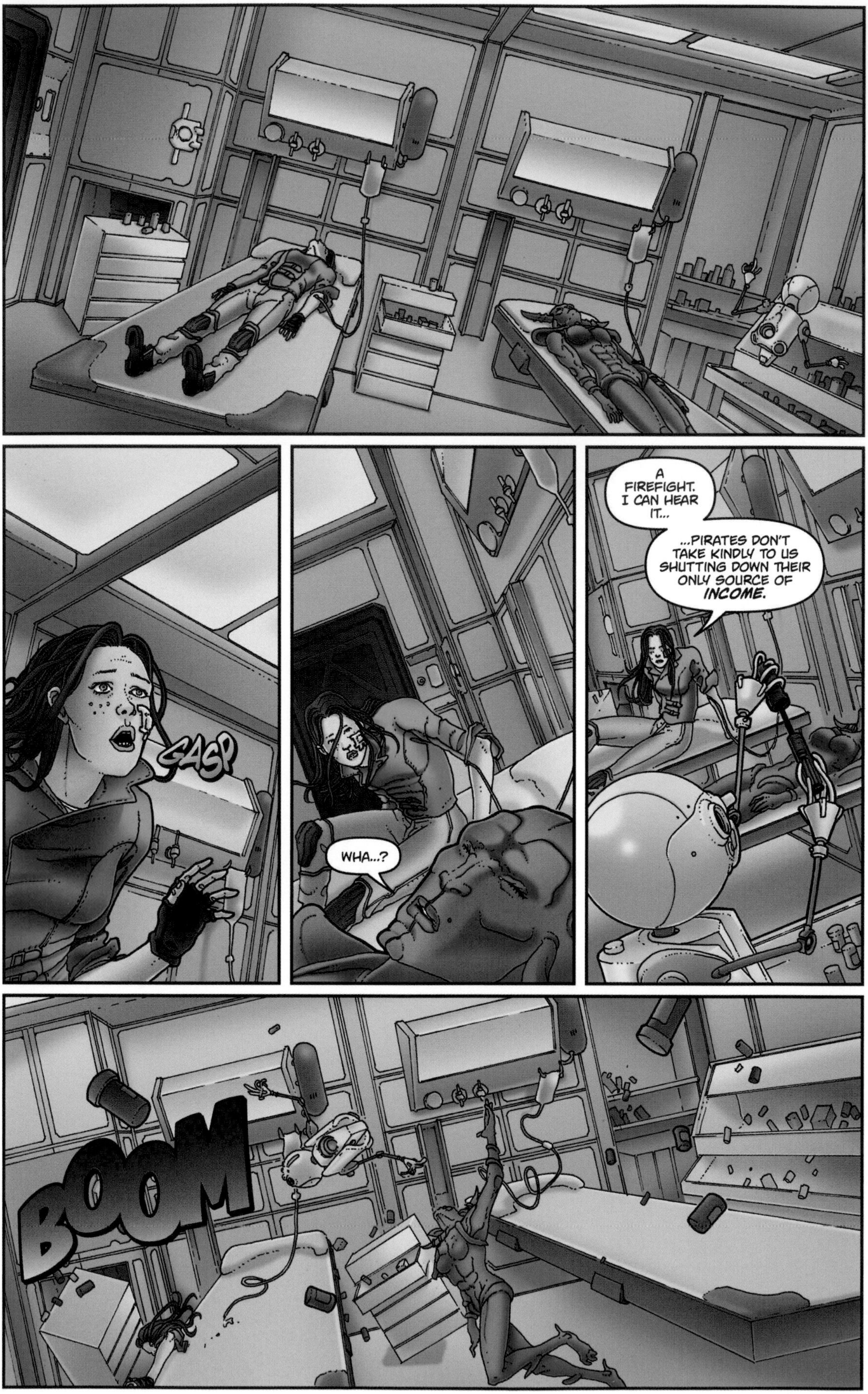
GASP
WHA...?
A FIREFIGHT. I CAN HEAR IT...
...PIRATES DON'T TAKE KINDLY TO US SHUTTING DOWN THEIR ONLY SOURCE OF INCOME.
BOOM

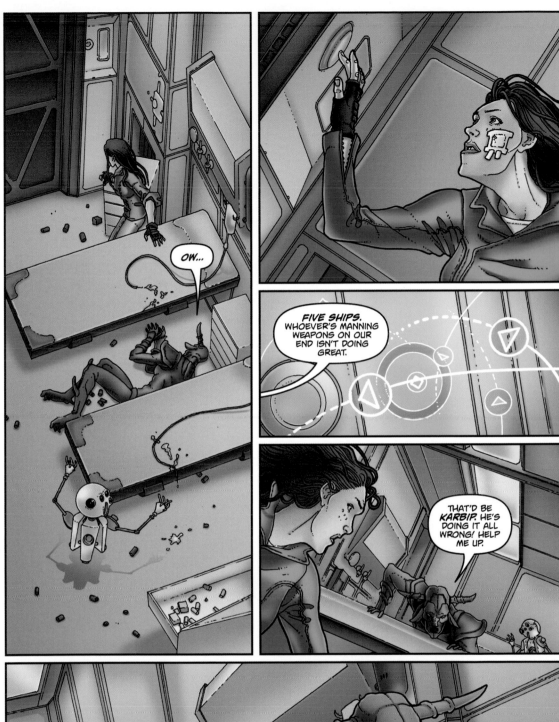

OW...

FIVE SHIPS. WHOEVER'S MANNING WEAPONS ON OUR END ISN'T DOING GREAT.

THAT'D BE *KARBIP.* HE'S DOING IT ALL WRONG! HELP ME UP.

WHAT?! YOU LOOK LIKE SHIT!

HELP ME UP!

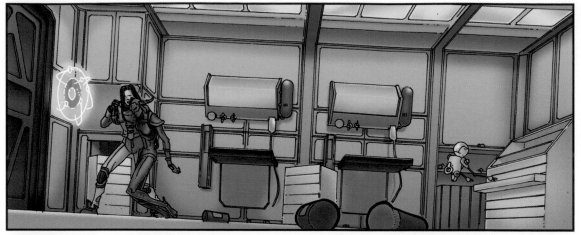

I'VE TAKEN **MANUAL CONTROL** FROM HERE.

EVASIVE MANEUVERS...

...SORRY. SHOULD HAVE GIVEN YOU MORE WARNING.

BOOM

GOT TWO. THEY'VE GOT **WEAK** SPOTS.

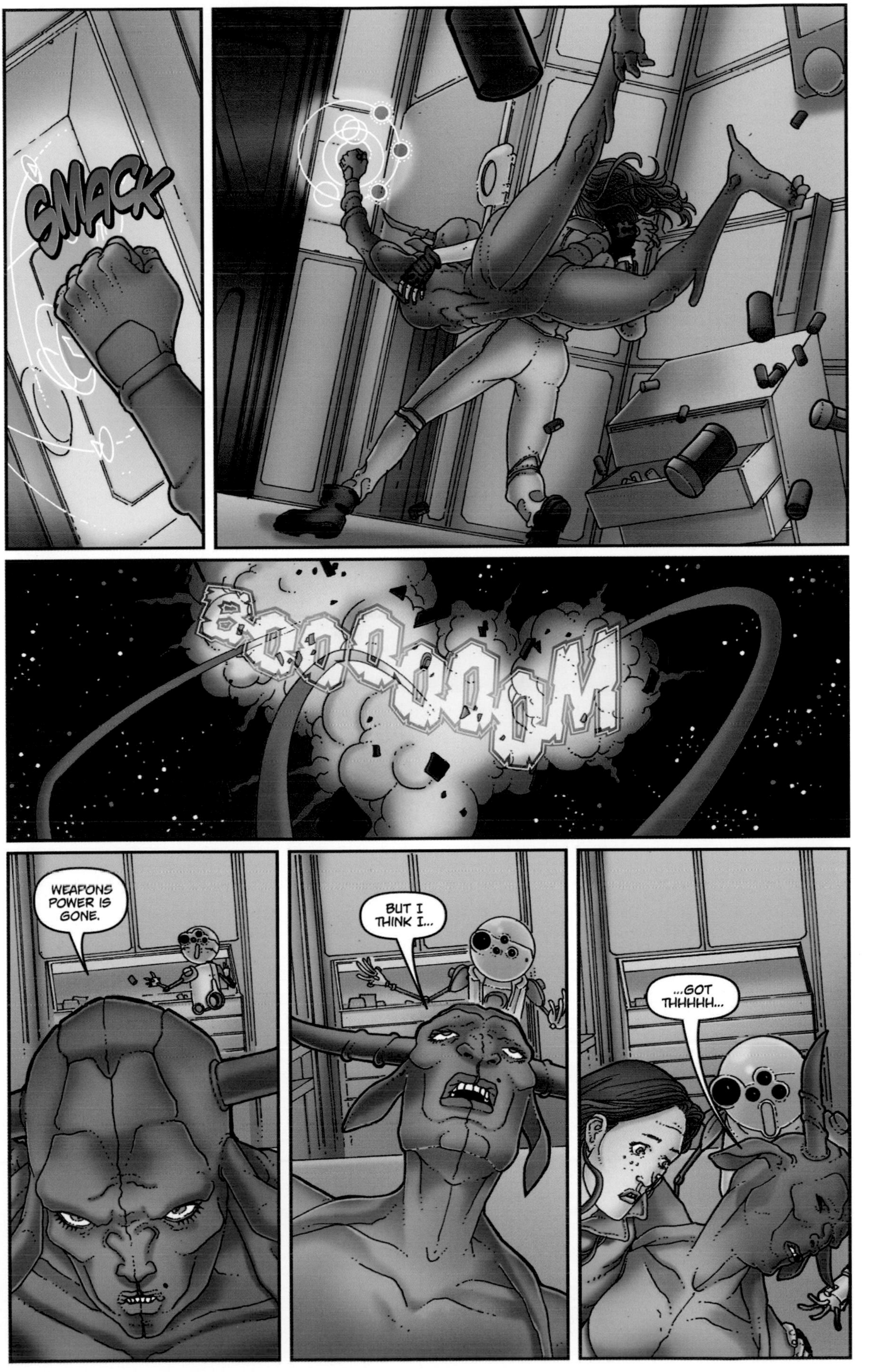
SMACK
BOOOOOM
WEAPONS POWER IS GONE.
BUT I THINK I...
...GOT THHHHH...

OKAY, OKAY. BACK TO BED. JUST LET ME TALK TO HOLDEN FOR A SECOND.
YOU WERE AMAZING. YOU... THAT WAS FUCKING UNBELIEVABLE.
I THINK...
I THINK I'M FALLING IN LOVE WITH YOU.
BACK TO BED.

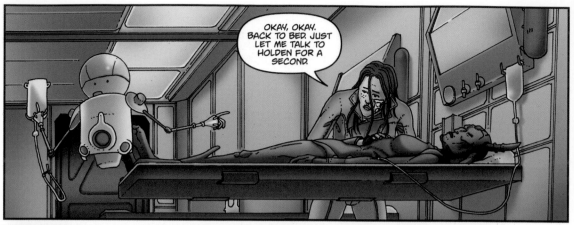

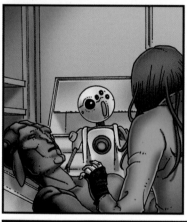

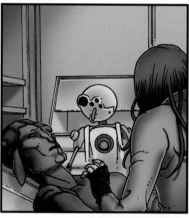

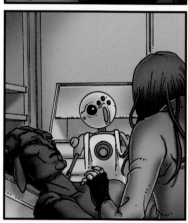

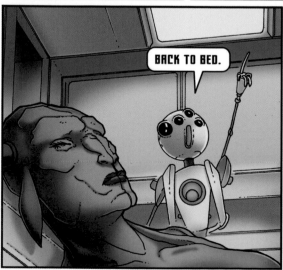

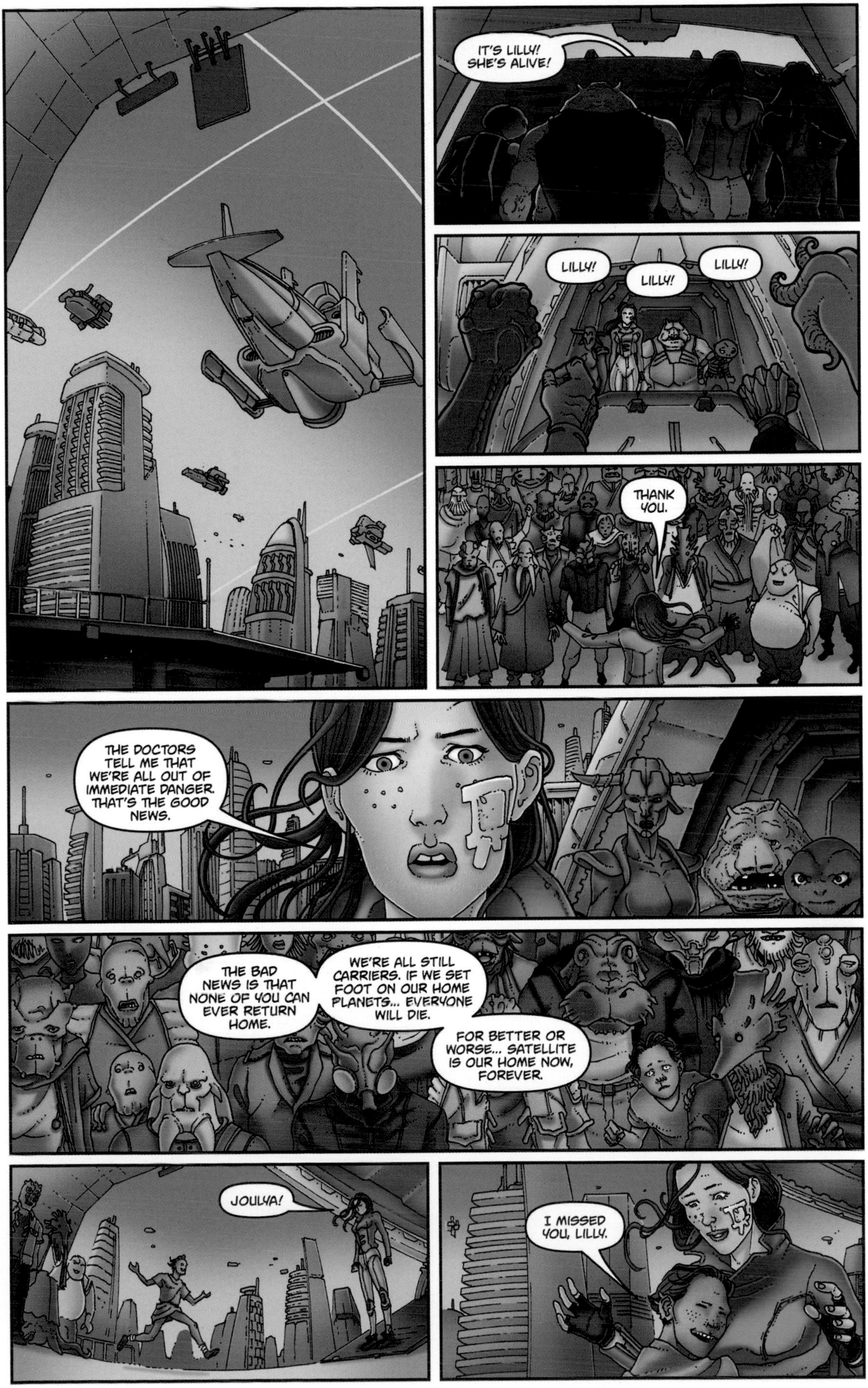
IT'S LILLY! SHE'S ALIVE!
LILLY!
LILLY!
LILLY!
THANK YOU.
THE DOCTORS TELL ME THAT WE'RE ALL OUT OF IMMEDIATE DANGER. THAT'S THE GOOD NEWS.
THE BAD NEWS IS THAT NONE OF YOU CAN EVER RETURN HOME.
WE'RE ALL STILL CARRIERS. IF WE SET FOOT ON OUR HOME PLANETS... EVERYONE WILL DIE.
FOR BETTER OR WORSE... SATELLITE IS OUR HOME NOW, FOREVER.
JOULYA!
I MISSED YOU, LILLY.

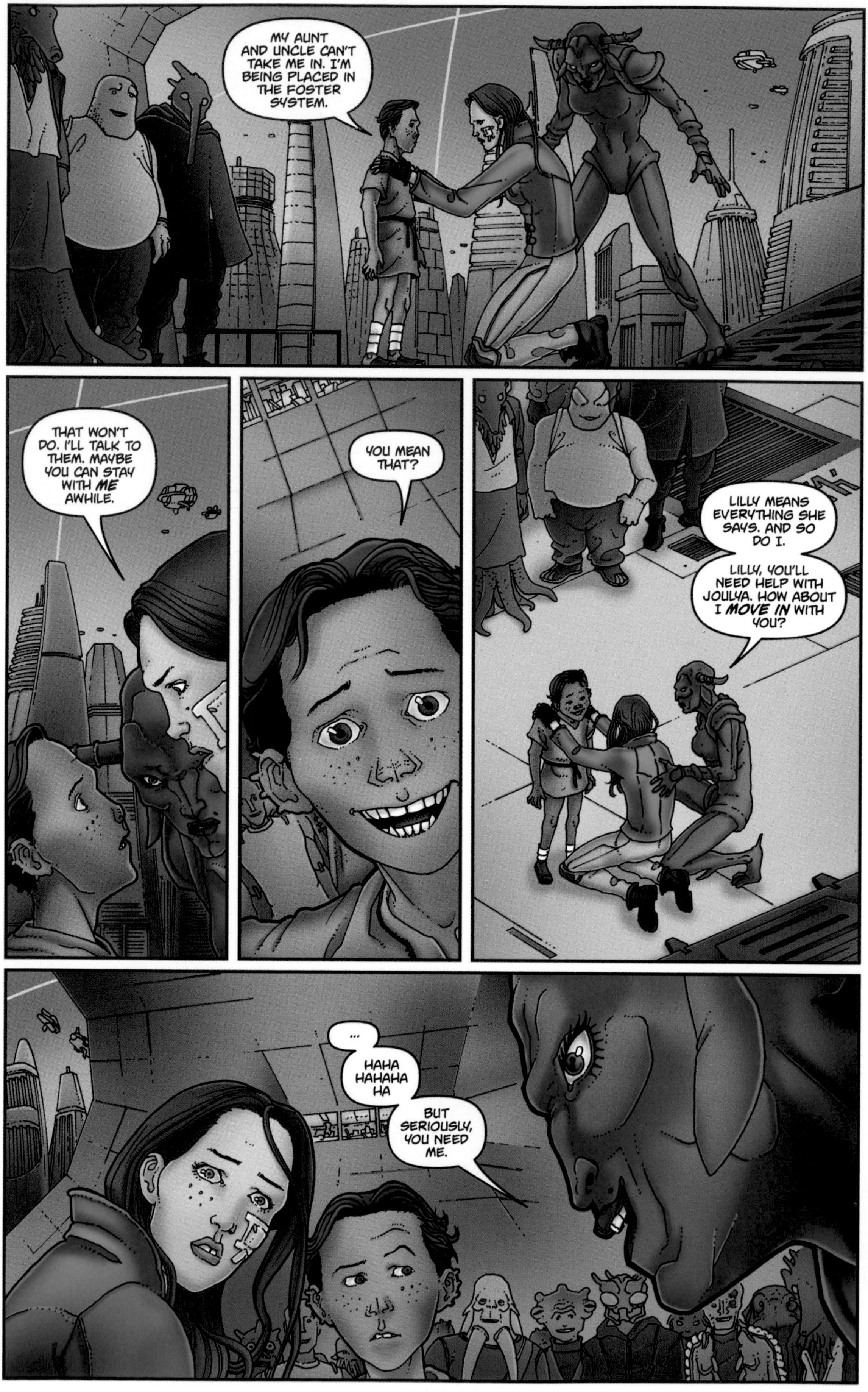
MY AUNT AND UNCLE CAN'T TAKE ME IN. I'M BEING PLACED IN THE FOSTER SYSTEM.
THAT WON'T DO. I'LL TALK TO THEM. MAYBE YOU CAN STAY WITH ME AWHILE.
YOU MEAN THAT?
LILLY MEANS EVERYTHING SHE SAYS. AND SO DO I.
LILLY, YOU'LL NEED HELP WITH JOULYA. HOW ABOUT I MOVE IN WITH YOU?
...
HAHA HAHAHA HA
BUT SERIOUSLY, YOU NEED ME.

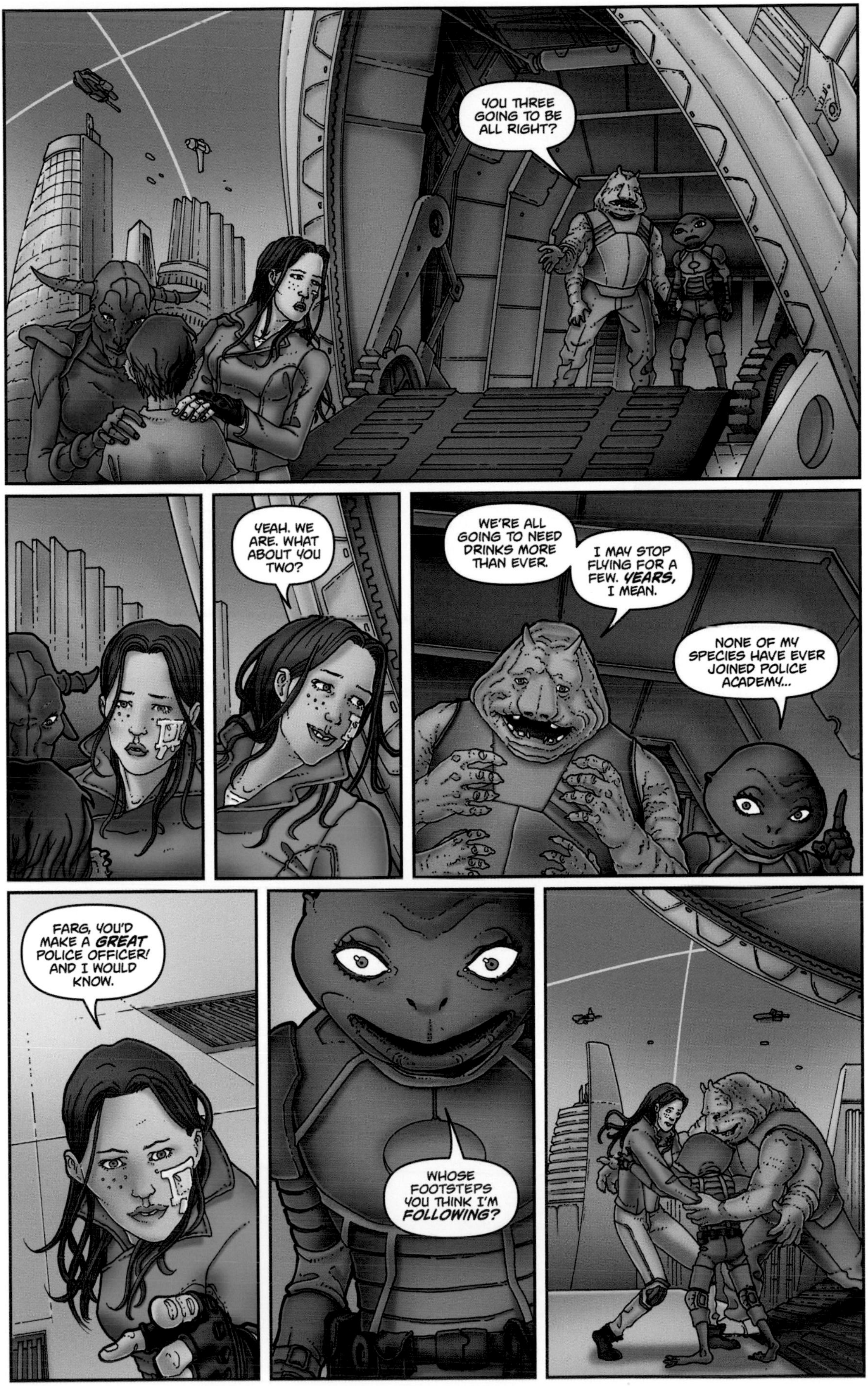
YOU THREE GOING TO BE ALL RIGHT?
YEAH. WE ARE. WHAT ABOUT YOU TWO?
WE'RE ALL GOING TO NEED DRINKS MORE THAN EVER.
I MAY STOP FLYING FOR A FEW. *YEARS,* I MEAN.
NONE OF MY SPECIES HAVE EVER JOINED POLICE ACADEMY...
FARG, YOU'D MAKE A *GREAT* POLICE OFFICER! AND I WOULD KNOW.
WHOSE FOOTSTEPS YOU THINK I'M *FOLLOWING?*

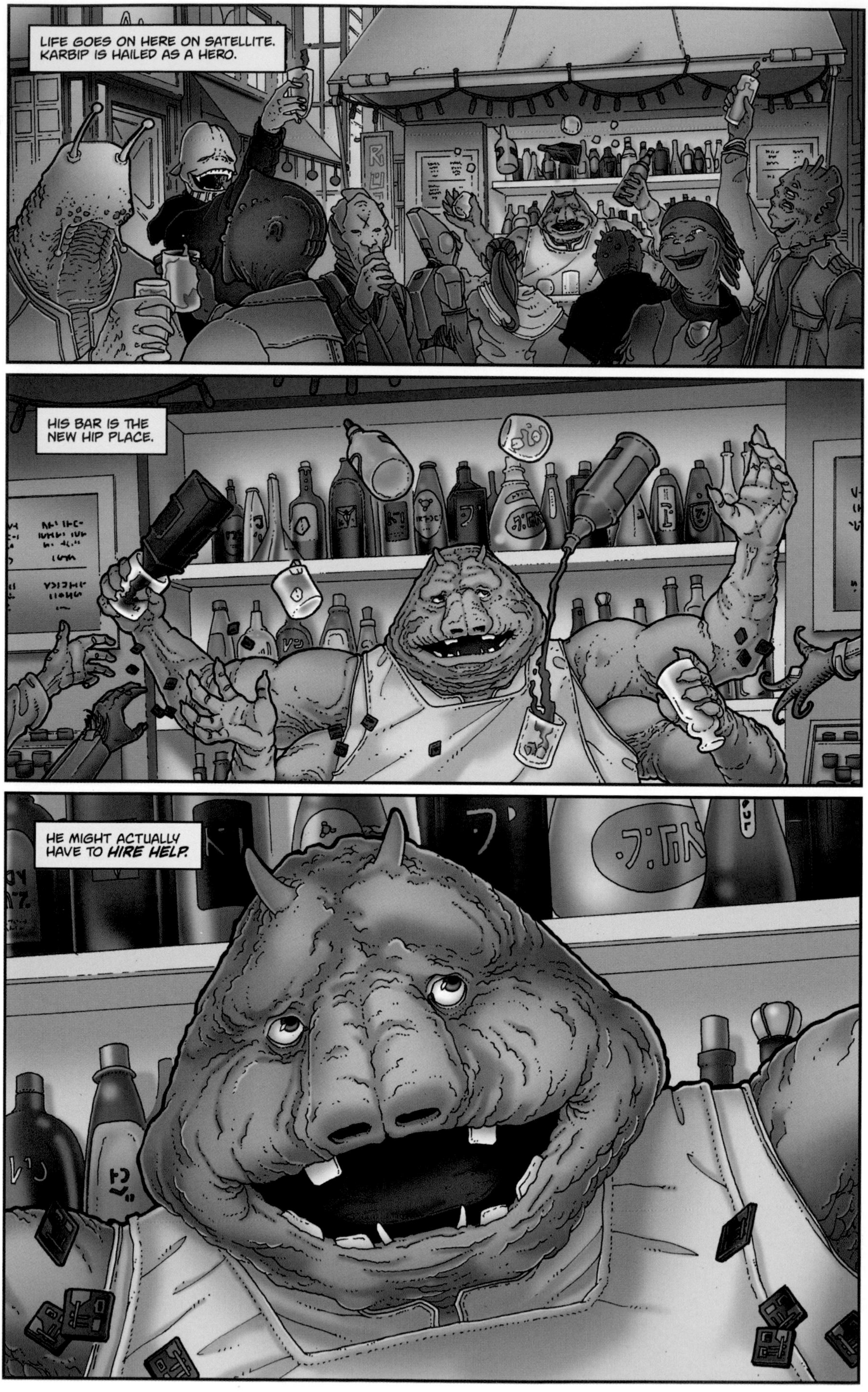
LIFE GOES ON HERE ON SATELLITE. KARBIP IS HAILED AS A HERO.
HIS BAR IS THE NEW HIP PLACE.
HE MIGHT ACTUALLY HAVE TO *HIRE HELP*.

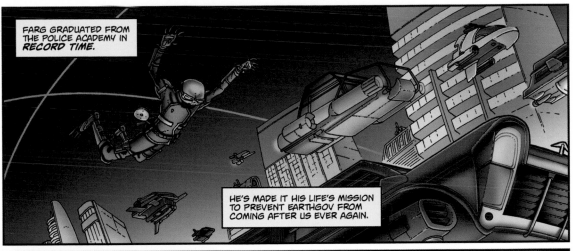

FARG GRADUATED FROM THE POLICE ACADEMY IN *RECORD TIME*.

HE'S MADE IT HIS LIFE'S MISSION TO PREVENT EARTHGOV FROM COMING AFTER US EVER AGAIN.

THEY SEND SPIES, SHIPS, WEAPONS...

...AND ARE NEVER HEARD FROM AGAIN. ALL THANKS TO THAT LITTLE GUY.

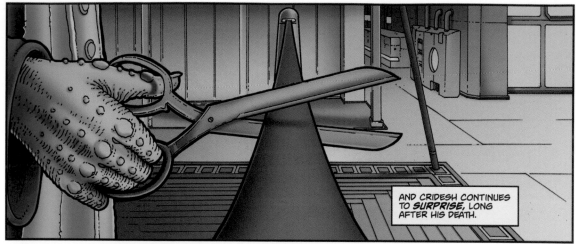

AND CRIDESH CONTINUES TO *SURPRISE*, LONG AFTER HIS DEATH.

HE ROUTED HIS SHARE OF THE PAY INTO SATELLITE'S FIRST HACKER DOJO. BOOKED SOLID.

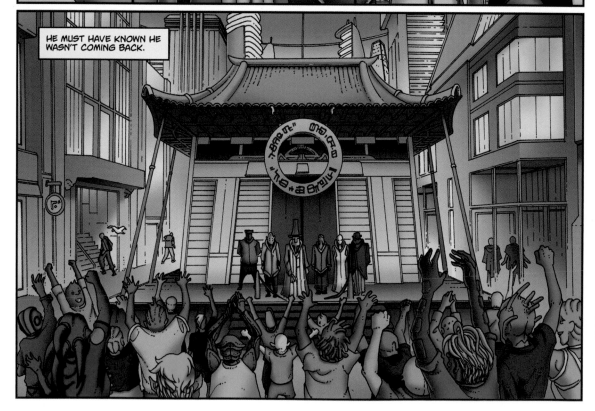

HE MUST HAVE KNOWN HE WASN'T COMING BACK.

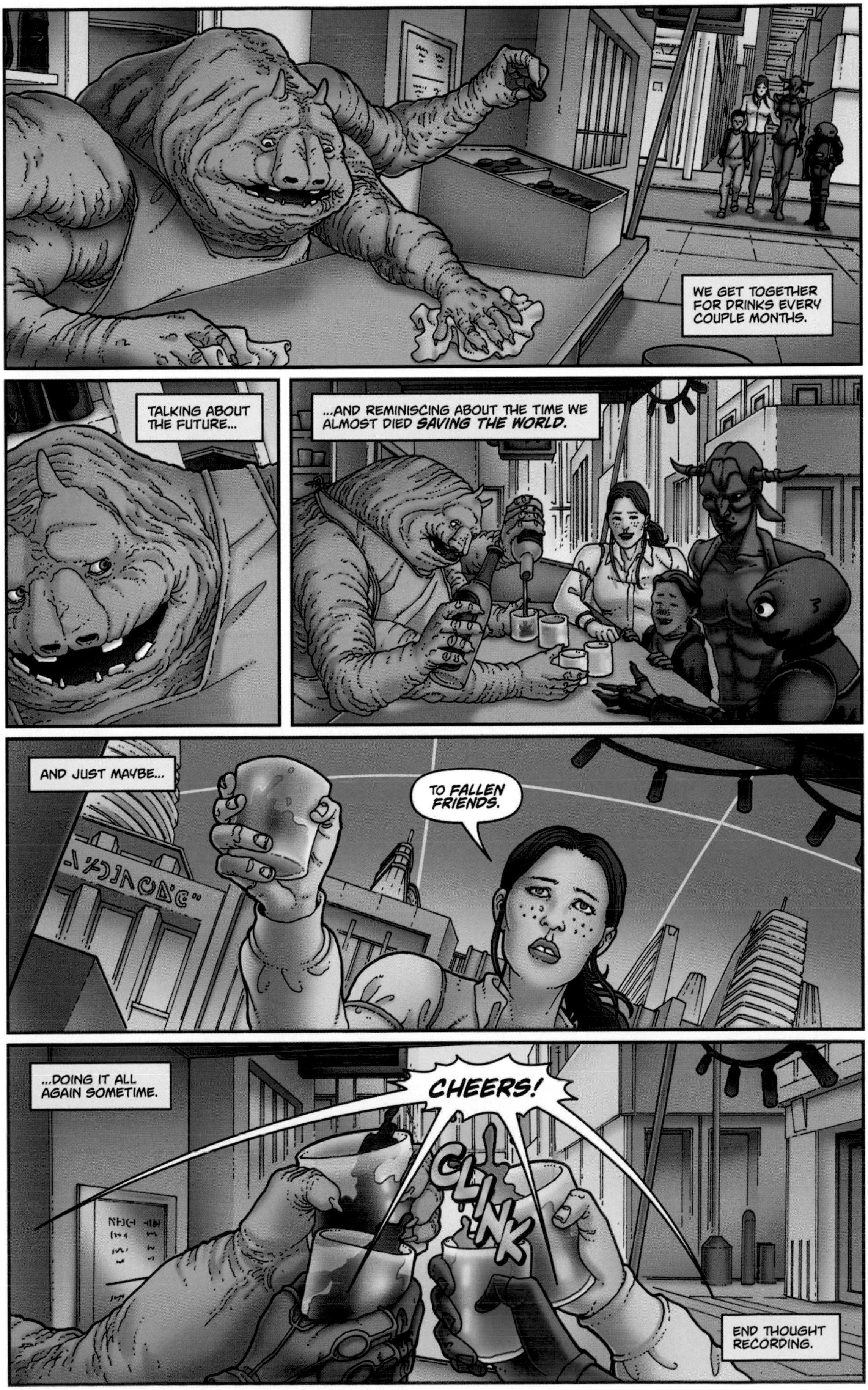
WE GET TOGETHER FOR DRINKS EVERY COUPLE MONTHS.
TALKING ABOUT THE FUTURE...
...AND REMINISCING ABOUT THE TIME WE ALMOST DIED SAVING THE WORLD.
AND JUST MAYBE...
TO FALLEN FRIENDS.
...DOING IT ALL AGAIN SOMETIME.
CHEERS!
CLINK
END THOUGHT RECORDING.

MONTHS LATER...

SKREEEEEEEE

LET'S NOT DO THAT AGAIN.

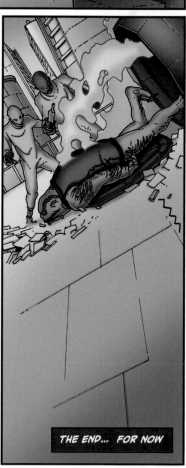

THE END... FOR NOW

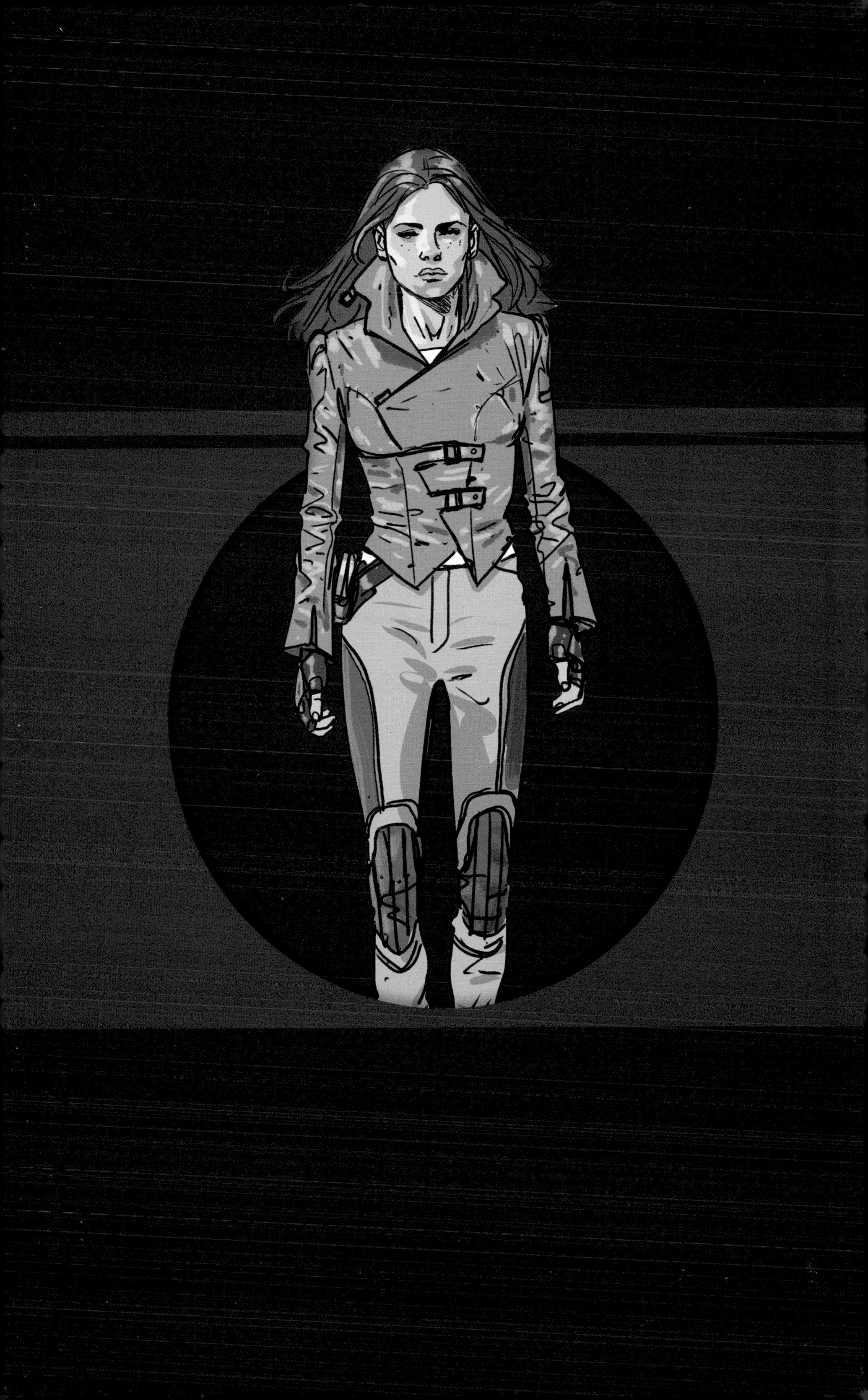

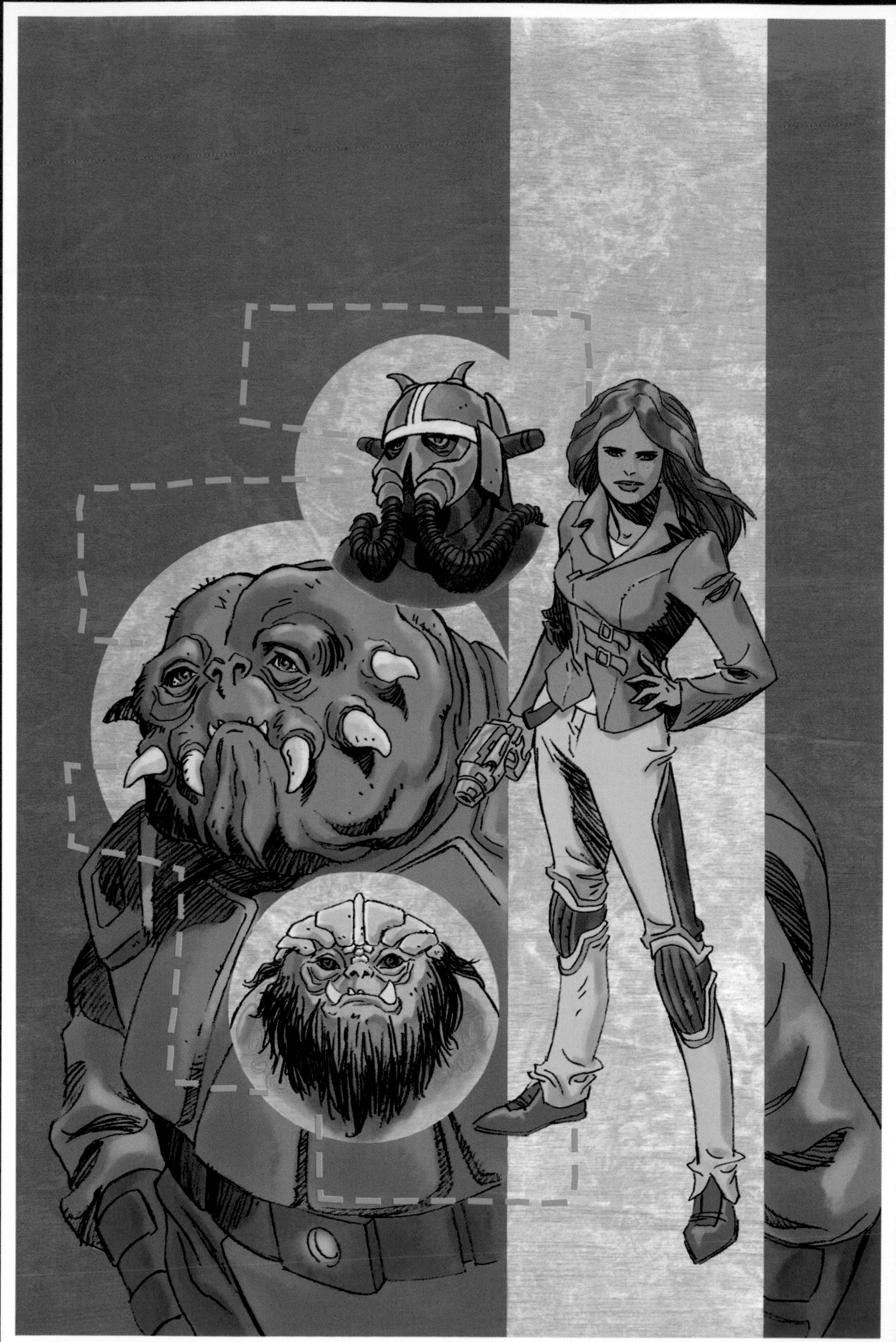

ART BY JUNE BRIGMAN

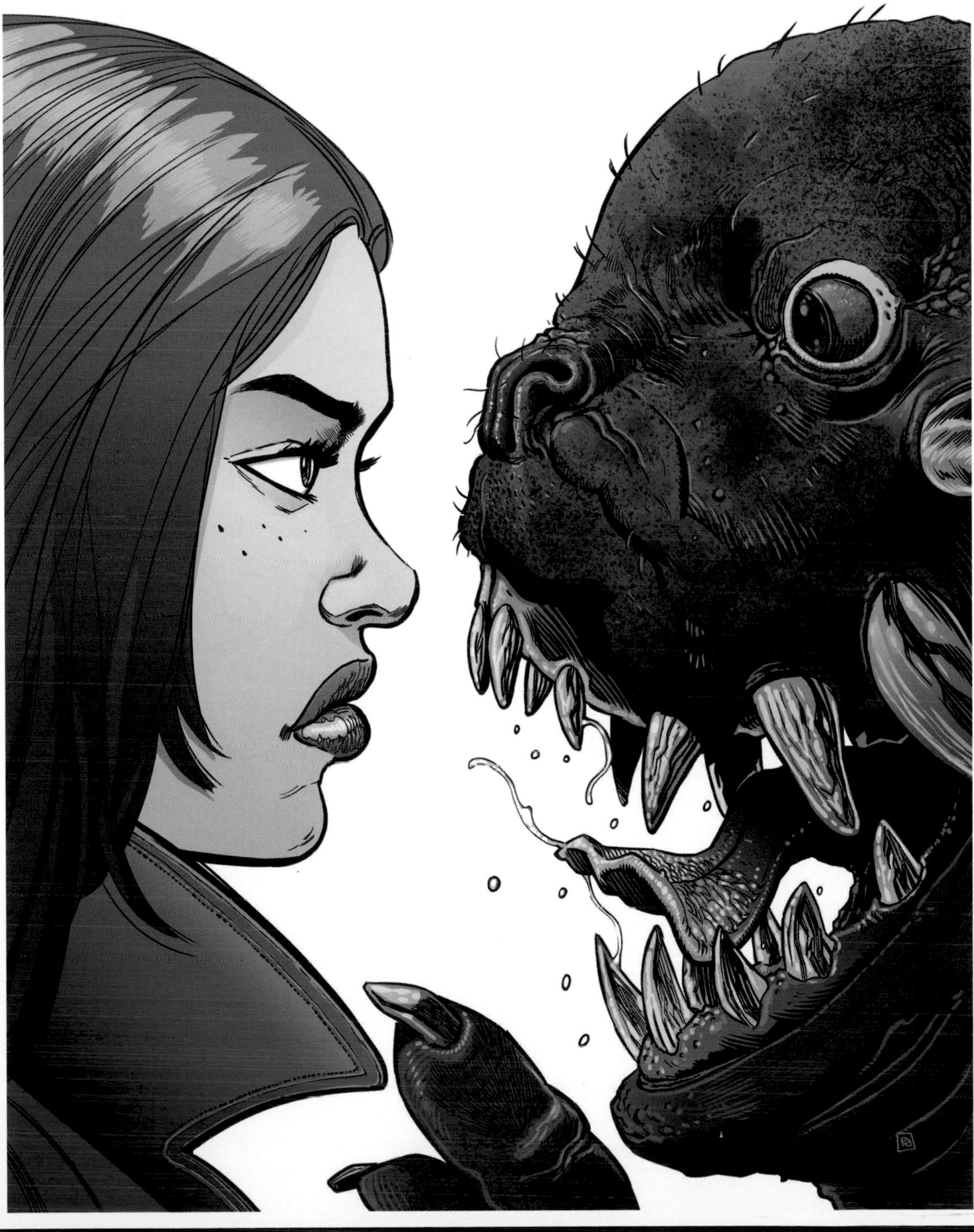

ART BY PJ HOLDEN

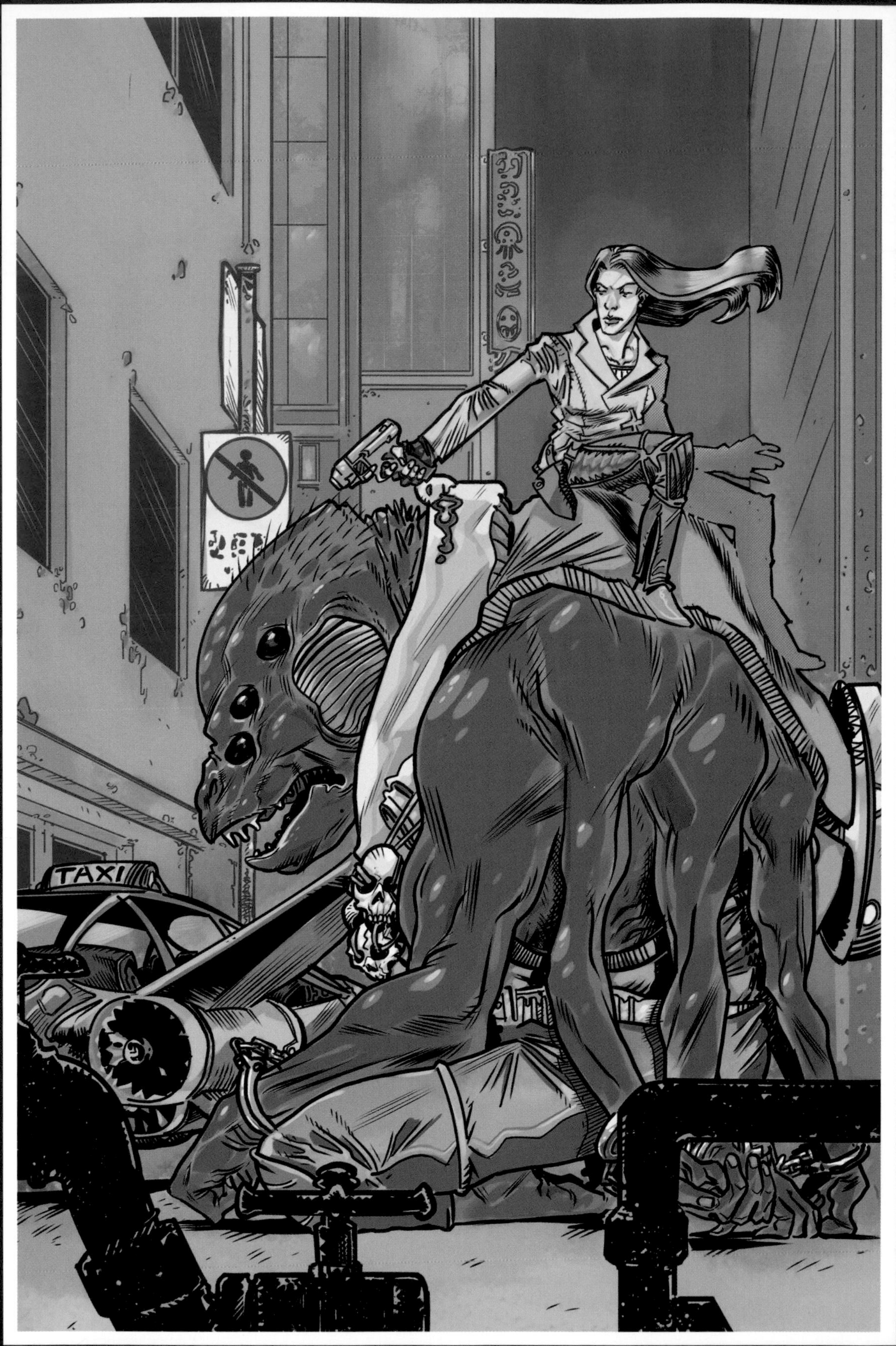
TAXI

ART BY JOHN BIVENS

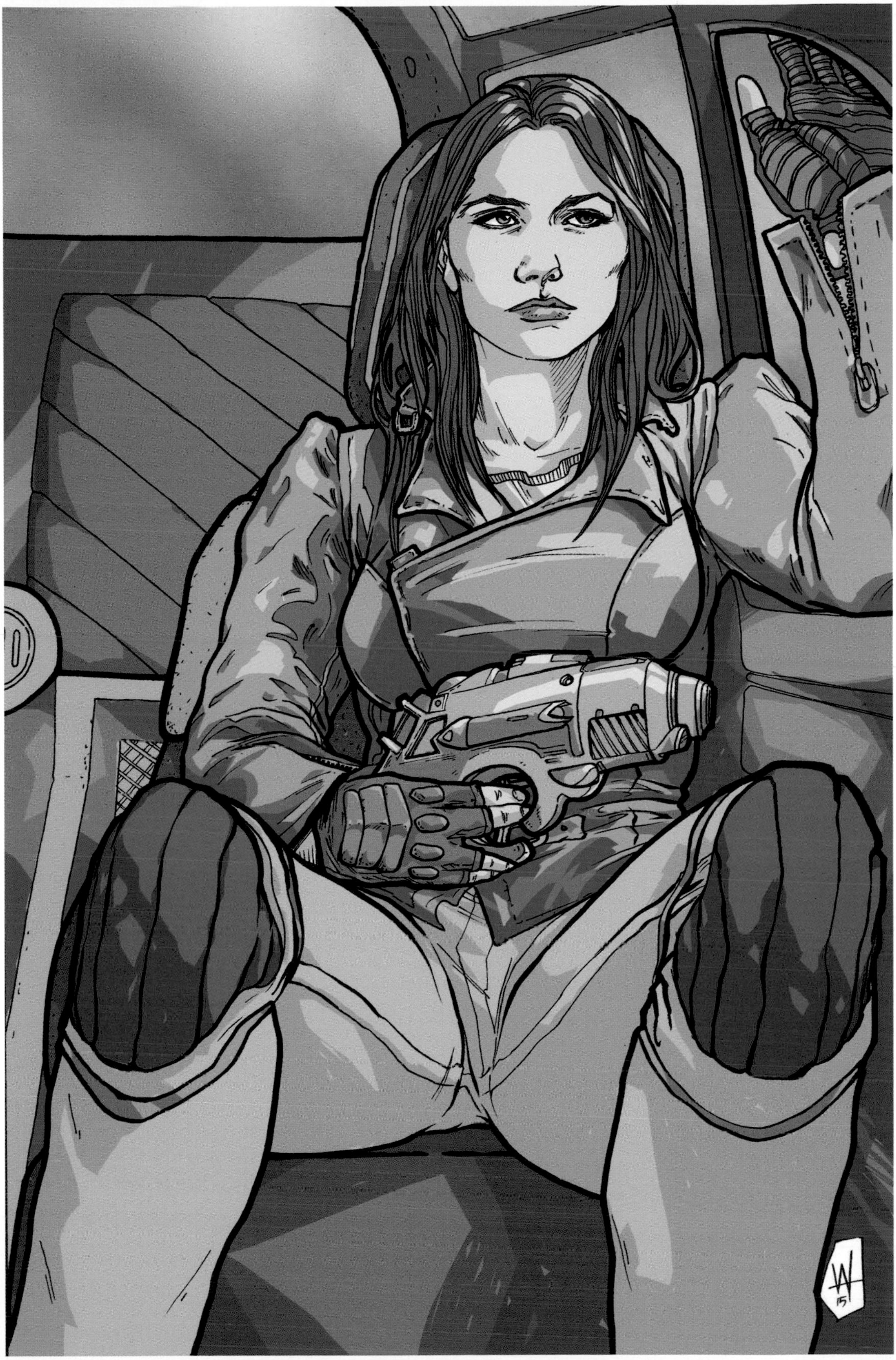

ART BY WESHOYOT ALVITRE

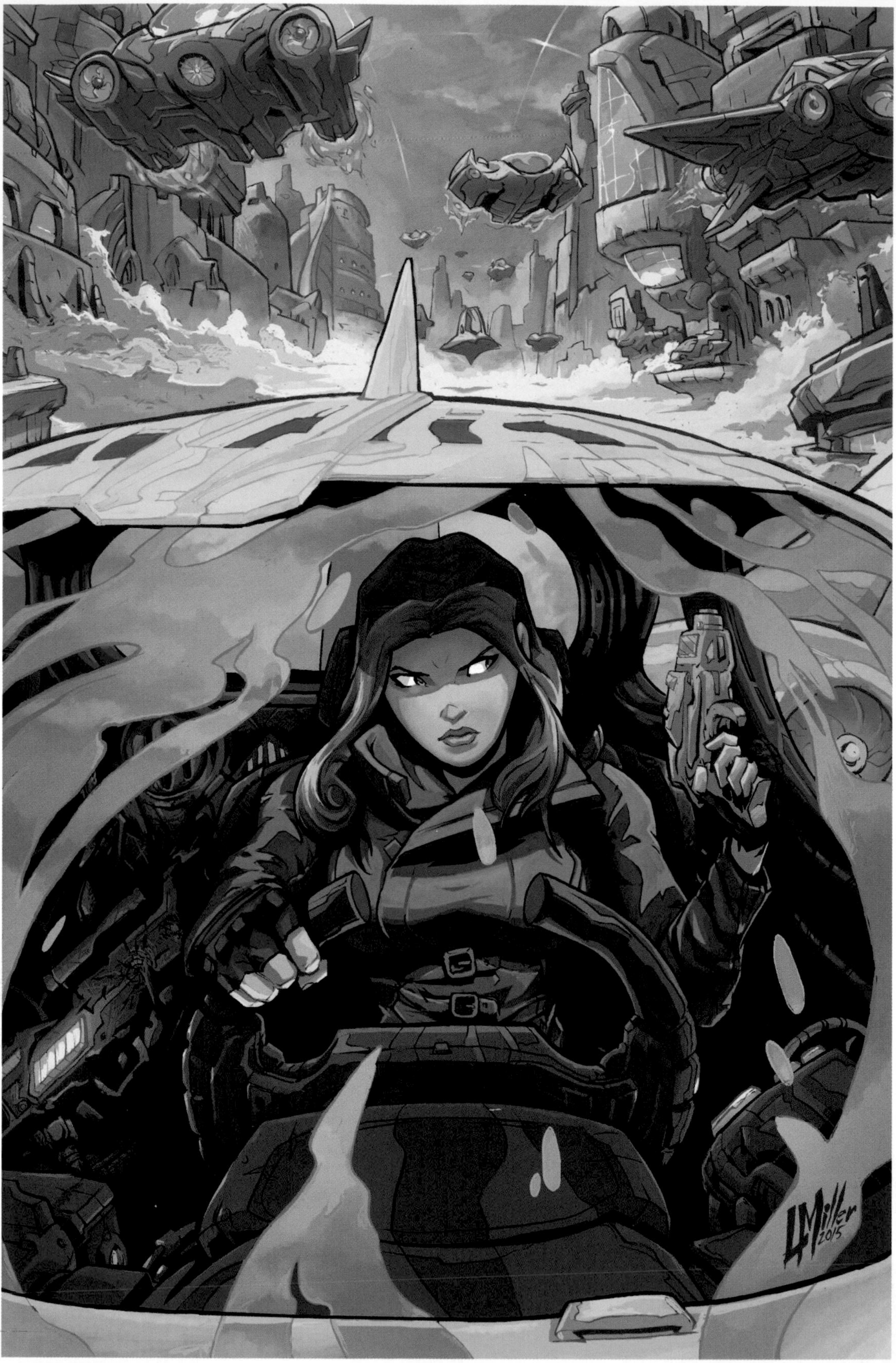
LMiller 2015

ART BY LOGAN MILLER

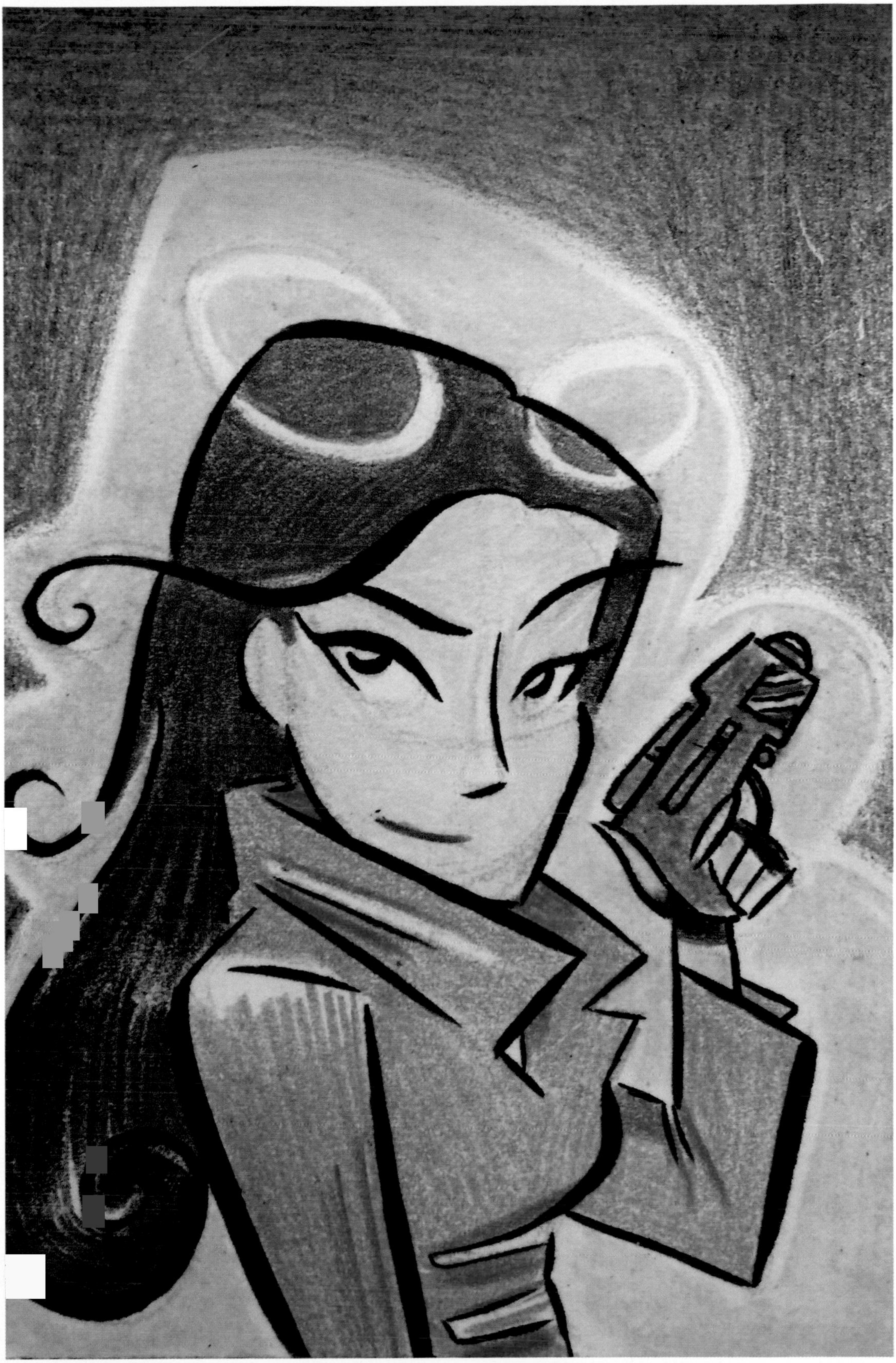

ART BY TOM BELAND

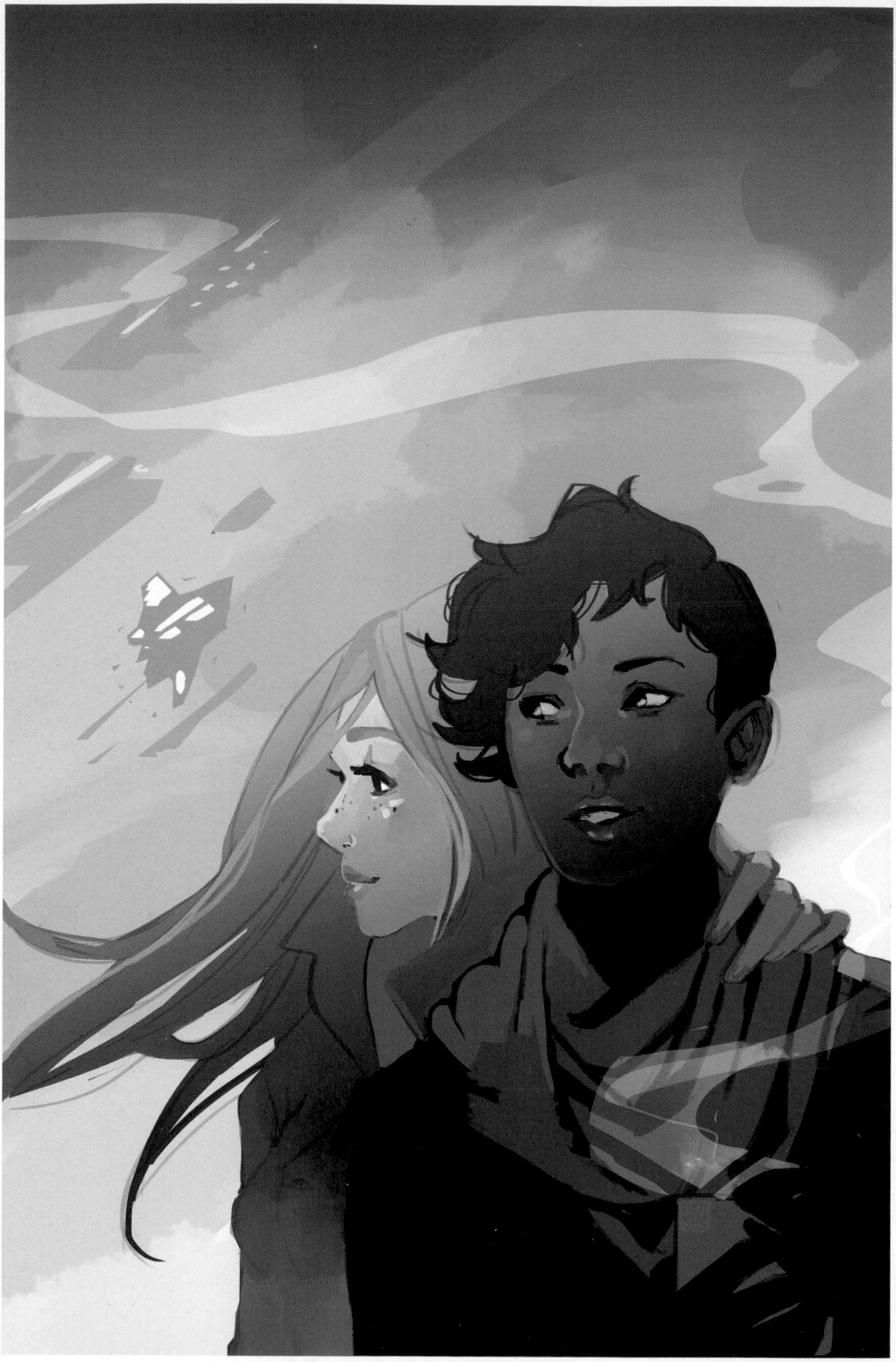

ART BY KEEZY YOUNG